MYSTIC MAYHEM

ASH FITZSIMMONS

MYSTIC MAYHEM

FORTUNE'S CHILD, BOOK ONE

Print Edition ISBN: 978-1-949861-63-1

Cover design by MiblArt.

www.ashfitzsimmons.com

CHAPTER 1

People who say that summer is their favorite season have never lived in the Deep South. Summer there is a season one endures, a long stretch of humid hell between the riotous blooms of spring and the relief of fall. Children enjoy it simply because of the freedom afforded them by the school break. For the rest of us, summer is a season best spent neck-deep in a body of water or hidden away in a building air conditioned roughly to the temperature of a meat locker.

I say this as someone who had it better than many. While I'd spent all but the first month of my life in Georgia, I grew up in a mountain town tucked into the stretch of the Blue Ridge where the land begins rising from the Piedmont into the peaks of the Smokies. Summers were cooler in the northeastern corner of the state—and unlike some of our more southerly neighbors, we saw snow in the winter—but my absolute favorite time of year was fall, when the apple harvest kicked off and the hills turned red and gold. Labor Day weekend marked the seasonal transition point on the calendar, even if the weather wasn't *quite* with the program yet.

That Saturday morning during the long weekend, I was parked in the town square beneath my tent as per usual for Market Day. Ragged Gap wasn't much more than a haphazardly assembled hamlet in the grand scheme of civic design, but as the hills around us were pocked with rental cabins and little else, we were the closest thing to civilization and a decent place to find provisions, and so we had our share of visitors with time on their hands and money to burn during the summer and fall. The Ragged Gap Tourism Board—aka Dolores Crichton and Benny Stamper, who met in the basement of First United Methodist once a month to steal the church's coffee and brainstorm—had hit on a winner a few years back with the idea of a weekend market for local vendors. "Local" had become a somewhat nebulous term over time, as I recognized merchants from places closer to Blue Ridge and Helen among our number, but the market was sufficiently successful to merit a blurb on the regional websites and draw in curious tourists, who left with too much produce and upcycled wind chimes. And since Labor Day was a "last hurrah" of sorts for families with kids young enough to miss a day or two of school, the town square was packed to the curb with vendor tents, unsheltered tables, curious browsers, and little children whining for ice cream.

As I'd seldom missed a Market Day since the program's inception, I'd been given my preferred plot near the ice cream truck, where foot traffic was high. I'd stacked my table with boxes and bottles of my products— well, the ones that weren't at risk of melting—and kept the rest in a long cooler in the grass. My lotion and body spray testers were set out in small bowls of ice, which seemed to increase their appeal on warmer days, and I'd decorated the display with bouquets of dried lavender.

Having parked both her kids on a bench with double scoops and their sunburned father, a woman came up to investigate my wares, and I smiled. "Morning! Let me know if you have any questions," I said, and stole a swig from my water bottle.

She carefully examined the items on offer—soaps, bath soaks, candles, sachets, the chilled lotion and body spray— then lifted the lotion from its ice bath. "May I?"

"Please." As she rubbed it into her hands, I said, "That's made with local goat's milk. I've got a farmer about thirty miles away who has the *sweetest* little goats."

She perked. "Does he do goat yoga?"

"Uh...I don't think he's gone that route just yet," I replied, wondering yet again about the insanity prevalent in larger cities. Yoga was fine and dandy, but I couldn't imagine how adding goats to the mix would increase my flexibility or help me achieve inner peace. "But they're great milkers, and I've been using them from the get-go. The honey's also local," I said, pointing to one of my soaps, "and most of the herbs and flowers I use are ones I've either grown or foraged around here."

The woman sniffed the back of her hand, presumably caught a whiff of the honeysuckle scent I'd added to the lotion, and smiled. "You make all of this yourself?"

"Every bit," I said with a grin. "And my house is small enough that it's a literal cottage industry."

Another woman, a well-coiffed blonde sporting overpriced athleisure, hurried up to the table. "Oh! I'm *so* glad you're here today," she said, and mimed wiping her brow. "I love this," she continued, reaching for a bag of my bath soak, "and the store up the street said they're out, but you'd probably be around...how much?"

"Ten dollars for that size, but I do have a larger one, if you'd prefer."

"Yes, please." She put the bag back and nodded to my other customer. "The owners of my cabin left a whole basket of these products in the bathroom, and I *need* more. Do you have a website?" she asked me. "Please tell me you ship."

"I sure do," I said, and made a show of putting one of my cards into a purple tote bag with her purchase. Reusable bags weren't terribly expensive to have customized, I'd found, and they served as continuing advertising. "Here you go. Cash or card?"

As I fiddled with my card reader, she took a look at the bag. "'Fortune's Fancies.' That's a fun name. Where does it come from?"

"Well," I said as her Visa finally cooperated, "I'm Jane Fortune, so…"

"*Perfect*. That's adorable." Her hand splayed toward me as if she were showing off her pink manicure. "This is just what I wanted. Thank you, dear," she said, taking her card, and strolled off down the square.

"Why don't you give me one of the small bags of the soak?" the other woman said. "And the lotion. I can use them both."

I rang her up and thanked her, and she slung my bag over her shoulder, logo facing out, as she headed back to her family. Free advertising—I'd take it.

Much of my business had started off this way, making small sales to curious passersby. But it had grown in its five short years from the days of me sitting at a folding table with hand-labeled boxes, hoping to sell a bar of soap or two, to a regular delivery route to shops and properties in the area. Ragged Gap Mercantile, the general tourist store with a bit of everything on the shelves, was my biggest single customer, but I also sold to some of the B&Bs and rental owners at a bulk discount in hopes that their guests would come to me for more. Heck, I'd even begun a monthly subscription service, which I was still fine-tuning and so limited to customers within driving distance. I wasn't rich by any means, but I was reasonably proud of my one-woman operation.

I mean, I had to do *something* with my business degree.

A few minutes after my pair of customers left, a brunette in oversized tortoiseshell sunglasses approached my booth. "Hi," I said with a smile. "Step in the shade—it's free."

She lifted her glasses, peered at my wares, then cocked her head. "Sorry…are you the, uh…the tarot reader?"

Suppressing a sigh, I replied, "No, you want Mystic Mountains. Four tables down, I think…yeah," I said, rising from my chair to look past my neighbor's racks of quilts. "The silver tent. If she's not there, she'll be in the store," I added, pointing to the shop across the street.

The woman thanked me and moved on, and I sipped my water. I'd learned years ago to scope out where Mystic Mountains had set up at Market Day, as at least one confused soul inevitably wandered up to my table, looking for incense or a palm reading. My surname created confusion, and some of the Mystic Mountains staff had remarked to me that setting up a "Fortune" tent so close to their shop seemed like deception, but I brushed them off. I always gave good directions and never badmouthed the place to tourists, no matter my thoughts about it. Frankly, if anyone was cheating, it was the business with the prominent downtown storefront that still insisted upon putting up a booth and taking space from a smaller merchant.

Some may wonder why a little town in the Bible Belt would support a New Age store only two blocks from the public library and the municipal offices. The truth is that mountain hamlets can have weird, split personalities. I knew plenty of people in Ragged Gap who never touched a drop of liquor, seldom swore, and lived and died by the calendar of events on the back of the church bulletin—the "God, guns, and grits" crowd one might expect. Some of them had come by our house relentlessly when I was a kid, encouraging my dad to send me to Wednesday-evening programs or summer vacation Bible school. They were decent folks, more or less, overwhelmingly conservative in their dress and politics but the first to stop and help if they caught you with a flat on the side of the road.

And then there was the woo-woo brigade.

Fun fact: north Georgia is Bigfoot country. Whether Bigfoot *exists* is up for debate, but the presence of the Bigfoot museum over in Blue Ridge goes to show just how many people in this part of the state want to believe. Along with the sasquatch hunters, the region has its share of mystics, hippies, magic-curious, and neopagans, some as deeply spiritual as the church crowd, others seemingly in it for the pentacles and crystals. The former didn't bother me in the slightest—if you feel closer to the divine while out in the woods, more power to you. The latter, however, at least in Ragged Gap, were a cliquish lot, quick to push back if questioned. Their domain was Mystic Mountains, which did a *killing* among the tourists who came in and poked around when it was too wet to hike. Their wares were the expected—polished rocks, jewelry, ceremonial items, books, candles, incense, all at a premium—and they'd added a "vegan" café while I was off at college. I stopped in once, discovered that the smoothie blender was broken, pointed out that egg salad is in no way vegan (even if the eggs came from hormone-free chickens), and was given death stares until I left the premises.

I'd tried to make friends with the Mystic Mountains crowd when I was thirteen, a gangly homeschooled kid in too-short jeans and a messy ponytail who'd been given the freedom of the open road courtesy of a new Huffy. The staff and hangers-on talked a good game, especially to a newly minted teenager who thought she'd finally found her tribe, but something told me to proceed with caution. I attended a few of their hangouts, sipped bitter herbal tea, and listened to twenty- and thirty-somethings talk about channeling their inner power and charging their crystals. Eventually, at the end of one such meeting, I approached the owner of the store, Stephanie Love—I never could tell whether that was her real name—and requested to speak to her alone. I said that I was having a focusing issue and asked if she had any suggestions.

Sure, Stephanie told me, all warmth and smiles. Her brown eyes crinkled, and her pink-streaked blonde ponytail bobbed as we chatted. She talked to me about developing a mantra and pointed to a display of polished stones corresponding to my chakras. I listened and nodded, and then I asked if I could show her what I was doing and get some feedback.

Of course, she said, and sipped her tea.

So I whispered one of the spells I'd been working on that week, and after a brief lag, a rose quartz sphere lifted off its base and flew into my hand. I was weaning myself off my wand, I explained, but without that focusing tool, my spells were taking longer than usual to work. What should I do differently?

Stephanie's teacup fell and shattered, sending porcelain shards flying across the wood and splashing my jeans, and I realized then that the so-called expert was not, in fact, magically gifted. She'd mumbled something about being unable to help me, and I'd quickly taken my leave, riding home with flaming cheeks and a sick knot in my gut.

I didn't tell my dad about my misstep, and to my knowledge, he never learned of it. He'd told me since I was little that humans lacked magical talent, but I'd been so *sure* that I'd proven him wrong...or perhaps I was just desperate to meet someone other than him who understood what it meant to be a teenage sorcerer not fully in control of her abilities.

I tried going back to Mystic Mountains after that, but the people who'd been so friendly before now avoided me, whispering to each other and cutting their eyes in my direction. I'd just grabbed a cookie when Stephanie came over and quietly but firmly told me that this meeting wasn't for me.

I might have been thirteen, but I wasn't an idiot, so I left.

Fourteen years later, Stephanie still owned and ran Mystic Mountains, offering her pretty trinkets and workshops and readings from self-proclaimed experts in tarot and reiki and past-life regression. Occasionally, we'd see each other on the street or at Market Day and nod, an acknowledgement of the other's presence but nothing suggesting friendship.

I wondered sometimes why she hadn't taken to me. She was a practicing witch, after all, and I'd been stupid enough to demonstrate actual power in her presence—why hadn't she asked me my secrets and paraded me in front of the others as proof that magic *could* be learned? Perhaps she was afraid she'd lose clout if people saw that the woman who'd been studying magic for two decades couldn't hold a candle to a kid. Perhaps she was just afraid of me. In any case, I seldom darkened her door, and we maintained the status quo.

I'd just packed a bag full of soaps and candles for a trio of college-age girls when an elderly man approached my table. Tall, sun-weathered, and bald as an egg, Grover Wilcox was a deacon at Ragged Gap Baptist, a pillar of the community, and a *very* familiar face.

"Good morning, Jane," he said, leaning down to take a glance at my offerings. "How are you today?"

"Fine, Mr. Wilcox," I replied. "Yourself?"

"Still standing, ain't I?" He smiled, exposing yellowed teeth. "Gonna need a bag of your soak for the missus and a tub of that goldenrod salve, if you've got any."

"One left. It's your lucky day." I retrieved a pot about the size of a tin of mints from the cooler and popped it in a bag. "Thought I'd go looking for more goldenrod tomorrow. The season's almost over, so it's iffy, but I'll make a new batch if I find any."

"Good, good," he said, and pulled out his wallet. "Speaking of new batches…anything coming up from your dad?"

I bit back my smile. Even Ragged Gap's most pious patriarchs and matriarchs knew that Dad made the best moonshine for miles. It had taken some of them a while to piece together that we were related—he was Coby Hewt, after all, while I was a Fortune. But once they understood that I had the intel on Dad's distillation, I suddenly found myself selling hand cream to alleged teetotalers who needed an excuse to ask a quiet question or two. I'd been shocked at first to see just who Dad's customers included—hell, the town's entire police force bought from him—but he made good product, and I didn't mind keeping his fans apprised of availability.

"Bottling next weekend, he thinks," I murmured. "Should I have him put one back for you?"

"Two, if you don't mind."

"Yes, sir," I said, and shot Dad a quick text while Mr. Wilcox watched.

"You ever think of taking it up?" he asked me. "'Shine?"

I grinned at him. "Nah. Dad's been brewing and distilling for a long time. I much prefer soaps."

He grunted. "Well, thank him for me, will you?"

I promised I would and shook my head as he walked off through the crowd.

On paper, my father was a blacksmith and farrier, a respectable profession if not a particularly lucrative one. He fit horseshoes and made decorative railings and the odd bit of yard art for nearby cabins, but most of the locals knew him for his moonshine. His *real* funding came from his work as a potion brewer—Dad had a greenhouse and workshop hidden on his property in which he grew plants unknown to humans and ground, mashed, and cooked them down into elixirs with miraculous effects (and often nasty tastes). But no one in Ragged Gap other than me knew of Dad's primary occupation, and as he kept a fair number of thirsts quenched with his mundane distillation, folks tended to leave him alone and let him work in peace.

When I was a teenager, I asked Dad what the secret was to his moonshine—was there a spell he used while the mash was fermenting, or did he add a splash of some exotic potion to the final product to improve the taste? He denied it. The secret, he told me, was a century of practice and experimentation. His work in a government greenhouse had afforded him ample opportunity to brew, and like many with his skill set, he took up recreational brewing and distillation along the way. "Start with good ingredients, know what you're doing, pay attention, and you'll make good product," he said. "But *never* adulterate. People have a right to know what they're consuming." His dark eyes had narrowed then, focusing in on mine. "I don't *ever* want to hear of you slipping someone a potion without their knowledge. Even if you think it won't hurt them, even if you think it's for the best—don't do it unless it's an emergency. Understood?"

I took that to heart. My products' ingredients were clearly labeled and perfectly ordinary, and I'd yet to hear of a customer with so much as a rash. My business was growing, and I'd begun to consider hiring a teenager or two to help with the shipping and deliveries, even though the Mystic Mountains clique continued to avoid me as if they feared my lavender linen spray might turn them into frogs.

Still, to my knowledge, they never badmouthed me to potential customers. By then, locals with even a peripheral connection to the witchy crowd knew that I was someone who could get things done when the situation called for…well, let's just say an *unorthodox* approach.

The automated bells at the Baptist church chimed noon, signaling the end of Market Day, and I stretched in my chair. Most of us would loiter for a few minutes while we packed, catching the late sales, and as I had nowhere in particular to be that day, I took my sweet time reloading my wheeled cooler and dismantling my tent. I had just finished finagling it back into its carrying case when a stranger approached me.

"Um, hi," she murmured.

I considered her briefly. Maybe my age, somewhere in her mid-twenties, but probably a few years younger. Blonde hair like mine, but hers fell almost to her butt, and the frizzy final inches seemed badly in need of a trim. Green eyes, which would be pretty if not for the shadows below them. Light makeup—drugstore, I guessed, nothing fancy. She wore a baggy long-sleeved T-shirt over powder blue leggings, but the extra fabric did nothing to disguise her swollen abdomen. Pregnant, obviously, and pretty far along.

"Hi, there," I said, and smiled. "Can I help you? I've packed just about everything, but you're welcome to take a look in the cooler."

She worried her bottom lip with her teeth. "Uh…" she began, hesitating, then blurted, "I heard you know something about magic."

"Oh, you want Mystic Mountains. It looks like they've already gone inside, but their store is just across the street—"

"No," she insisted, and gripped my wrist. "Friend of mine told me that you can *fix* things. You're Jane, right?"

I stood there and studied her more closely. She seemed exhausted, but the look in her eyes spoke of something more akin to desperation.

"Do you want to get some lunch and talk about whatever's bothering you?" I asked quietly.

"I ain't got the money to eat out."

"It's okay," I said, and patted her hand until she released me. "Let me get my stuff loaded, and we'll have ourselves a chat."

She tried to help me tote my gear to my truck. I let her carry my folding chair—I generally didn't ask people for help cleaning up my messes, especially heavily pregnant people—but pitching in seemed to make her feel better about the situation. Once I'd locked the old truck, we walked up the street to Mama Hen's Café, one of Ragged Gap's handful of downtown eateries. The owner of the place was Henrietta Grange, who had leaned in to her nickname and littered the walls with every bit of poultry-themed décor she could thrift, and her brood of daughters and sons kept the restaurant running. It wasn't fancy by any stretch, but she offered chicken salad made without celery, which kept me coming back.

My quiet companion and I snagged a booth near the kitchen, and once our waitress brought giant plastic cups of sweet tea, I said, "I'm Jane Fortune. What's your name?"

"Emma," she whispered.

"Nice to meet you. Now, what's going on?"

She waited until the aisle beside us was clear, then pushed up her sleeves, revealing a patchwork of fresh and healing bruises, many of them finger shaped. "My husband."

I sipped my tea while she covered her arms again. "Did this just start?"

"No." Emma shook her head. "He can be a real nice guy, but when he drinks too much, he gets *mean*, you know?"

I nodded.

"And it wasn't so bad when he was just hitting on me," she continued, staring down at the laminated menu. "I can take it. But he got laid off *again*, and he since he ain't working right now, he's home all day, and he drinks, and…"

When she raised her head, I saw the anger beneath her fear. "We got two little girls and one on the way. He's started hitting the babies. Knocked our oldest down the porch stairs yesterday and broke her arm. She's with my mama and daddy right now, and so's her sister. I didn't come home last night after I took them to the hospital. Don't know if he's sobered up yet or still drunk off his ass."

I waited until she fell silent, then asked, "Would you like some help getting out? I've got a friend down in Atlanta who works for a battered women's shelter, and she's got connections all over the state. I'd be happy to call her and see what they can do for you. She knows some lawyers who can help with restraining orders and divorces, too."

But Emma began to tear up as I spoke. "He says if I

leave or try to take the girls, he'll kill us."

"You believe him?"

She nodded, and her face crumpled as she tried not to cry.

"Hey, hey, it's all right," I soothed, taking her hand across the table. "Are you hungry?"

"A little," she admitted.

That was an understatement. She'd tried to order a side salad, and I'd added a chicken sandwich and fries, which she wolfed down like she hadn't eaten in a week. I gave her my onion rings as well and wondered when she'd last had a full stomach. Pregnancy was hard enough without worrying where your next meal was coming from.

As Emma's pace slowed, I asked, "What do you want from me?"

She didn't hesitate. "I want him gone. Forever. I don't want to be fighting him for custody, worrying about whether he's getting physical with my girls."

"Understandable. That said, I don't know what you've heard, but I don't kill people. Haven't yet, and I don't plan to start now."

"That's what my friend told me," she mumbled, and wiped the onion ring grease from her mouth. "But could you, like…could you send him a message? Scare him?"

I nodded. "Yeah, I could do that."

"How much would it cost? I ain't got a lot, but you can have this damn thing," she said as she started to wriggle her tiny engagement ring off her swollen finger.

"It's okay." Covering her hand with my own, I said, "I don't charge. Just tell me where I can find him and where you'll be waiting."

And for the first time since I met her, Emma smiled.

Sunset comes early in the mountains, and the shadows were growing long when I drove up to the secluded cabin around seven-thirty that night. Just as Emma had predicted, Hal's beloved Chevy was parked in the driveway, and at an angle that suggested less than full sobriety. The man himself I found sitting on his porch with a half-empty bottle of cheap whiskey beside his chair. He stood as I climbed down from my truck and raised a shotgun, which swayed erratically in his unsteady hands. "Where are they?" he slurred.

"Safe," I called back, folding my arms. "You must be Hal."

"Damn right." He squinted down at me. "The hell're you?"

"No one of importance."

It took him a moment to process that. "You CPS? You trying to take my kids? What'd that bitch say?"

"I wouldn't worry about Emma," I replied. "Or the girls. You're in a heap of trouble, Hal."

His response was to rack the shotgun, but I held my ground.

"Get out of here," he ordered.

"No. What's going to happen now is that *you* are going to get in that truck of yours and get out of Ragged Gap. And you're not coming back. *Ever.*" I shrugged. "I'm letting you off easy, friend. But if the sun rises and I catch you in this county, you'll wish you never laid a finger on them."

Hal began to laugh, and his gun pointed seemingly everywhere but directly at me. "You can't make me do nothin'," he proclaimed.

I looked back at him for a long moment, then barely smiled. "Oh?"

With a whisper, the porch burst into flame.

I had the fire well under control—this wasn't my first rodeo—but drunk, stupid Hal sure didn't know that. Screaming like a cheerleader in a slasher film, he tripped down the stairs, dropped his gun, and scrambled back to his feet. I sent a little jet of flame to wrap around the gun, keeping it out of Hal's reach, but he didn't even try to retrieve it. With fire sweeping across the weedy lawn behind him, he ran in terror for his truck, fumbled with the door, and managed to climb inside.

Keeping the door open with a quick spell, I strolled up to the truck while Hal scrambled toward the passenger seat, whimpering. "Mark me," I said, holding his wide-eyed stare. "You ever come back, you ever bother Emma again, and I won't be so nice."

He shrieked when I let my arms and shoulders burst into flame.

"Run," I whispered, then retreated before I could set his truck on fire and slammed the door.

He fishtailed out of the driveway—I'd parked on the other end of the property for a reason—and peeled off down the mountain, driving like he was trying to qualify for NASCAR. Hoping the deer had sense enough to stay out of his way, I extinguished the blaze on myself and the house, considered the scorched ground and blackened porch, then closed my eyes and tried to concentrate, willing my focus to a laser point. Fire was easy, but reconstruction was always a pain in the ass.

As I coaxed the scraggly Bermuda to crawl up from the dirt and across the yard, I heard the distant sound of a police siren in the valley. It would be too damn bad if Hal got slapped with a DUI and locked in the drunk tank overnight, I mused. Pickled though he was, I knew I'd made an impression, and I could imagine him pacing the cell, begging to bail out so he could flee.

Or maybe the cops had pulled over another tourist doing fifty in a thirty zone, which was tantamount to shooting fish in a barrel. Either way, I wasn't bothered.

Night had fallen in earnest by the time I finished, and I called Emma's cell as I started home. "He's gone," I said. "You let me know if he comes back, now."

"What did you do?" she whispered.

"That's between us," I replied, and cut the conversation short.

A girl's got to keep a few secrets, after all.

CHAPTER 2

I awoke to a shaft of light in my face Sunday morning and groaned, reminding myself once again that I *really* needed to either get some Velcro for the curtains or invest in real shades.

Home ownership is romanticized when you're young and living with your parents. You want to strike out on your own, be independent, and get a place in which you make all the decorating decisions—a place in which you set the rules and no one can stop you from eating string cheese and Oreos for dinner. An apartment sounds sweet, but a *house*, now—a real house without thin walls between you and your neighbors, somewhere you can turn into an extension of yourself—that's the dream, isn't it?

I did the apartment thing while I was in college, first in Athens, then in Griffin, and enjoyed my early foray into freedom. Sure, I couldn't repaint the walls or change the light fixtures, and my upstairs neighbor was a freaking clogger, but it was liberating to live away from my dad and the confines of his roof and rules. As much as I loved my father and our house in the woods, I'd been homeschooled all my life, and we generally avoided people. I wanted to make friends with my neighbors and grill on my porch and have company in to watch movies and eat pizza. And that's what I did: for four years, I lived on my scholarships and generous stipend from Dad, met people my age who, incredibly, couldn't tell poison ivy from kudzu, and tried to decide how I wanted to fledge. The world lay open before me, and Dad suggested that a few years in Atlanta might do me good.

But the mountains had their hooks in me, and though I considered internships in Atlanta and Nashville and even Los Angeles, I ended up packing my truck and going home after graduation.

Of course, I needed a place to *land* once I returned to Ragged Gap. Dad offered my old bedroom, but coming back to your childhood house, where you're surrounded by your poor adolescent decorating choices and can still hear the echoes of the Saturday morning cartoons you used to devour, feels a bit like failure when you're desperate to make it on your own. Instead, I took what I'd saved up during college, searched through the foreclosure auctions, and found a midcentury cabin for a steal. It was a definite fixer-upper, but it squatted on a decent patch of wooded land that sloped down to a creek, abutted only by a hunting property. I bought it, did my happy dance, then began the restoration process and realized just what I'd gotten myself into.

The problem with being a sorcerer in a small town is that you've got to keep the extent of your abilities quiet. Sure, people knew by then that I wasn't someone to be trifled with, but I still couldn't just ensorcell my cabin into a five-bedroom chalet. *Subtlety* was the name of the game, as Dad had stressed all my life, so I pulled up home improvement videos, drove myself to the hardware store, and put in the hours that long, miserable summer.

Oh, I didn't do *everything* the hard way—I fixed the plaster and let the paint apply itself one night as I swore at the cheap air conditioners I was trying to install in windows that probably hadn't had right angles on the day they were built—but I kept up appearances. I hung shutters, power-washed a couple decades' worth of grime off the cracked cement portion of the mostly gravel driveway, and removed rotten boards in the front porch. With Dad's supervision, I climbed up on a ladder and replaced missing shingles. I installed gutter guards and plugged mouseholes and called out an expert to inspect my septic system. I needed a new water heater on day one, the ancient refrigerator died on day ten, and by the end of the first month, the washer and dryer had likewise given up. While Dad helped me install the replacements, he stepped back and made me do the work of finding appliances and figuring out how I was going to pay for them and get them home.

I *did* cast a spell around the place to keep out termites, but as Dad had done likewise, he had no room to complain.

By the end of that August, I collapsed on my thrift-store couch, looked around at my habitable if somewhat undecorated living space, and decided that interior design could wait.

In the five years since, I hadn't exactly gotten around to turning my house into a showplace. The couch and bathroom had been upgraded—magically, though I didn't tell Dad—and I'd installed ceiling fans and hung a television over the fireplace. My apartment furnishings from college were a functional mishmash that did the trick, and I'd splurged and bought a plush bedside rug so I wouldn't wake to a cold floor in the winter. The cabin's other bedroom served as a storage unit, as Dad had surprised me on my twenty-third birthday with a prefabricated shed large enough to do me for a workshop. He'd even paid for my new outbuilding to be rigged for power and water, though he'd left me to find the tables and sinks and bins and yet *more* air conditioners I'd need to get it up and running.

With most of my time and money going right back into the business, I let the dream of a photo-ready home go by the wayside, happy just to have a place to crash and a reasonably reliable roof overhead. And so the paint peeled until I got around to patching it, the small paved portion of the driveway cracked anew each winter, and I kept putting off the ordeal of hanging bedroom shades.

I rolled out of bed and shuffled to the kitchen for a cup of tea, which, as usual, I groggily muttered into existence by floating the kettle under the spigot and then onto the stovetop while the teabag unwrapped itself. I liked my tea as iced and sweetened as the next Georgian, but first thing in the morning, a hotter, more concentrated dose of caffeine and tannins hit the spot. While a mug removed itself from the cabinet and the brew came together, I pulled out my chair, scrunched my eyes closed against the dawn, and ordered the bread into the toaster and the butter to the table.

Look, if you're going to have magical powers, you might as well let yourself be lazy in the morning.

As I sipped and chewed, I made my plans for the day. First thing would be foraging while it was still nice and cool. I wanted mushrooms for my pantry, but I was also eager to hunt for late goldenrod and maybe the very last of the lavender. While my property wasn't all that large, my neighbor didn't mind when I picked flowers on his hunting land...or if he did, he never told me about it. Frankly, since I'd planted the garden on my side of the creek to begin with, I figured that anything growing on his side was a bonus. Once I'd poked around close to home, I had a few prime foraging spots in the hills to visit, which could take me a few hours. I'd pack a sandwich and make a full morning of it, then have time to visit Dad in the afternoon and bring him dinner. He was brewing that day—just *what* he was brewing, he hadn't told me, but he'd said it was one of those brews that required round-the-clock supervision to ensure the final product turned into a useable potion instead of a fireball. I'd offered to help on brews like that, which would at least give Dad a chance to sleep during the process, but he was a stubborn perfectionist who insisted on overseeing the brew himself.

That, and letting me help would have violated the terms of his licensure. Even in his second career, Dad remained a government man, and his authorization to grow and brew said nothing about bringing in an uncertified relief sorcerer. Thus, while Dad had taught me a fair bit about the theory of potion assemblage and creation, he wouldn't let me near the stuff he made for exportation.

Fortified with toast and tea, I brushed my teeth, pulled back my hair, and changed into my mucking-around jeans and long-sleeved shirt. Hiking boots offered a modicum of protection against snakes. I threw together a sack lunch, which I left in the fridge to take with me once I'd searched my backyard and the creek area for useful produce, then grabbed my canvas foraging bag and headed out into the morning.

September can be muggy—summer sometimes clings with a vengeance—but that morning was crisp and lightly breezy, just under sixty degrees and cloudless. I hunted through my flowerbeds, pulling a few useful blooms, then started down the sloping hardwood-dotted yard toward the creek for a bit of light trespassing. The creek was seldom more than a rivulet, maybe six inches deep and a couple feet across, though I'd seen how quickly it could rise during heavy rains—never enough to put my house in jeopardy, but to a level where I recognized the awesome power of water to scour and shape the land.

As I looked down the creek's length, I noticed what appeared to be a furry brown lump lying on my neighbor's side and paused. If anything with teeth had come over for a drink, I didn't want to interrupt, and I assumed the animal would soon catch wind of me and amble off. But the lump didn't move, which suggested a less charming alternative. I'd found my share of dead critters by the creek—decomposing birds, a headless squirrel, a bloated raccoon—and while I normally let nature take its course, I didn't want anything as large as that corpse seemed to be to sit and rot out my back window for weeks. Praying that I wouldn't get down there and find a dog with a collar and tags—no one wants to have to make *that* phone call—I left my bag on the ground and jogged over for a closer look.

Well, it sure as hell wasn't a dog.

What I'd seen was a pair of legs—goat legs, to be precise, covered in curly brown hair. The hooves were lightly muddied, nothing unusual. The rest of the body had been covered with a black garbage bag, which someone had taken the trouble of weighting down with fallen tree limbs and haphazardly camouflaging with leaf litter. I didn't want to know what was beneath the bag—whatever was awaiting me wasn't going to be pretty—but since there was no way I was going to leave the goat there to skeletonize, I steeled my nerve, gave my breakfast firm orders to stay down, and pulled aside the covering.

And then I took a few steps back, stared at the corpse, and swore while my brain tried to catch up with my eyes.

The goat...*wasn't*.

Where the rest of its belly, head, and forelegs should have been was a body that seemed way too close to human. Arms with tanned skin and short-nailed hands extended from the sleeves of a faded Lynyrd Skynyrd T-shirt. Like the legs, the head also bore a dark mop of curly hair, but from the protruding forehead rose a pair of thick horns that curled back and around the ears. The corpse's mouth was almost closed, but its wideset eyes were open, revealing brown irises and rectangular pupils. Its ears were slightly pointed and pierced, with what appeared to be a sapphire stud in the right and a diamond in the left.

After a moment's stunned reflection, I realized I'd stumbled across a dead faun.

That alone would be cause for concern—we may have Bigfoot in the mountains, but fauns aren't native to Georgia—but the fact that the faun appeared to have a bloody gunshot wound through its shirt suggested I'd wandered upon a crime scene. This was a homicide.

Faunicide, my overwhelmed brain so helpfully offered.

Common sense and an adolescence of *Law & Order* reruns told me what I needed to do next: call 911 and let the police handle it. But since the apparent victim was a freaking faun, I couldn't very well invite the local cops to take a look around. Instead, I went with plan B, which was pulling out my phone and taking photographs of the scene, just in case something happened to it before I could find a more responsible adult to clean up the mess.

I put the garbage bag back in place and started with wide shots, trying to capture exactly how the faun had been dumped, then removed the bag again and focused on the body. When I prodded at the corpse with a stick, the limbs seemed stiff—rigor mortis, I thought, making a note on my phone. It was just after eight, so maybe someone who knew about decomposition could work backward from that. I needed to get in closer for documentation, but that meant *touching* the body, which necessitated a trip to my workshop. I kept plenty of nitrile gloves on hand for cleanliness when I mixed and packaged, and I double-gloved and tucked in the cuffs of my sleeves before handling the faun.

Thus shielded from contact and having locked my phone, I returned and resumed the glamour shots. I took pictures of the faun's pale face and mismatched earrings, moved to the torso, then turned my attention to his arms.

Wasn't there something about bagging hands?

After another trip back up the hill, I taped sandwich baggies around the faun's stiff fingers, then looked for anything distinguishing on his arms. The right one was just dirty and purplish in patches underneath—livor mortis, I guessed—but the left had a tattoo on the bicep, a heart encircled by two dates with the letters KII in the middle. A memorial, I guessed, and the second date was only about ten months past. I puzzled over the letters in the heart while I took pictures, then recognized them as a transliteration of a Pactish word: *mouse*.

He got ink done over a dead mouse?

At forty-eight, though, it would have been the world's longest-lived mouse, so maybe it was a nickname. And that might explain the ring the faun was wearing on his left hand—not gold, nothing so expensive, but maybe tungsten or steel.

I moved down the body, turning my attention to the goatish legs. Having zero experience with fauns, I was grateful to learn that his *equipment* seemed to be of the retractable variety—or if it wasn't, it was small enough to be hidden within his hair, and I sure as heck wasn't going to poke around for it. With that photoset finished, I wriggled his T-shirt upward, exposing the bloody hole in his chest, and tried to get good photos before something started eating the corpse. Finally, with the shirt returned to its place, I rolled the body over—no easy task, as it was literally dead weight—and photographed his splotchy flip side. I noticed a wider hole through the back of the shirt where the bullet must have exited, and then I caught sight of his stubby little tail, which was as unyielding as the rest of him.

Putting the faun back as I'd found him, I made yet another trip up to the house and returned with the big tarp I used for raking leaves. I covered him as well as I could, weighting the edges down with rocks and limbs, then stepped back, caught my breath, and cast a spell around the area to hide the body from view. I could still see it if I looked properly—the spot seemed to shimmer like a haze—but the average human would walk right on past.

Still, I knew this wasn't a long-term solution. The faun wasn't going to recover and amble away if I left him alone, and I *really* didn't want to try to mask the stench of decomp.

I could have incinerated the body with ease. Fire had always come naturally to me, much to my dad's chagrin when I was an angry toddler, and I could have made a little funeral pyre without setting the woods ablaze. But I had the sinking suspicion that the guy had been married. Even if this Kii person was dead, maybe the faun had family looking for him. Parents, in-laws…kids, even.

I couldn't leave him to rot in my backyard, and I couldn't make him vanish without letting his loved ones know where he'd gone. Besides, since I didn't see a gun anywhere near him, he'd obviously been murdered. Forget the fact that there was a faun in Ragged Gap—we had ourselves a killer, and that was a much more concerning proposition.

With a sigh, I put my phone in my pocket and started back to the house, knowing full well that Dad was *not* going to be amused.

I took my sweet time stalling. The gloves needed to be tossed, of course, and I carried the few flowers I'd picked out to the workshop for drying, and then I made another bracing cup of tea...but soon, I ran out of excuses to put off ruining Dad's day, and I dialed.

He picked up on the third ring. "Janie?"

"Hi, Daddy."

He hesitated, then asked, "What's your bail?"

"I'm not in jail," I hastily reassured him, and grumbled, "Don't plan to start now."

"Uh-huh. Did you forget that it's brew day?"

"No, and I'm sorry, but, uh...there's a dead faun in my backyard, and it looks like he was shot."

Silence stretched across the line for a moment.

"Are you *sure* it's a faun?" Dad finally asked.

"I mean, it's either a faun or else someone stitched half a dude to half a goat and glued on some horns. Oh, and he's got goat eyes, too, so unless someone in Ragged Gap has been buying costume contacts—"

"Really?"

"Hang on," I said, and scrolled through my camera roll for a good overhead shot. "There," I said as I texted it to Dad, "you tell me."

What I heard next was the ding of a received message, followed by quiet profanity.

"Yeah. I've got the area as secured as I can make it, and I left him where I found him," I continued, "but we've got to do something."

"Burn the body," he replied without hesitation. "Keep the fire small, but get rid of the evidence."

I scowled at the kitchen cabinets. "*No*, are you crazy? That's a person with a family and friends and stuff, and he may have been murdered, and I can't just cover this up and leave them to wonder!"

"Janie, listen to me," said Dad. "An unmasked faun running around out here is up to *no* good at all."

"Maybe he had masking jewelry, and whoever killed him stole it."

"Unlikely. He's not even wearing pants! Honey, you need to make this go away."

I took a deep breath, hastily collecting my thoughts. "Ignoring for a moment that his family surely has a right to know what's become of him," I said, pacing the kitchen, "there's a decent chance that whoever killed him is still around. The body's within sight of my back door, Dad."

"Maybe it was your neighbor. That's hunting property, isn't it? Maybe someone mistook the faun for an animal."

"Dove season just started," I countered—the Baptists had been advertising a weekend outing—"and I *know* that whatever hit the faun in the chest isn't the sort of ammo you use for birds."

"Birdshot."

"Whatever. So either there's someone in town who killed a faun, now knows that fauns *exist*, and is probably freaking out, or else there's someone in town who killed a faun and *doesn't care*." I paused for that to sink in, then said, "You need to call this in, Dad. Getting rid of the body would just be slapping a bandage on the situation."

He grumbled, but I waited him out.

"Can you keep the body hidden until Tuesday?"

"*Tuesday*? I don't have a deep freezer that big!" I protested. "And if I leave him sitting out, he's just going to rot and attract scavengers. We need a professional *now*."

"I understand," he said, "but this brew's just getting started, and I can't leave. It's going to be at least Monday afternoon before I can handle a detective—"

"I can handle one."

Again, Dad fell silent, but I pressed on that time. "I'm not a little girl anymore," I reminded him. "And the faun's by my property, anyway. Surely I can talk to a cop without the world coming to an end. You babysit your brew, I'll take the fuzz out to the body, and we'll all go on about our day, yeah?"

"Janie…"

"I'll be careful," I insisted. "I can do this, Daddy."

"Janie," he murmured, "if they find out about your mother…"

He had a *good* point, and so I chose my words carefully. "Wouldn't it be worse if they found out that you'd covered up a murder, too?"

Dad said nothing for a few seconds, then softly sighed.

"If someone catches on, you can fib your way out of this," I pressed. "Just tell them that she ran away before she could take the draught, and you couldn't find her. If they want to go hunting for her and drag her back, *fine*. Maybe then she'll have the decency to look me in the eye and tell me why she split," I muttered. "Not your problem."

"Until I'm asked to testify. Or given truth serum."

"Okay, so you opted not to kill someone. Wow, what a monster," I deadpanned, and leaned my back against the counter. "You've got a real bunch of winners running the Pactlands, don't you?"

"It's…complicated."

"Not where I'm standing."

"You've very young," he replied, but sounded resigned. "I…I have a friend at Laws. We worked together on a few cases. I think I can trust them to be discreet, but…"

"But?" I prompted.

"Once your existence gets out there, I won't be able to hide you again. There are going to be some uncomfortable questions."

"I'm ready," I told him, trying to sound confident. "It's all right, Dad. I'll keep you safe."

After another long, silent stretch, he said, "Okay," and cut the call.

CHAPTER 3

The rule hadn't changed since my earliest childhood: if Pact agents came around, I had to hide.

When I was a little girl, Dad sat me down and explained how the game was played. He came from a place called the Pactlands, an artificial world created as a refuge for beings humans might otherwise hunt to extinction: elves, trolls, fauns, and even sorcerers like him. Judging by his descriptions, the Pactlands was nice, at least as pocket worlds went—the air was breathable, the water was potable, and the weather was mild, even if the topography was more utilitarian than aesthetically interesting. Unfortunately for the peoples of the Pact, they couldn't completely sever themselves from the world they'd escaped because plants grew extremely poorly in the Pactlands, and no one had yet discovered a feasible workaround. Much of the uninhabited land was little more than prairie, trees rarely grew taller than hip high, and the dedicated agricultural regions were magically tethered to the outside world, a complicated and expensive undertaking. Thus, master growers and brewers like Dad were licensed to operate outside the Pactlands, where they could keep greenhouses full of useful plants and ship their wares back across the border.

Of course, not everyone with a license was always on the up and up, so the Division of Plants and Potions sent its agents to make quarterly inspections of the facilities. Since Dad wasn't running a magical meth lab, he received glowing reports and got to keep his license—convenient for us, as no one within the Pactlands knew of my existence.

Our saving grace was that DPP's people didn't make the trek out to Ragged Gap more than once a quarter. The nearest portal into the Pactlands was hidden near Central, over the state line in South Carolina, about an hour away. The agent assigned to Dad's facility always called ahead to schedule convenient inspections, which usually kicked off around dinnertime or shortly thereafter. Thus, four times a year, Dad had to hide every trace of me, but he had plenty of advance warning.

When I was a baby and he was a sleep-deprived single father, he'd taken the easy route and added a small dose of a sedative potion to my bottle that would knock me out until morning. I'd awakened none the worse for wear, or so he said, but when he overdosed me at three and I slept for two days straight, he became unduly cautious. For the following inspection, Dad cut the potion to what he thought was a safe level, only to sneak upstairs after the agent left that night and find me sitting on the rug with my dolls, wide awake and *very* chatty.

From that point on, Dad simply removed me from the house. Since he sold 'shine to many of the local families, he knew which had daughters of babysitting age who might be persuaded to watch me at their homes in exchange for pizza money, rented movies, and substantial compensation for their time. My babysitters never complained, and since I got a cheese pizza and any movie with a rating less than R out of the deal, neither did I. But that only worked until I was twelve, when I protested that I wasn't a baby in need of supervision, so Dad changed tactics: he drove me up to North Carolina, where the closest real movie theater was located, then left me with five twenty-dollar bills after extracting my promise that I'd stay put and meet him when he called. Armed with enough cash to make myself sick on popcorn and Snowcaps, I would chill in the theater all night, usually sitting through a double feature of my own design before Dad returned to take me home. Whatever I didn't spend was mine to keep, a little recompense for the fact that Dad was temporarily kicking me out of my house.

I knew Dad hated the arrangement—I could see the guilt in his eyes when he dropped me off and sped away—which is why I never gave him hell over it. Dad wasn't always the most emotionally demonstrative of fathers, but I never doubted that he loved me and was proud of me. He was my sole teacher, and he was both quick to praise when I mastered concepts and patient when I struggled. And while our house wasn't anything fancy, I knew that Dad would provide me with whatever I needed. I wasn't an *embarrassment* to him by any stretch.

The problem was that my existence was evidence of a crime.

I don't remember a time when I didn't know I was adopted. Dad never made a secret of it, and he tried to give me age-appropriate answers to my inevitable questions as I worked through my place in the universe. My biological dad had died, he explained, and my mom had to leave for a while. He couldn't tell me when, if ever, she'd be back, but he assured me that he would always be my dad. But while he had my birth certificate and Social Security card to prove my identity, he lacked the first shred of evidence of a legal adoption—one reason that Dad opted to educate me himself instead of taking his chances with public school.

Dad's answers were truthful enough, but I nagged him for more, and when I was thirteen, he finally told me the full story of where I'd come from.

In the decades before I was born, Dad had been the chief of DPP's growing facility in rural Virginia, an agency-run operation that supplied its niche and highly regulated botanical needs and still found time to come up with unique cultivars. He'd forged an impressive career of nearly a century by that point, and so he had the pick of the litter when prospective horticulturalists came up as agency hires. In 1991, he took on a promising trainee of forty, a pretty blonde sorcerer named Essa Nerin who had one of the greenest thumbs Dad had ever seen on anyone who wasn't a full-blown floramancer like he was. She was a natural, the sort of person who happily spent hours on her knees tending the beds and kept dirt in her cuticles, and despite her youth, she possessed an almost encyclopedic knowledge of exotic plants.

(Yes, Dad had insisted, forty was quite young. Sorcerers, the shortest-lived of the Pact races, often saw three centuries, and mandatory education for all children in the Pactlands lasted until thirty-five. Most government agencies wouldn't even consider applicants under forty, and Essa had made the cut at DPP because of the recommendation she'd received after her five-year internship with Dashom Brothers, an experimental greenhouse operation in the capital.)

The greenhouse in Virginia was its own community, its membership leaning heavily toward the young and unattached. The facility straddled both worlds—according to Dad, you could unlock the greenhouse door within DPP's office tower, open a second door within the suite, and step through to the Virginia side. To minimize the regulatory nightmare of people coming and going across the border, the agency strongly encouraged greenhouse staff to live outside the Pactlands. While life on the far side could be interesting, the rules were necessarily strict: no displays of talent in public, required approval for any trip more than ten miles off the property, and of course, mandatory masking for anyone who couldn't pass for human. Sorcerers were fortunate in that regard, but everyone else lived with false faces—sometimes more—so as not to accidentally spark rumors of, say, centaurs frolicking in the woods.

Once off the clock, the staff weren't exactly spoiled for choice concerning external amusements. The greenhouse was remote by design, and the nearest hamlet was barely more than a post office, two churches, a volunteer fire department, and a bar called Bobby's Place—or Bobby's Disgrace if one were the sort of patron who disapproved of sticky floors and gross urinals. The bar wasn't even great by dive standards, but when you're desperate enough, proximity trumps class, and so the greenhouse staff made semiregular forays down to Bobby's to drink cheap beer and play pool.

It was there, or so Dad said, that Essa met Aaron.

Essa was a friendly woman, able to chat with a fencepost if left with no better companion. Aaron was a local boy, a blond with dark eyes and a dimpled grin who tended bar at Bobby's. He was handsome, Dad allowed, perhaps twenty-five or so, and he could make a shockingly good martini from the bottles on offer.

After a few months, Essa didn't care that Aaron was going nowhere fast, that he was a decade and a half her junior, or, far more importantly, that he was human. She fell hard…which left Dad in an awful position.

Pact law was clear: romantic entanglements with humans were strictly forbidden. Anyone who dared to love a human was given a miserable choice, and by virtue of his position as her chief, Dad had to present Essa with her options when he caught her with Aaron in the back of the bartender's steamed-up car. The smart choice would be to return to the Pactlands that night and accept a transfer into another group, something that would keep her safely chained to a desk. The other choice—the fool's choice—would be to take the death draught.

Dad had been given several vials of the stuff to keep on hand as a warning to his more wayward employees, and he'd brought one out to drive home the point to Essa. The draught had no antidote. It would block her power, rendering her functionally human, and while it was designed to speed up her aging to human levels, anyone who spent time with the draught knew that it was *too* effective. No one who took it lasted more than thirty years, and most of the documented deaths were due to common illnesses.

If Essa gave up Aaron, she could enjoy maybe another two and a half centuries and build a solid career and a good family in the Pactlands.

She decided that price was too high.

That night, Essa tendered her resignation, turned in her credentials, and swallowed the slow-working poison to be with the man she loved…or so the official reports said.

Dad was a well-respected chief and a longtime DPP employee with barely a scuff on his file, but he couldn't condemn Essa to death. Instead, as she stoically awaited her fate—the alternative was making Dad call for backup, and she couldn't fight off the whole greenhouse—he poured the draught into the dirt, told Essa to act sufficiently queasy until she was out of the facility, then drove her back to Bobby's, where Aaron was waiting to whisk her away. He bade them good luck, gave them a few hundred dollars toward their new life together, and suggested that other towns might hold better opportunities for them. While he hated that Essa had sacrificed her life in the Pactlands for a fleeting chance at romance with Aaron, he hoped they'd have many happy decades together.

They had about eighteen months.

By then, Dad had resigned from DPP—losing a grower to the draught wasn't his fault, his colleagues insisted, but he still decided that it was time for someone new to take the helm. Having easily secured a brewer's license, and having long been a certified master grower, he moved down to Ragged Gap and built his own greenhouse. Semi-retirement suited him nicely, and he appreciated the quiet of solo living in the mountains.

Somehow, Essa found him, and she didn't come alone.

She showed up on his doorstep one cold night in March 1994 with heartbreaking news: Aaron was dead. He'd taken a job as a late-night convenience store clerk because the money was better, and a robber had shot him for two hundred bucks in the register and a few dozen packs of cigarettes. Essa had begged him to stay on the day shift, but Aaron was determined to support them because she had to quit her job.

After all, someone had to look after me.

I was only a few weeks old, a chubby, brown-eyed baby with a thatch of cornsilk hair, or so Dad told me. Essa knew that her forged papers wouldn't withstand the scrutiny of a police investigation, so she'd taken me and fled South Carolina, loading Aaron's car with just the necessities. She'd spent nearly everything she had to pay that month's rent and buy diapers and formula, and despite the risk, she'd resorted to magic to keep me clothed.

Dad never had children of his own, but he saw how desperate Essa was, and so he let us stay.

In the days that followed, Dad took over my care while Essa alternately slept and cried. He knew she was depressed—postpartum hormones plus the loss of Aaron must have sent her into a tailspin—and he let her be, leaving food outside the guest room door and occasionally knocking to see if she needed anything. But on our fifth morning there, as Dad carried me into the kitchen to start the coffee, he found a note waiting on the table. Essa apologized, but she said she couldn't handle a baby, especially without Aaron. She'd left my few things and Aaron's belongings behind, but she gave him no phone number, nor any indication of where she was going and when she might return.

So that was us, then: Dad and an infant of unknown talent.

He called me by the name my parents had used, the one gift they bestowed on me before disappearing from my life.

I wondered sometimes if Dad ever wished I'd taken after Aaron.

Apparently, there's no way of knowing how any given hybrid is going to turn out. Most of the folks in the Pactlands stuck to their own kind, which sort of made sense—I mean, I couldn't exactly see a naga and a troll getting freaky, and I could hardly imagine what their offspring might look like. When Essa dropped me on Dad like a crying hot potato, he had no idea which of my progenitors I might favor. Would I end up with a sorcerer's power and a human's lifespan? No talent at all but impossibly slow aging? Something in between?

At twenty-seven, I was still a cipher in some respects, but one thing had become clear to Dad when I was just a toddler: I had power, and not merely ordinary sorcerer abilities. For reasons Dad could never explain, I was a born pyromancer, unusually gifted with fire.

Let's just say that my tantrums were the stuff of *legend*, and Dad invested in multiple fire extinguishers to keep the house intact.

If I'd been untalented, then Dad could have passed me off as a random human baby left on his doorstep, or even as the unfortunate child of Aaron and poor draught-weakened Essa. After all, the draught snuffed out talent in the drinker's children, too. Instead, he had a baby pyro on his hands—a half-human pyro, sure, but one in need of training nonetheless.

Beyond the lack of paperwork establishing him as my father, Dad couldn't risk sending me to school for fear that I'd lose control. In a perfect world, he'd have shipped me off to the Pactlands to get a proper education, or at least to place me with a family better equipped to handle me. But since revealing my existence would almost certainly lead to the discovery that Dad hadn't forced the draught on Essa, the best he could do was teach me himself, both in ordinary academic pursuits and in magic. While I did well enough on the scholastic side to get into college, my magical education was somewhat patchy, far more practical than theoretical in its focus, and limited in scope. I mean, I could change my appearance on a whim and start fires with barely a thought, but Dad *still* hadn't taught me to brew.

We both knew that as long as I stayed hidden in Ragged Gap, I'd never reach my full potential as a sorcerer. Dad wanted the best for me, but he had to balance that against the possibility of prosecution—all scruples aside, he'd broken the law. Besides, if Dad were incarcerated, who would look after me? As the years passed, he feared the specter of imprisonment less and less, but he and I both doubted that anyone who would arrest him for sparing my mother's life would welcome me into the Pactlands.

But I was grown now—maybe not a full-fledged adult by Pactlands standards, but capable enough to live on my own in Georgia. By almost any metric, Dad had done a damn fine job of bringing me up. Now that I didn't need his care to survive, however, Dad's calculus was shifting. What were a few years on a penal farm if I finally got the opportunity to study under real teachers and fully master my abilities? Still, Dad didn't jump to turn himself in, and he could breathe more easily during his inspections since he no longer had to worry about hiding me. But I schemed. Surely, I reasoned, I could throw together a cover story that would get me a glimpse across the border without inculpating Dad.

Well, whether I was ready or not, this was my big chance. There was a corpse in my backyard, and I was determined to do the right thing.

Around eleven that morning, about an hour and a half

after Dad made a call to the Pactlands, I peeked out from behind the dining room curtain as a black Jeep pulled up to the house.

"I've known Detective Birrid for a long time," Dad murmured beside me, squeezing my shoulder. "The Division of Laws liaises with DPP as needed, and Liogh's been handling DPP cases for at least fifty years. They're only about thirty years older than I am, so we sort of grew up in our agencies together."

The mention of DOL made my stomach flop, but I tried not to show it. "Nymph, right?"

"Yup."

I'd never seen one in person—not that I knew of, at any rate—and Dad hadn't shown me pictures to prepare me. The extent of my knowledge of the species was that they were born with elemental powers, were one of only four of the Pact races with the ability to brew potions, and were functionally immortal. I'd asked about a language barrier, but Dad had said that this wouldn't be a problem. He'd taught me Pactish, the Pactlands' standardized creole, from a young age, and he insisted that Liogh was fluent. "Hell," he'd added, "they come out here enough that they probably speak English. Don't worry about that."

Thus reassured that it wouldn't be taken as a slight if I couldn't string together basic greetings in Nymphic, I mentally rehearsed my plan. Be cool. Be professional. Don't stare.

And be wary of nosy cops.

"I did mention that's Liogh's nonbinary, right?" Dad asked as the Jeep's door opened.

"Yeah."

"It's common among nymphs, more like a third gender than 'none of the above,' but Pactish doesn't have good terminology for it. If you use the wrong words, they probably won't be upset. Just do your best, eh?"

I nodded and peered through the glass as the detective walked around toward the door—then quickly ducked behind the wall when I realized I was in view.

Dad left me to wait by myself when the doorbell rang, and I heard him greet the detective in Pactish, his voice warm but slightly strained. "Liogh. Thanks for coming. I'm sorry to drag you all the way out here, but—"

"It's no trouble," the newcomer replied, their tone higher but equally friendly. "Good to see you again, Yacovi."

It made sense that Dad's colleague would use his real name, but since he'd always been 'Coby' to me, it struck me as strange.

"I'm sorry it's under these circumstances," said Dad.

"Of course. But since you saved me from a day of case reports…"

Dad hissed. "No weekend for you, huh?"

"Not right now. Nor for you, either," they added with an exaggerated sniff. "What's brewing?"

"Healing potion—my brew room is at the back of the house, but the smell permeates. Just be glad it's not Happy Juice."

I silently concurred. Healing potion was a pain to brew, but it smelled like cinnamon and vanilla with a touch of lime as it came together, and the house smelled more like a bakery than a lab. "Happy Juice," a potion that was more or less an energy shot on steroids, smelled potently of sauerkraut, a stench that could linger for days and was impervious to all air fresheners.

Liogh chuckled. "Are you still distilling?"

"I am, and I'll send you home with a bottle for your pains," said Dad. "Last I checked, 'random murder' wasn't your beat, but—"

"Not my first body," Liogh assured him. "I may not be the detective who ultimately handles this case, but I'm certainly willing to take a look. A *faun*, you said?"

I heard the front door close and footsteps start in my direction. "Wouldn't have believed it myself if I hadn't seen the photos. Come with me, I've got your witness in the dining room."

This was it. I took a deep breath, tugged my shirt straight, and tried to radiate calm.

As Dad escorted Liogh through the doorway, my first thought was that they made an odd pair. Dad was—well, *Dad*, a middle-aged man of average height and build. He kept his brown hair short, which did nothing to hide the gray that had begun to sprout at his temples and spread. He wore what I'd come to think of as "brew couture," a long-sleeved gray T-shirt and wash-faded jeans, both of which were decorated with a rainbow of stains and splashes. While stain removal via magic was easy enough, Dad never bothered. The detective, on the other hand, was a solid head taller than Dad and thin—*willowy*, I thought, fluid in their movements. On first glance, they struck me as Middle Eastern in descent, or perhaps South Asian: brown skin, large brown eyes with a thick fringe of lashes, a slightly crooked nose, and long black hair pulled back in a ponytail. With their blue polo shirt and khakis, they could have been heading to the golf course. But what seemed strangest to me was that this person, though several decades Dad's senior, appeared to be about my age.

Liogh gave me a quick once-over, then looked to Dad for an introduction.

"Jane," he said, continuing the conversation in Pactish, "this is Detective Birrid from DOL. Liogh, this is…"

He paused only long enough to meet my stare.

"This is my daughter," said Dad. "You're going to want to talk to her."

Liogh's eyes widened as they glanced back and forth between us. "You never told me you had a family, Yacovi!"

"Just Jane," he murmured. "It's the two of us."

"Hi," I said, approaching, and reflexively stuck out my hand.

Liogh shook it and smiled, some of the gravity of the situation they'd been called to investigate momentarily forgotten. "A pleasure." They studied me more carefully as they released their grip, and a small wrinkle formed between their eyebrows. "I admit that I'm no great judge of sorcerers' ages, but you're rather young, are you not?"

"Twenty-seven."

They cut their eyes to Dad. "You managed to get permission to raise a child outside the Pactlands? I'm impressed."

Dad smiled but said nothing.

"I mean, I probably shouldn't be surprised," Liogh continued. "Anyone who could keep the DPP greenhouse going for as long as you did must know how to get by over here. But...huh. Well," he said, turning back to me, "better to meet you late than never. Now, what's this about a faun?"

"He's at my place," I replied, and cocked my thumb toward my truck, parked in front of the house near Liogh's Jeep. "Want to ride or follow me?"

"I'll follow," they said, and headed for the door. "Yacovi, can I give you a lift?"

"I can't come," Dad told them. "The brew shouldn't be left unsupervised..."

"*Ah*. Of course," said Liogh, though they sounded a little disappointed.

"But you're in good hands with Jane. I'll let you get to it."

I nodded to Dad as I passed him, and he pulled me in for a quick hug as Liogh stepped outside. "Be careful, little girl," he whispered, then pushed me on my way.

CHAPTER 4

As I parked in front of my house, I told myself this would be fine. This was absolutely not the worst idea I'd ever had. Nothing would go wrong, and I'd handle myself beautifully in front of Dad's colleague.

The detective. With at least a century's experience.

Trying to convince myself that I wasn't going to make a mess, I shaped my face into what I hoped was a sufficiently neutral and not at all suspicious expression and stepped out of my truck.

Liogh was right behind me, and they unfolded themself from the Jeep and slid a black leather messenger bag across their chest as I hurried to unlock the cabin. "Come on in," I called over my shoulder. "I left a box of gloves in the kitchen if you didn't bring your own."

"Much appreciated," they replied, and paused on the mat to wipe their shoes clean—hiking boots, I noticed, a practical choice for the mountains. This was absolutely not Liogh's first time in the field.

"So, uh…" I began lamely as they latched the door, "do you want to see the body?"

"In just a moment. Gloves?"

I beckoned the detective into the kitchen, and they glanced around the room with polite interest. "Here you go," I said, thrusting the cardboard box toward them. "There's plenty more in my workshop, but I'm afraid they're all the same size."

They chuckled and pulled out a pair. "We'll make do. Now, help me out…Jane, was it?"

I nodded, internally bracing myself.

"This is your home?"

A softball. I could handle that. "Yes…uh, Detective," I replied, catching myself as I fought the southern instinct to end every utterance to an elder with *sir* or *ma'am*. Dad only affected the practice when necessary to blend, just like he put on a convincing accent, but I'd somehow absorbed the linguistic tic. "I bought it after college. Been fixing it up. Slowly," I admitted, considering the horribly dated cabinetry and scuffed Formica countertops.

"I see." They snapped their gloves into place. "Rather young to move out on your own."

That was a question disguised as a statement, and I trod carefully. "Not around here. It'd be kind of weird if I still lived with Dad."

They grunted. "Keeping up appearances, then?"

"Something like that." I gave them a moment's consideration, conscious that the silence stretching between us just might be deliberate. "Dad said you're a nymph."

"He's not wrong," Liogh replied with a little grin. "Masking is a necessary evil out here, you understand."

"Sure, sure," I said with feigned confidence. "Uh…what kind of nymph? Or is that a totally rude thing to ask?"

To my relief, they didn't gasp in horror. "Water. Not the flashiest of talents, but at times, it's useful." Once again, they studied me, and I could practically see the gears turning. "You've never met a nymph?"

"Not unless they were masked and didn't tell me."

"Hm." They opened their bag and rooted through it, then started piling items on the counter—a laptop, a charger, what seemed to be a power converter. "No sense in bringing the full kit to the site," they explained. "So, have you lived here your whole life?"

"Most," I replied. "I was born in South Carolina, but Ragged Gap is home."

At that, their dark eyes focused on mine, and I realized I'd said too much. "You've never lived in the Pactlands?"

"No," I said tersely, and started gloving up. "Uh...I took some pictures earlier, just in case. You can pull them off my memory card if you want."

"That would be great, thank you. But you've never lived there? Not even for school? Which you *should* still be attending," they added disapprovingly, then dropped me a wink when I met their stare again. "Of course, I'm not a truancy officer, so your secret's safe."

I could lie, I mused. Tell the detective that I'd commuted or some such. But then they'd surely ask me details about my school and classes, and I'd be out to sea.

"I've never been to the Pactlands," I murmured, then quickly insisted, "But I'm okay. Dad homeschooled me, and he's got a sweet collection of grimoires, so I can handle myself."

Liogh considered that in silence, then grunted again and closed their bag. "Well...I suppose you'd better show me this faun."

I didn't know if I was off the hook yet, but the corpse out back was definitely a more pressing problem than my educational situation. "This way," I told the detective, heading for the kitchen door. "He's technically on my neighbor's land, but it's a hunting property, and my neighbor seldom comes this close."

"I should hope not," they replied, following me into the yard. "That sounds dangerous."

"At least he hasn't mistaken me for a deer yet. See the hazy bit? That's where the body is."

Liogh and I walked quickly down the slope to the creek, and I broke the camouflaging spell. "There you go," I said, awkwardly hanging back as the detective approached. "Uh...like I said, I took pictures..."

"Is this how you found the body?" they asked, gesturing to the weighted tarp.

"No. I didn't want to leave him exposed out here...did

I screw up?" I asked, my anxiety spiking.

"Doubtful." They removed the rocks, then methodically pulled back the tarp, revealing the hooves and legs of the deceased. "Did you touch the body? Move it?"

"Just for pictures, and I was wearing gloves. I didn't know how soon anyone was going to get here to examine him, and I was trying to collect evidence in case the bugs got to him or something started scavenging, and—"

"Calm down." They turned briefly to flash me a grim smile. "I just need to know so we have the full story. Now, let's see your face," they muttered to the corpse, and flipped back the rest of the tarp.

To my surprise, the detective recoiled almost immediately, then collected themself and crouched for a closer look.

"He had a garbage bag over part of him to start with, plus some leaves," I said. "There's a hole in his shirt, and it's wider in the back, so there may be a bullet in the dirt."

"And the bags around his hands?"

"I thought that's what you're supposed to do," I mumbled.

"Good impulse." They gently brushed the faun's hair from his face, then noted his bicep tattoo and moved his arm back and forth for a better view. "You say you found him this morning?" Liogh asked, standing.

"Yeah. I came out here to forage and saw him."

"Forage?"

"I, uh...I make soaps and lotions and stuff. Toiletries. Hence the gloves and the workshop."

One corner of their mouth ticked. "I didn't *think* you were brewing with Yacovi."

"He won't let me. Says his license won't allow it," I added, hoping to score Dad some brownie points with the fuzz.

"Mm. Were you here last night?"

I wasn't about to confess to magical arson. "After dark.

I slept here."

"You didn't hear gunfire?"

"No…" My eyebrows rose. "You think it's a dump site?"

"Perhaps. It will bear investigation."

"Any idea who might have killed him? Or who he is? I don't exactly know how many fauns are around…"

"Thousands," Liogh replied, "but I do know this one. Daniot Frim," they said, folding their arms as they stared down at the corpse.

"Friend of yours?" I asked, praying I wasn't about to step in it.

Liogh sighed. "Not exactly. Frim was a producer," they said, keeping their gaze on his discolored remains. "Groups of them sneak out here illegally to make their product. Potions, drugs, anything that can be used to get high. He wasn't a big-time player, but his group produced for Silver."

"Is that an organization?" I ventured.

The detective glanced at me, momentarily surprised, then seemed to recall his audience. "No. That was the *business* name, if you want to call it such, of a high-ranking elf who's now doing considerable time. He was the kingpin, if you like. Anyway, we were tracking Frim's group with a farseer. Do you know what that is?"

I quickly racked my brain. "Farsight's a wild talent, right? Like floramancy?"

"Exactly. Our farseer could follow things remotely in real time. Most of Frim's group was savvy enough to take the blocking potion—it stymies farseers," they explained before I could ask—"but Frim's dose degraded, and his human girlfriend was unprotected. Did you see his ink?"

"Something about a mouse, right?"

"That was her nickname, Kii. Legally Melanie Pickett, as I recall. And since there are two dates here, I think it's safe to say she's deceased…" They squatted by the body again and squinted at the tattoo. "Fairly recently. This puts her death at last November. Forty-eight," they said softly, and shook their head. "I realize humans are short-lived, but she went *young*. Wonder what happened."

"Rival gang or something?" I suggested.

"Maybe another of Silver's groups. If those two ended up on a hit list, I wouldn't be shocked. Leaving Frim like this is almost certainly a message." Seeing my bemusement, they straightened and asked, "Has Yacovi told you about the death draught?"

"Yeah," I replied, resisting the urge to hug myself. Playing it cool was significantly harder than I'd imagined while chatting beside a corpse.

"We caught Frim and Kii in Georgia about a year and a half ago. Given his file, he was looking at substantial prison time, the sort that wouldn't see him free again until she was long dead. So we gave him a choice: return to the Pactlands and face justice, or give us the information we needed on the rest of his group, take the draught, and go live out his days with his lady."

I fought to keep my face still. "Suicide, you mean."

"Yes," they said simply. "They fucked us over in the end. Once we let them go, they called their little friends to warn them, we were careless, and by rights, we should be dead now."

"What happened?"

"Short version, if you're arresting a siren, make sure at least one member of your party is wearing earplugs. It's the only good thing my snoring has ever done. Life tip," they added with a smirk, tapping the side of their nose. "Try not to get punched in the face."

I frowned. "Huh?"

"My colleagues who've overnighted with me compare my snoring to heavy machinery. On that trip, my boss made everyone earplugs. The farseer was using them to focus as we approached the producers' camp, and when the siren surprised us, she wasn't overcome because she couldn't hear him. Managed to wake the agent who's currently her fiancé, and *that* became a mess unto itself, but…well, I digress. We took the rest of the group back to the Pactlands, and Silver had almost all of them killed in custody. The lone survivor was the siren, and he's in solitary now for his own protection." Nodding to the faun, Liogh said, "I wonder if Frim regretted the deal we made. He was young enough—he could have done his time and still had plenty of life to enjoy. Instead, he chose this. Less than a year with Kii, and less than two all told."

"It was a shitty choice."

Liogh cocked an eyebrow.

"Either kill yourself slowly or never see your girlfriend again? What sort of choice was *that*?"

The detective stared at me, and I forced myself to hold their gaze. After a moment, they said, "Speaking as an agent of the Division of Laws, Frim knew the risk."

"And speaking unofficially?"

"Unofficially, you're right. The more I see of the draught, the less I like it. The farseer I mentioned, both of her grandfathers took it. If you want to talk about messed-up families…"

"Shit," I muttered, then turned my attention back to the corpse. "You said that leaving him like this is a message?"

Liogh grunted. "That's what I'm afraid of. Before we let Frim and Kii go, we put a permanent mask on him—he passed for human when he left. If you're an elf or sorcerer and you die having masked on your own power, the mask falls apart, but if you die with a permanent mask on, it's not supposed to break. Frim certainly couldn't have done it. And look at him—no necklace, no rings, no masking jewelry to change his appearance back."

"He's wearing earrings," I offered.

They shook their head. "He had those when I last saw him. They're ordinary studs. So what this suggests is that someone *knew* he was masked, killed him, and took the mask off before dumping the body here. At the very least, it tells me his killer wasn't human."

"And you think it's just a dump site? He wasn't killed here?"

"No. Come here," they said, and carefully rolled Frim onto his side. "Look at the dirt below the body."

I bent closer and peered at the forest debris...and then it clicked. "There's not enough blood."

"*Exactly*. I see the exit wound," they said, pointing to the bloodstained hole in the faun's T-shirt, "and given the location, I'd expect to find a pool. His back should be covered, and the leaves should be bloody. But since there's little to no blood here, it looks like someone cleaned him up, and you tell me you heard no gunfire behind the house last night..." They eased Frim back into position, then dug in their bag for a camera. "I do want your photos, but let me take my own."

I stepped back, giving them room to work. "Do you want help?"

"Well," they said, pausing to snap a picture, "that depends. Please tell me Yacovi has taught you to levitate objects."

I might not have had the most extensive magical education, but I was able to save Liogh the trouble of hauling their victim up the hill. Once they'd finished taking pictures, they jogged back to their Jeep for a blue body bag, and I muttered my familiar spells until the faun floated into the bag, then out of my yard.

I crunched across the gravel driveway. My cabin was sufficiently remote that I didn't worry about folks spotting us while the body bag glided along in front of me. "So...back seat?" I asked the detective, eyeing their vehicle—good for rough terrain, but not exactly a hearse.

"Not quite. Hold him there for just another moment, won't you?" they asked, then opened the trunk and pulled up the black carpet to reveal a metal trapdoor. I leaned closer when Liogh turned and started climbing down a ladder into a space that couldn't have existed without serious magic at play. Breaking the laws of physics wasn't a new concept to me—I mean, Dad's greenhouse was almost as long as a football field, but from the outside, it looked like an ordinary storage shed. Still, I'd never seen the trick worked on a vehicle before, and as Liogh flipped on the lights in the hidden compartment, I could tell that no expense had been spared on the Jeep.

"If you could send him feet first, that would be great," said Liogh, wheeling a gurney into position.

I did as they asked, then climbed down after Frim, only to find myself in a mobile laboratory. Gray tile floors, black workbenches, basins and beakers and a whole cabinet of colorful potion bottles secured to one wall...the place was several times larger than the SUV and as well-equipped as Dad's brew room.

"What the *hell*?" I muttered.

Liogh chuckled briefly as they maneuvered the laden gurney to a latched black case the size of a refrigerator. "I don't always take agency vehicles, but they can be pretty useful." When they lifted the lid of the case, a cloud of fog rushed out—cold storage, I gathered. Liogh slid the corpse inside and latched the lid, then turned to me and shrugged. "When Yacovi called and said there was a potential murder, I took one of the mobile morgues. Easier to transport Frim home."

I could have poked around in the lab for an hour, but I climbed out of the hole and scooted down from the Jeep's trunk. As Liogh closed the trapdoor and fixed the carpet, I said, "Hope you find whoever did this soon. If I've got a killer on the loose in Ragged Gap, especially one with magical talent..."

The detective grimaced as I let that thought die unfinished. "Question."

"Shoot."

"You don't have any cameras at the rear of the house,

do you?"

"No. The only traffic I get back there is from wildlife. However…"

Liogh followed me as I walked away from the Jeep. "Idea?"

In response, I pointed past the side of my cabin toward the shallow creek and woods around it. "See the big oak down there? The one with the lightning damage halfway up?"

"I…think so, yes."

"Do you see the camo-colored bands going around the trunk? Two of them, skinny."

They stepped closer to me and shaded their eyes as they squinted into the distance. "Yes…"

"Trail camera. My neighbor's got them all over his property. He likes to know what's out there—deer and trespassers both. *That* one," I continued, pointing to the creek camera, "used to face my backyard, and we had words about it. The angle's not great for our purposes, but if our victim was dumped down there, the camera might have caught something. If we can pull the rest of the footage, maybe we can get enough to ID the shooter."

"Good plan," they replied with a curt nod. "And how do we access the pictures?"

I turned and cocked my thumb toward my truck. "We negotiate. Hop in."

If you opened the dictionary to the word "curmudgeon," you might find a full-color picture of my neighbor, Jerry Parker, in lieu of a definition. Jerry was a bald, eternally frowning Vietnam veteran who'd mostly kept to himself since coming home from Asia. I'd heard that his wife, Sandy, was a sweetheart, but she'd died when I was a little kid. Jerry had a son and daughter, and grandkids besides, but he generally divided his time between his cabin halfway up a mountain and Junior's, a hole-in-the-wall bar where the tourists never ventured. Junior's had little to recommend it but cold Bud and cable, so if football was on, Jerry could be found bellied up to the bar in his ratty camo jacket, enjoying a modicum of human companionship and saving on his TV bill.

My path might never have crossed Jerry's but for three peculiarities.

First, despite all logic, Jerry had found...not *friends*, exactly, but people willing to listen to him while sober at Mystic Mountains. His gruff exterior was, I gathered, a protective measure; Jerry had seen some shit during his tour of duty, and he'd brought a fair bit home with him. I don't know who dragged him into that store in the first place, and whatever they sold him was no substitute for therapy, but he'd been a loyal customer for years. And because he'd stuck around for a while, he'd heard the usual rumors about me.

Which brings me to the second point. Jerry's hunting property was fairly large, but it was bounded on all sides by neighbors with no inclination to sell. When my cabin had become available, Jerry had apparently been primed to buy it until he got to the auction and saw me there. I hadn't tried to look threatening that day, but I suppose my reputation was sufficient to make him back down and let me have the property. I'd tried to thank him on his way out, but he'd just grunted and marched off to his truck.

As for the third, Jerry and I had seldom spoken in the years since, but he'd been to my house exactly once. I hoped I wouldn't have to dredge up that visit, but it was ammo nonetheless.

I'd visited his place only twice: once to discuss the trail camera aimed at my kitchen, and the other to deliver a bottle of moonshine that one of Jerry's buddies had ordered for him from Dad as a Christmas gift. Thus, while I had his address, I let the GPS guide me. Roads in my neck of the woods could be winding and poorly marked, and I didn't always trust my memory.

As I drove, I gave Liogh the sanitized version, explaining only that Jerry was a reclusive grump who wasn't altogether fond of me. They considered that, and as the GPS directed me onto a narrow trail up a hill, they asked, "Do you anticipate violence?"

"No," I replied. "Jerry's got guns, but he never waves them around." I paused then and cut my eyes to Liogh, who couldn't have passed for a local if their life depended on it. Even if they'd masked themself as a stereotypical good old boy, their accent was unplaceable—presumably normal for the Pactlands, but definitely not Georgian. "Listen, I know you're the cop and all, but let me do the talking, okay?"

"Sure." They glanced at me, faintly smirking. "Does Mr. Parker not like strangers, law enforcement, or both?"

"Any and all of the above, I think."

"Shocking. I'll follow your lead."

A few turns later, at the top of a little road dearly in need of fresh asphalt, I parked in front of Jerry's cabin, which was substantially larger than mine but in far nicer shape. Jerry's hobbies included hunting, watching football, and home improvement, and I followed the buzz of a power saw and the smell of fresh sawdust to the open door of the workshop shed adjacent to the house. I waited for him to finish his cut, then knocked twice on the doorframe and stepped back.

Jerry turned, then raised his plastic safety goggles and peered at me. "Fortune?"

"Hi, Mr. Parker," I said, raising a hand in greeting— and to show him my lack of weapons. "I'm really sorry to bother you, but could I talk to you for a second?"

He sighed but walked out from behind his workbench, sawdust coating the arms of his plaid flannel shirt like snow. "What is it?"

"There's been a…"

I paused, not wanting to say *crime*. Jerry had little use for police, but if someone was committing crimes on his land, he might take it personally and do something stupid.

"An injustice," I told him. "One I've been asked to look into."

He shoved his hands in the pockets of his jeans and stared at me.

"The person responsible may have cut through your property," I continued. "I need to see your trail cameras."

At that, his bushy eyebrows rose. "Which ones?"

"All of them. If you can give me a map, I'll go pull the photos. Save you a trip, and I'll put the cameras right back like I found them."

"*Hell*, no. I'm not letting you screw around with my gear."

I sighed, digging deep for patience. "Please, Mr. Parker. This is *sensitive*—"

"And who the fuck are you?" he interrupted, looking past me at Liogh.

The detective nodded. "Leo Beard," they replied in a surprisingly good American accent—not nearly southern enough to escape scrutiny, but passable.

"Friend of mine," I hastily told Jerry. "He's helping me with this…issue."

Jerry's eyes narrowed. "You some kind of foreigner?"

"Leo's Romanian," I improvised. "We went to UGA together. He got a great tan in Florida while lifeguarding this summer. Doing a Master's down there, right?" I asked, turning to Liogh and silently pleading with them to play along.

To my relief, they flashed a winning smile. "Accounting."

I wasn't sure if Jerry fully bought our story, but his xenophobia dropped from a near boil to a slow simmer. "Look, I don't know what you've gotten yourself into," he said, looking back at me, "but it ain't my business, and I don't want no part of it. Stay off my land."

I hoped nymphs weren't mind readers, as what went through my thoughts at that moment was hardly what one would consider ladylike. The asshole was forcing my hand.

"Mr. Parker," I said, keeping my voice low, "I know you don't want trouble, and I'm not trying to make any. But there's someone who needs my help. Like your Bethany did when her ex was beating on her. Remember that? You came to me, and I fixed her problem, and I didn't ask for a dime."

"That's *my* land—"

"And *this* is when you pay it forward," I snapped as flames sprung to life and licked down my arms.

Jerry jumped back, bumping into a worktable, and gawped at my display.

"You know what I can do," I murmured. "I don't want to threaten you, Mr. Parker. I won't hurt your cameras, but I need to see what's on them. That's all I'm asking. Give me a map so I can find them, and we'll be out of your hair."

"Put that out," he ordered. "Are you crazy? There's enough sawdust here to set the mountain on fire."

I obliged, then pushed up my sleeves to show him my unburned skin. "Map?"

He stormed into his workshop, where he yanked a notepad and pencil off a metal drum. "Y'all stay where I can see you."

Liogh and I held our positions in silence, waiting for Jerry to finish his work. After a few minutes, he tore a sheet of paper free and emerged from the shed, then thrust the map into my hands. "Get lost, Fortune."

"Thank you, sir," I replied, and started for my truck with Liogh.

"Hey, boy," Jerry called after us. When Liogh turned around, he asked, "You some kind of freak like her?"

"I wouldn't go that far," they replied, and hopped into the passenger seat before Jerry could press them for details.

CHAPTER 5

"**S**orry about that," I muttered as I sped away from Jerry's house. "Should have warned you. He's low-key racist, and he definitely has suspicions about anyone born outside of the state, so...thanks for backing me up. If you've got a better cover story in mind, I'm all ears."

"No, yours was perfectly acceptable," Liogh replied. "I'm not upset about that."

Feeling the pressure of their eyes, I turned and found them studying me again. "But you *are* upset?"

"Not upset. Surprised." They waited while the GPS barked an order, then said, "You're a pyromancer."

"Uh...yeah."

"Interesting."

They fell silent as we drove down a gently curving road lined with hardwoods. The leaves were still green that early in September, but within a month, the wash of reds and yellows heralding full autumn would be upon us. Glancing to my left, I spotted a deer standing in the shade and willed it to stay on its side of the street.

After a time, Liogh cleared their throat. "Your father has a wild talent, I believe. He's a floramancer, yes?"

I nodded. "So he tells me. I've peeked in the greenhouse, and I'd believe it."

"Does he not grow the plants you use in your products?"

"He's never offered, and I wouldn't ask." Catching Liogh's raised eyebrow, I explained, "Dad's particular about the greenhouse—he only grows plants for export in there. Says he doesn't want to do anything to risk his license."

"That's wise, even if it leaves you somewhat inconvenienced."

"Eh." I shrugged. "I like foraging, and it makes the job a little more exciting. Gets me out of the house."

Liogh waited for a quarter mile or so, then said, "Must have been challenging for Yacovi to raise a pyro."

"He trained me well," I said, gripping the steering wheel. "It's under control."

"Having seen that display, I'd agree…though I *am* curious as to why you thought it was prudent to do that in front of a human."

Shit.

"I…fucked up," I admitted. "When I was a kid. I thought some people in town had talent like mine, and it turns out they just play at magic without having the first bit of actual ability, so I scared them, and they didn't want me to come around after that. But rumors spread, you know, and when folks are desperate enough, they do crazy things like come to me."

"You help them?"

"What else am I supposed to do? This is my town, and if people need help, and I'm the only one who can make a difference…that's an obligation. What use am I otherwise?"

"This may come as a surprise," they replied dryly, "but you're not required to cure the ills of the world just because you were born a sorcerer."

There was a scenic pull-off by a creek a few yards ahead of us, and I swung the truck over and put it in park. "The first person who asked me for help was Sara Crow. We were seventeen. She caught me when I came into town to grab a pizza. Her mom hadn't been in the picture in years, and now that she was growing up, her dad was trying some shit with her that no father should do to his kid."

Liogh winced.

"Yeah. She wanted to run away with her boyfriend, but Daddy Dearest told her he'd shoot the kid if she tried—and since Daddy was a sheriff's deputy, he had pretty good aim."

"What did you do?"

"Waited until Sara was out of the house, then went up to the door, stood on the welcome mat, and remotely applied pressure to that asshole's testicles until he was on the floor, begging for mercy. Told him I'd take them and his dick besides if he ever touched his daughter again. Then I blew up his truck for good measure. Not the patrol car—that's taxpayer money—but he had a sweet F-250 with plenty of chrome and custom wheels. Can't exactly explain *that* to your insurance company."

"Did he listen?"

"Well enough, I'd say. I saw Sara about a month later. He'd given her the keys to the house and left town. She and her boyfriend were married by the time I came home from college," I added. "Couple of kids. I doubt they see much of their grandpa."

They considered that, absently rubbing their chin. "And…no one raises an alarm about you? No one tries to get rid of the sorcerer in their midst?"

I shrugged. "No one knows I'm a sorcerer—they just know I've got some abilities that I employ selectively. And this is a small town. Folks talk. I've only done favors for about a dozen people, but since everyone knows everyone else…people don't mess with me." When the detective continued to stare, I folded my arms. "You probably think I'm an idiot. I've never told Dad about this—he may know by now, but we don't talk about my vigilante side hustle. Not really a hustle, anyway. I don't get paid for it."

Liogh's gaze didn't waver, and I squirmed. "Okay, yes, I do understand that it's a bad idea to start throwing fireballs around normies, but some of the things I've heard and seen…I can't just sit there and do nothing. 'Thoughts and prayers' don't do much when your wife gets pissed at your toddler and almost drowns him, or the nice deacon who lives next door and hangs out with your parents starts loitering outside your bedroom window, jerking off. If people are so desperate that they're willing to ask me for help, they need it." I waited for the detective to chastise me, then asked, "What, no lecture?"

"Perhaps later. We do have more immediate problems…"

"Right," I muttered, and pulled back onto the road. "Are you up for a hike, or do you want me to get the photos and meet up later?"

"I'll come with you," Liogh replied. "This *is* my investigation."

"Lucky you." I slowed at a four-way stop, then rolled on through. "Question."

"Sure."

"What's Beukal like?"

They chuckled softly beside me. "It's home, I suppose. I was born in the city, and I've spent most of my life there, so I know it fairly well. The districts have their own personalities, but overall…it's livelier than anywhere else in the Pactlands. Museums, artists, decent nightlife. Fewer solo-species pockets than elsewhere in the hinterlands. I mean, you've got some apartment buildings specifically designed for trolls, say, or gnomes, but it's more or less well mixed." They shifted slightly in their seat to better face me. "Have you never wanted to further your education there? You mentioned college…"

"UGA. I graduated five years ago and came home."

"Why?"

"Why?" I echoed, and laughed to myself. "Good question. I guess it comes down to the fact that Dad's here, and he's all I've got, and I know Ragged Gap, so…it's not great, but it's familiar."

"I'm sorry to hear that," they murmured.

"What," I asked, "that I got sucked back to my

hometown?"

"That your mother is gone. I…I don't mean to pry, but I've been friends with Yacovi for a long time, and he never mentioned a wife or a daughter…"

Clearly, I had to give him *something*, and I prayed he'd be satisfied with what I had to offer. "There is no wife," I murmured. "Dad's never married. He's not my biological father, either. *That* guy died, and my mother dropped me with Dad and split. I couldn't tell you if she's alive or dead. Anyway, that's why he goes by Hewt, and I'm a Fortune. He didn't even legally adopt me—he just took me in and brought me up."

"I see," said Liogh, and mercifully let the matter drop.

I cut my eyes to them, saw them watching the woods go by, and flipped on the radio.

Jerry's property was about fifty acres—not the largest hunting preserve in the region, but not a small patch of land—and unfortunately wasn't level ground. The Appalachian foothills weren't impressive as mountains went, but when you were traipsing up and down them on a mission, they were steep enough for my legs, at least.

The map Jerry had made us was decent. He'd drawn a rough circle with a dozen Xs around its border, plus one in the middle—the cameras, I assumed—and scrawled in notes about landmarks. My neighbor might not have liked me, but he *feared* me, which, while not ideal, served our purposes that afternoon. Since he'd gone as far as to mark my house at the edge of the map, I could orient myself to the first camera, and I suggested to Liogh that we grab sandwiches before going for a hike. They seemed amenable to that idea, and foregoing my premade lunch in the fridge, I fixed grilled cheeses while Liogh transferred the photos I'd taken to their computer.

Glancing over my shoulder from the stove as they worked, I asked, "What kind of laptop is that? I don't recognize the logo."

They grinned, then reached over the top to point to the emblem in the lid, an eight-pointed star with a recessed purple circle around it. "That's the DOL insignia. There's a tech team that designs computers and such for those of us who spend any time out here. They make sure our machines are compatible with human equipment...and then there's this," they said, flipping the computer around to show me.

I left the sandwiches sizzling on the griddle and squinted at the screen. "Is that...Windows *95*?"

"Decoy," they said proudly. "It's like a skin that can run over the real operating system—"

"But why *that* OS? It's ancient!"

Liogh's confidence faltered. "Ancient? It's only—"

"Twenty-six years old. Dad held out until the bitter end, but even he let me upgrade his computer eventually. Have your tech folks not been over here in, like, my lifetime?"

Their brow puckered as they considered the screen. "Well, yes, but this was the program they put on my first laptop, and I've just transferred it with every new machine..."

"Wait there." I quickly plated the grilled cheeses, then brought in my computer from the den and unlocked it. "If you want a decent decoy, it should look something like this. See the difference?"

"Noted," they mumbled, and quickly finished uploading my pictures while I pulled together a jar of dill spears and a bag of relatively fresh chips.

As we ate, Liogh remarked, "You're taking all of this well."

"Taking what?" I asked, biting the end off a pickle.

"Don't tell me this isn't the first body you've discovered."

"Oh, no. Definitely the first. I mean, I've had dead animals back there, but no fauns to this point." Trying to read their expression, I asked, "What, should I be balled up in the corner or something?"

"Not necessarily," Liogh replied. "People react in a variety of ways. Some panic at the scene and break down. Some hold it together. If I may offer you a piece of advice?"

I gestured for them to continue.

"Camp with your father tonight. Everything may hit you once you sleep and let your guard down, and if that happens, it would be best not to be alone. I've seen this play out with plenty of witnesses," they added, reaching for the chips.

"Thanks," I mumbled. "I was going to bring him dinner, anyway. He can't leave his brew unsupervised."

Liogh smiled to themself. "Once, for about a week, I considered handing in my badge and taking up brewing. Don't know what got into me, but I'm glad it worked itself out."

"Aw, come on, you don't like dealing with caustic plants and explosive liquids?" I teased.

"Not particularly. I'm grateful for people like Yacovi who have the patience and steady hands, but...no." They sipped their water. "You don't want to follow after Yacovi?"

"Not really. Dad's taught me the basics, and that's enough to know I don't want to make a career of it."

"Mm. Come to think of it, I don't suppose I've ever known a pyro who went into brewing or horticulture. Their talents tend to lead them in other directions."

"Beyond soapmaking and vigilantism?"

They snorted into their glass. "Yes. *Far* beyond. But that's a conversation for later," they said, and shoveled down the rest of their sandwich. "Shall we take a walk?"

I quickly washed up, stowed my computer in a tote bag as a backup to Liogh's, and led the way down the embankment toward the woods. "The first camera is there, the oak I showed you earlier," I told them as I hopped the creek. "Here, let me get the card out…"

Liogh was waiting with their laptop at the ready when I produced the memory card, but they frowned as I handed it over. "What, um…how do I…"

"And *that* is why I brought mine," I said, unpacking my machine. "Hold on, let me get it set up…"

Balancing my computer in my arms, I slotted in the memory card, waited for the computer to read it, then opened the folder to see the pictures. "Okay," I muttered as Liogh looked over my shoulder, "deer…deer… raccoon…squirrel…another deer…"

"Can you limit the pictures to the last day or so?"

"The new ones are at the bottom, and this…aw, shit. Timestamp on the last one is Friday, and that's just a possum."

"So you think our killer didn't come this way?"

"Not necessarily. They didn't step in front of the trail cam. It's a static view, and it only triggers when there's movement. See? No videos in here," I said, scrolling through the images. "Jerry's gear isn't exactly top of the line. Does the trick, I guess, but that's a bust for us. Give me a minute and let me download these, just in case."

As I leaned against the tree with my computer, waiting for the files to finish transferring, I took stock of my surroundings. The day had warmed a bit since that morning, but the temperature remained comfortable and the humidity low. A pair of phoebes called at each other, one close by, the other deeper in the trees. Glancing toward Liogh, I saw them staring into the distance as if trying to spot the next camera.

"Want the map?" I offered. "If you're anxious to get going, I'll catch up."

The detective turned back to me and shook their head. "No, thank you. What would I do until you arrived, look at the card and try to guess what's on it?"

I grinned. "Fair. Almost finished…"

A few minutes later, I'd stowed my gear and slotted the

memory card back into the camera, and I pointed up the hill on Jerry's side of the creek. "That way."

While the terrain was a tad on the rough side, it wasn't impassable by any stretch, though I was sweating through the back of my shirt by the time we reached the top of the hill. I paused for a second to catch my breath and review the directions to the next camera, then continued eastward until I spotted the landmark Jerry had identified, a lichen-laced boulder beside a pair of oaks that had germinated so close together, they'd grown up entwined around each other. He'd affixed the camera to one of the pair, and I extracted the card and plopped onto a fallen log to transfer the files.

To our disappointment, that camera offered us nothing useful, but after the uphill hike, Liogh didn't complain about the break we took while my computer worked.

The ground leveled out somewhat as we pushed onward toward the third camera, and then the fourth. By the time I was dumping the files from the fifth, I was ready for the water bottle I'd stuck in my bag on the way out the door. I took a deep gulp, grateful for the relief, then looked up to find Liogh watching me. "I'm sorry," I said, recapping the bottle, "do you want some? I'm not contagious."

"Brought my own, thank you," they replied, patting a bulging pocket on the outside of their bag.

Still, they continued to regard me like I was a particularly interesting pinned beetle, and my stomach started to knot. "Is something wrong?" I asked, hoping I sounded nonchalant. "Sorry, the computer's working as fast as it can."

"I don't mean to be rude or insensitive, Jane," said Liogh, "but the pieces aren't adding up."

"You don't think our killer came through the woods?"

"Not that. You."

I sat very still, cognizant of the humming computer and the rustling of the leaves overhead, and deployed my best poker face. "Oh?"

They slowly walked closer, keeping me in focus like a herding dog staring down a recalcitrant lamb. "Something's missing. Yacovi has never married. He has no biological children. No nieces or nephews, either—he used to lament being an only child. I understand that he might have tired of running DPP's operation, but to move here, without any close connection to the Pactlands, and spend the last twenty-seven years raising an adopted daughter…"

I willed myself not to be the first to look away.

"A daughter who's clearly a sorcerer," they continued, "given your apparent talent, but no kin to him. So tell me," they said, stopping a few feet away, "who *are* you?"

I sat frozen on the rock where I'd landed, trying my best to stay calm and think through this. Fire and the computer on my lap would be a poor combination. But as Liogh watched me, I realized that this—*this* right here—was the dumbest decision I'd ever made. Yes, the dead faun deserved justice, but to have thought that I could breeze through this day with a freaking *detective* and not get the third degree about my cover story was just stupid.

As I struggled to find a way out of the mess I'd made, Liogh's expression softened. "It's all right," they said, slowly dropping to a crouch. "I'm not here to hurt you. All I came here to do was investigate a murder—you're not part of my assignment."

Silence, at that moment, seemed like my best bet.

"Jane," they murmured, "whatever it is, I'm not going to report you. Unless you've been kidnapped and need help—"

"I don't need help."

They held up their hands in surrender. "Okay, okay," they soothed. "That's fine. But until I know who you are, I have to assume that you were brought here against your will."

They had me, and they knew it.

I sighed and put my computer on the ground, protecting it in case my nerves made something ignite. "I wasn't kidnapped or trafficked, or anything like that," I said. "My mother used to work for Dad at the DPP facility. That's their connection—they weren't lovers or anything. He was just her boss. So when she decided she didn't want to be a mother anymore, she tracked him down, left me with him, and split. The end."

Liogh's brow had furrowed as they listened to me, but a few seconds later, the tumblers fell, and their dark eyes widened with comprehension.

"Can we talk about something else, please?" I said in a rush, trying to distract them. "Like…how far do you think the next camera is? We're starting to make a more northerly turn, I think…"

Their expression didn't change, and I knew my attempt was for naught.

"I recall," Liogh said in a low tone, "hearing about a…an *incident*…in the greenhouse. About thirty years ago, shortly before Yacovi retired. It was quite the scandal at the time. A black spot on his record that none of us saw coming. It was unfair that some tried to pin the blame on him—Yacovi was always the consummate professional, the sort of chief who cared about the mission but refused to sacrifice his underlings' well-being. I'm sure he tried his best with…her…"

My shoulders stiffened under their unblinking gaze.

"He had a trainee," Liogh continued, "a sorcerer who chose a human and took the draught."

I folded my arms and stared back at them, praying for a sudden hailstorm to cut this conversation short.

They seemed to take my measure as they watched me in silence for a few seconds, then said, "You're half human, aren't you? That's why he's kept you hidden away."

A wild, reckless part of me suggested denying everything, but that wasn't likely to work. "Yeah," I admitted. "I know damn well how you people feel about folks like me, so you can cut the concerned act."

"It's no act," said Liogh, sitting back on their heels. "And I have no quarrel with you. That farseer I mentioned, the one who helped us catch Frim and his girlfriend—she's partly human, too."

"*Partly?*"

They shrugged. "Elven in all but her looks. She was born and raised in Virginia. And since you've at least heard of the Pactlands and speak this language well, you're ahead of her."

I grimaced. "Yikes."

"Exactly. Rose got Pactish from a potion, and I can't imagine how long it will take her to smooth out her accent. She's intelligible, mind you, but it's obvious that she's a native English speaker. Bizarre to hear an accent like that inside DPP," they added with a little smile, "but that's where she landed, and they're fortunate to have her."

The detective was obviously trying to set me at ease, but I didn't drop my guard. "Okay, so you've a token humanish friend. Colleague. Acquaintance. Whatever."

"I have no problem with humans in general," they replied. "But since they have a history of attacking my kind…you understand the tendency toward wariness, yes?"

"Sure," I mumbled. "If it makes you feel any better, to this point, I've only gone after humans, so…"

"Should you change your mind, I can hold my own," they replied with a brief grin. "Laws *does* train its people. But something still doesn't make sense to me," they continued, sobering. "If you're half human, then how are you so talented?"

"Y'all are the experts in this, not me," I replied. "And weren't you just telling me about your quasi-human *farseer?* Looks like I'm not such a freak, eh?"

"I might concur if not for the draught. Rose is two generations removed from it, and given that potion's instability, perhaps her existence shouldn't have been such a surprise. But you, now—your father was human, your mother took the draught, so you shouldn't have talent at all. It neutralizes power in the drinker's offspring..." They paused. "Unless..."

I sat still, watching them and saying nothing.

"Unless," Liogh said quietly, "she *didn't* take the draught."

The silence stretched between us, marred only by the snapping and rustling of a squirrel passing between the trees to my right.

Liogh broke first with a long exhalation. "I *knew* he didn't have it in him."

"Huh?"

"Yacovi. He cares about plants and people, maybe not in that order. I was *stunned* when I heard that he'd had to give the draught to one of his team. That's...not a pleasant experience, regardless of the circumstances, but to give it to a kid her age..." They shook their head. "The last time I gave someone the draught was Frim, and I had several sessions with a counselor following that. Getting ambushed by a siren didn't do nearly as much to mess me up as did putting that potion in his hand." Their mouth tightened briefly, as if they'd tasted something unpleasant. "I understood why Yacovi retired after the incident. But seeing you here, an admittedly half-human *pyromancer*...that would only be possible if your mother didn't take the draught after all."

To my supreme annoyance, my eyes started pricking. This was no time for tears and weakness—this situation called for a show of strength, maybe a thinly veiled threat to ensure the detective's silence. Instead, as my tears began their rapid escape, I blurted, "You can't tell on him. *Please*. Dad's all I have."

Liogh's face shifted from its blank professional mask. "Jane—"

"He was afraid of this," I said, picking up speed. "He didn't want to call anyone out to see the body, but I insisted, and it's my fault, and please, *please*, don't turn him in—"

"*Jane*," they said more firmly, rising. "Listen to me."

"He's my dad. He didn't want to hurt anyone," I blubbered, my vision blurring. "I'll go away, I'll stay out of the Pactlands, but leave him alone…"

I sobbed in earnest at that point, panicking and furious with myself for thinking I could handle this situation. I was supposed to be smart, a capable adult, or at least savvy enough to make up a few convincing fibs to explain myself. And *this* was the best I could do? Freeze like a deer in front of a semi and cry?

The next thing I knew, someone was gently pulling my hands away from my wet face, and I found that Liogh had knelt in front of me. "Jane," they murmured, "I won't say anything, little one. Okay? Calm down."

It took me a few ragged breaths to bring myself under control, and Liogh held my hands until my tears stopped. "You're not…you're not going to arrest him?" I managed.

They shook their head. "Technically, perhaps I should. Yacovi understands the law as well as anyone. But…you see, the people who make laws aren't usually those who have to *enforce* them. I know your dad, I *respect* your dad, and if he decided he couldn't bring himself to condemn someone barely older than a child…I can't blame him. DPP put him in that position to run a greenhouse, not kill his own people." Giving my hands a firm squeeze, they said, "Dry your eyes. Secret's safe."

My face felt like it was burning from the force of my flush, and I wiped my tears and snot on my sleeves. "You're *seriously* not going to say anything?" I pressed.

"You have my word," they replied, and pointed to the computer. "Has the transfer finished?"

"Oh, uh…" I'd forgotten about it in the last moments, and I hastily pulled it back into my lap. "Yeah, we're up. Let's see…"

Liogh waited while I scrolled through the folder.

"Anything?"

"Fucking deer."

They groaned. "Again?"

"No, really," I said, and turned the computer around to show him the view. "These deer were fucking."

"Ah." They coughed. "*Well*. The majesty of life. That's...delightful."

I grinned and packed my computer away. "Are we a little squeamish?"

"*We* just think there are certain matters that don't concern us," they replied, "and..."

"And deer porn is one of them?"

Liogh grunted and gathered their things. "Certainly does nothing for me. Shall we press on?"

Not until we reached the ninth camera did we hit paydirt.

"Okay, check this out," I said to Liogh, plopping my computer onto a boulder and scooting aside. "Saturday night. It's all in grayscale because this is night vision mode, but..."

They muttered behind me, and while I couldn't make out what they were saying, I sensed it was profane.

Jerry had set up this camera, located in the northwestern corner of his property, to face a little clearing. It had taken several photographs on Saturday around ten p.m., and the series was telling.

The first photo showed Frim and another man. Frim faced the camera, and I recognized his Skynyrd T-shirt, though he was taller and wore jeans, and he lacked his naturally goatish attributes. He was masked, I realized—and had I seen him in public, I'd never have suspected he was a faun beneath it all. His companion, a few inches taller, wore camo pants—probably Army surplus, not uncommon around town—and an oversized jacket that fell at least to his knees, an item of clothing way too warm for the time of year. Frim's mouth was slightly open, perhaps in conversation.

"Recognize him?" Liogh asked, pointing to the taller man.

I shook my head. "Not from behind."

The second photo featured a burst of gunfire. Frim's body twisted at an odd angle, while the other man—who, damn him, continued to hide his face—extended a pistol with an unusually long barrel. No, not a barrel, I realized— that was a silencer. The bright muzzle flash showed that the gun had just been shot.

Well, that explained the need for the jacket.

"Is this the murder site?" I asked, looking to Liogh. "I don't see blood..."

"Simple enough to confirm. Let's look through the rest of the set."

I switched to the third picture. Now Frim was on the ground, his shirt bloody. I couldn't see his lower half—the other guy was kneeling between him and the camera, blocking the view—but Frim still didn't have horns, so the mask was on.

"See his hand?" said Liogh, tapping the screen. "Look, you can just make out a syringe."

He was right—the shooter was aiming a syringe at Frim—but I couldn't begin to guess at the color of the liquid inside. "What's he injecting?"

"I think I know. Any more?"

The final photo showed Frim, now unmasked, being dragged out of view by his hooves—well, I assumed. His legs were in the air, and several inches of denim hung empty below the place where the shooter had grabbed him. Given Frim's sudden change in form, I was surprised the jeans had held together as well as they had.

"Still no face," Liogh remarked. "We'll look at the other cameras in the circuit—maybe we'll get lucky. But first..."

I stood back as they reached into their bag and pulled out a stoppered bottle of dark purple liquid. "What's that?"

"This," said Liogh, giving it a vigorous shake, "will show us what our camera-shy friend must have cleaned up on his way out." Noting the camera's position, they stepped into the center of the area where Frim and his killer had been, then put the bottle on the ground and glanced at me. "You're going to want to retreat."

Once I'd reached an acceptable distance, Liogh pulled the cork from the bottle and sprinted through the trees to join me. Before I could ask what was going on, something in the bottle exploded, and a cloud of purple mist billowed from the neck. It rose about ten feet before spreading, thinning, and sinking onto the leaf litter.

"What the hell?" I demanded.

The detective smirked. "Patience."

They gave the potion a few minutes to activate, then started toward ground zero and motioned for me to follow. "Take a look. What do you see?"

Much of the area appeared untouched, as if the cloud of potion had been nothing more than ordinary fog. But as I neared the spot where Frim had fallen, I saw a massive splotch of sparkling purple on the ground, like someone had upended a vat of glitter in the middle of the woods.

"Bloodstain?" I asked.

"Precisely. A *cleaned* bloodstain. There's a potion that removes blood—great in hospitals, useful for restoring scenes, and popular on the black market to cover up crimes. What that purple one does is react in the first potion's presence. It leaves a residue," they explained. "And since it was used last night, that residue is *fresh*. Stay where you are, please. Let me photograph this."

While Liogh took pictures, my stomach clenched as I considered the size of the bloodstain. Shimmery purple was better than red, but still, Frim had lost a ton of blood.

"What about the bullets?" I asked as Liogh circled the scene.

"That's next on my list," they replied. "Just a few more snaps…"

Satisfied, they returned their camera to their bag and extracted a gray, palm-sized disc with a rubber strap across it. Sliding the strap onto one hand, they held the disc flat above the ground and began making slow passes across the bloodstain. Suddenly, I noticed a bright flash from the leaves, followed by a second one a few inches away.

"Two bullets," said Liogh. "The shooter has good aim—I only noticed one wound on the body, so perhaps the bullets followed similar paths. Come here, if you will. Grab my camera."

I followed their directions, taking pictures of the glow from the leaves. "How are they doing that?" I asked.

"Metal detector," they replied. "Useful in times like this. All right, if you'll reach in my bag again, you'll find gloves…"

They only needed one, and within a minute or two, they'd retrieved the bullets and wrapped them for transport. "These will go to our forensics unit," they said as they packed up. "Not much use without the gun, but should we find a likely weapon, we'll want to compare them."

The two of us stared at the sparkly purple stain.

"Were you planning to clean that up, or are we walking on and hoping no one sees it?" I asked.

They shot me a sly look. "Want to show me what you've learned?"

"Meaning?"

"Controlled burn."

I cracked my knuckles, then focused my will until a ball of fire sprang to life in my cupped palms. "You're sure you have everything you need from the scene?"

"Torch it," they replied.

"If you say so." With that, I spun the fireball into a thin rope, then tossed it like a lasso around the bloodstain. A few muttered words anchored the perimeter and sent flames racing toward the center, licking at everything in their path. My fire burned hot, and within a minute, the area was nothing but dirt and ashes. Satisfied, I willed the fire out and turned back to Liogh. "How was that?"

"Not too shabby," they said, and pointed toward the rough trail onward. "Let's get the next camera."

By midafternoon, we'd made the circuit, but we could have headed straight back to my place for all the good it did us. Whoever the killer was, he'd managed to avoid the rest of Jerry's trail cameras, leaving us with a grand total of four useful photos, plus a bunch of goldenrod I'd picked along the way.

"So what happens now?" I asked as Liogh packed their Jeep.

"Now?" They stowed their gear in the passenger seat and closed the door. "Now we handle this. I'll see that Frim's next of kin are notified, and I'll pass this information up the chain."

"And what about me?"

They frowned. "What *about* you?"

I jabbed one arm toward Jerry's property in frustration. "There's a goddamned murderer in my town, and he knows magic. And why would he unmask Frim? That's got to be a message, right? What's he saying?"

"Too early to tell. This will bear investigation. But as for you," they said, gripping my shoulder as they held my stare, "I want you to stay out of this. Pretend you know nothing."

"But—"

"Don't make me explain to Yacovi why you're in a body bag, Jane."

I huffed my indignation. "Maybe you didn't notice, but I've got a set of skills."

"Oh, I noticed. You've got an impressive gift, but you're also underage and undertrained. Stay alive," they said, leaning closer as they lowered their voice. "I'll be in touch if I need anything."

"And what if I need something from *you*?"

They tilted their head. "Fair point. Perhaps we could trade phone numbers—cut out Yacovi as the middleman."

Once I'd put Liogh's contact information into my phone, they climbed back into their Jeep and sped away, leaving me with my unsettled thoughts. Frustrated, I grabbed my keys and headed for town. Dad would have to make do with takeout, as I sure as hell didn't feel like cooking.

CHAPTER 6

Labor Day dawned sunny and warm, perfect weather for the tourists who'd come to find a lake upon which they could float and day drink. I rolled over in my childhood bed—a full-sized mattress, not the queen to which I'd treated myself after college—and squinted at the light peeking around the old shades, wishing for a winter rain to justify sleeping in.

Either nymphs were prescient or Liogh had spoken from long experience, as I'd seen the clock about every ninety minutes since I'd first closed my eyes the night before. Frim haunted my dreams, but so too did the shooter, rendered a faceless apparition in a black duster by my imagination, a nightmarish gunslinger with improbably good aim who stalked me as I slept. I'd managed to suppress the urge to jump out of bed and run down to the cot where Dad was camping by his potions—I was a grown woman, for God's sake, not a six-year-old freaking out at monsters in the closet—but somehow, I *had* felt slightly safer attempting to sleep with him in the house.

Not that I would ever confess to such.

Grumbling, I pushed myself vertical and attended to my brief toilette, then shuffled downstairs, where I found Dad waiting on the gurgling coffeemaker. "Hey, Janie," he rumbled in his morning bass. "Sleep okay?"

"Eh," I muttered, pulling a second mug out of the cabinet for myself. "Long night. You?"

"Also long. One of the batches almost boiled over, and *that* would have been a solid gold disaster." The coffeemaker sputtered, and Dad poured for us both. "Why don't you take it easy today, girlie? Hang out here, watch some TV. I know it's not exciting, but…" He shrugged and raised his mug. "You had a hell of a Sunday," he said, and sipped.

"No rest for the wicked, I'm afraid," I replied, reaching for the sugar cannister. "And I've got plenty to do to distract myself. Unless you need help here…"

"Oh, I'll be fine," Dad assured me, "but you know you don't need an invitation if you want to come home."

"Much appreciated." I doctored my drink and smiled at him. "Love you, Daddy."

"Love you, too, Janie," he said, and kissed the side of my head. "And I worry about you, you know?"

"I'm *fine*."

"A likely story." Jutting his gray-stubbled chin toward the stove, he asked, "Were you thinking of having breakfast before you go? Because if you were going to cook, I might steal your leftovers…"

I carefully elbowed him in the arm, cognizant of the hot coffee in his hand, then dug a frying pan from the cabinet. Eggs and bacon wouldn't harm anything but our cholesterol.

Dad left me to work in peace, taking the opportunity to check on his brew, and returned just as the toast was popping up. He pulled the condiments from the fridge without asking, and I set the table, accustomed as we were to how breakfasts ran after my overnight visits. Soon, I slid a plate in front of him, then joined him with my own and reached for the butter, feeling much better with a cup and a half of Dad's cheap but effective coffee in my bloodstream.

"What's on the agenda, then?" he asked, opening the jar of peach preserves.

"Drive home, shower, and deliveries." I spread butter on my toast, then swapped condiments with Dad.

"Deliveries on Labor Day? Not even the post office

does that, girlie."

"Not to the rental management companies," I clarified. "I've got a list of mail orders to pack and ship, and then I need to go to town and talk to Bitsy."

His brow wrinkled. "Do I know Bitsy?"

"You should. Bitsy Prescott—skinny redhead, runs Ragged Gap Mercantile?"

"Oh, yeah," he said absently. "I keep forgetting that Darlene sold it." He bit into his toast, chewed contemplatively, and swallowed. "And it's *Bitsy*?"

I broke a bacon slice in half and popped a piece in my mouth. "If you were Mary Esmerelda, you might go by Bitsy, too."

Dad didn't press me for details of my time with Liogh, for which I was deeply grateful. I'd given him some vague answers the night before—we'd had to go for a hike, the murder was on camera, and Liogh had spoken highly of him—but I'd been sparse with specifics, and Dad hadn't pried. Granted, his brews could take up a ton of mental bandwidth, but I had a hunch that Dad had been around the Pact agencies long enough not to ask a civilian to rehash the details of the murder investigation she'd stumbled into.

And in all frankness, with Sunday behind me, I was more disturbed than I let on. Finding the corpse was bad enough—it's one thing to see actors with bullet holes on TV, but spotting the real thing in the wild, without the benefit of stylistic camera angles and well-placed commercial breaks, is another matter entirely. Frim wasn't a paid extra. He was dead, hours dead, and no matter what he'd done in his life, he deserved a more dignified end than being tossed by the creek for stray dogs to scavenge. Add to that the fact that I'd watched his murder play out on a trail camera, and that the killer could very well still be at large in my town, and...well, I really shouldn't have expected a solid night's sleep.

After breakfast, I told Dad goodbye and promised to

stop in for lunch—not to be social, but rather to ensure that he remembered to eat during the complicated final steps of the brew. I sped home, avoiding any road that led toward a decent-sized body of water where tourists might be congregating, and jumped into the shower for a most welcome few minutes beneath the pounding spray. I'd been judicious in my use of magic to renovate the cabin, but the master bath was the big exception. Having stared down the barrel of avocado tiles and rusty fixtures, I'd said to hell with it all and used spells to redo everything. Maybe the white marble counters were a tad ostentatious for the rest of the cabin, and maybe I didn't need twenty-five square feet of shower space with a rainfall head, a handheld head, a sound system, mood lighting, and a niche for my aromatherapy diffuser, but the way I saw it, there was no point in being a sorcerer if you didn't have a *little* fun with it.

Once I was clean and dressed, I considered my to-do list. Packing the mail orders could wait until the afternoon, I decided—it wasn't as if the post office was open, anyway. Eager for a distraction from my own thoughts, I loaded up the truck with Bitsy's order and headed down into town.

Despite the holiday, enough of the small stores had decided that the potential sales from the tourist influx were worth more than a day off, so I had to poke along behind a line of cars looking for the public parking lot before I could turn into the alley beside Ragged Gap Mercantile and zip into the loading space behind the store. Bitsy wasn't strict about delivery times, and I buzzed and waited. A minute or two later, the door opened to reveal the proprietor: five-foot-one on a good day and rail-thin, with large green eyes, a healing sunburn, and a mop of naturally red corkscrew curls, which she kept short for ease of handling. Grinning up at me, Bitsy said, "Hey, stranger! Come on in. I've got a few customers in here right now, but the stockroom is all yours."

She propped the door, and I began unpacking my

wares—a box of lotion bottles, another of soaps in three scents, a third full of packaged bath soak. Two at a time, I lugged the boxes into the stockroom and carried them to the shelf where Bitsy always kept my products. Grabbing a Sharpie from the pen cup on the counter, I rummaged through the old boxes in my section to see what remained after the last delivery, then consolidated what I could, wrote the contents on the front of the new boxes, and left the invoice on the counter beneath the paperweight Bitsy favored, a bright yellow smiley face under glass.

We had a system worked out.

I generally wasn't so hands-on with my customers, but Bitsy was different. For starters, she wasn't a native, but rather an Atlanta transplant. She'd told me her story one evening over drinks at Ragged Gap's lone wine bar. Bitsy grew up in a moneyed suburb, the daughter of a surgeon and his much younger wife. While she did her four years at UGA at her parents' insistence, her true desires were twofold: start a little calligraphy business and marry Taylor Donovan. The latter was accomplished in June following their graduation, just before Taylor started law school. The former was slower in coming, as Bitsy had taken any work she could find to support them. While Taylor crammed and pulled his hair out, Bitsy worked extra shifts and learned to economize, and her carefully budgeted earnings paid the rent and put food on the table. It wasn't a glamorous life, but Bitsy was deeply in love with her high school sweetheart, and when he wasn't trying to parse cases, Taylor was as kind as he'd ever been.

To their great relief, Taylor passed his classes and the bar, and they moved to Atlanta, where he'd found employment as an associate in a prestigious firm. Now Taylor was the one working at all hours of the day and night, giving Bitsy a breather and a chance to finally lay the groundwork for her company. Calligraphy had long been a hobby of hers, and with her rock-steady hands, she could produce beautiful invitations—and just in time, as several of her sorority sisters had recently become engaged.

Over the next four years, while Taylor traveled and stayed late billing, Bitsy built her little enterprise, one word-of-mouth recommendation at a time. She had plenty of work to keep her busy, but she made time to look after her husband, tidying their condo daily, running errands, and making sure there was a home-cooked meal in the fridge for him whenever he returned. When Taylor took her out to dinner on their seventh anniversary and presented her with an emerald tennis bracelet, he seemed tired and perhaps more distant than usual, but Bitsy told herself this would pass. Only a few more years, and Taylor would make partner—and then she would see more of him. Something *had* to give.

Two weeks later, when Taylor was pulling an all-nighter, Bitsy fixed up a plate for him and drove it to the office. A junior associate met her at the security desk, a young woman who'd lost her suit jacket after five and traded her pumps for sneakers, and chatted with her as they rode the elevator up. The associate was bubbly, practically effervescing about how nice Taylor was and what a great mentor he was shaping up to be, and Bitsy smiled with pride. *That* was the kind, generous man she'd married, helping the firm's babies find their footing.

The associate quietly laughed with Bitsy as she led her through the maze of tastefully neutral offices toward the one into which Taylor had been upgraded just a year before. Bitsy had helped him move his possessions and picked out a new rug for the space, and she was looking forward to sitting with Taylor for a moment, maybe enjoying the view of Atlanta's nightscape from twenty-three stories up. He would be so surprised and happy to see her, she just knew it.

But as they neared, Bitsy heard muffled voices behind Taylor's closed door and began to worry that she was interrupting something important. Maybe Taylor was with a client long after hours and would be embarrassed if his little wife in her capris and kitten heels walked in with dinner. The associate assured Bitsy that she wasn't barging in on anything, and she rapped a knuckle twice against the door before opening it…

…and quickly slamming it closed.

The look on the poor girl's face—the shock of catching Taylor with his pants down, fucking another associate over his desk—haunted Bitsy as she undertook the painful task of disentangling their lives. Taylor apologized, but he didn't fight for her. He didn't have the time or inclination for marriage counseling, and when he told her as much, Bitsy knew in her soul that Taylor's current affair was not his first. She wanted to rage and smash things one minute, and the next, she longed for nothing more than to curl up and hide so no one could ever know the depth of her humiliation. A love-blinded fool, that was all she was, and now she'd outlived her usefulness to Taylor.

It was her mama who drove her to an appointment with one of the best divorce attorneys in the city and paid the hefty retainer. Bitsy was brokenhearted, but her parents would be damned if their little girl was left destitute.

Taylor represented himself, which was his greatest mistake in the whole messy business. By the time the decree was finalized, Bitsy had her maiden name back and a six-figure lump-sum settlement, and since there were no children, she never had to see the cheating bastard again.

But she couldn't stay. She couldn't just find a new apartment and meet up with her girlfriends like nothing was amiss and her life wasn't in pieces—like she hadn't been played for years by the man she loved. On a whim, she rented a cabin in Ragged Gap for a week that autumn, where she could take in the changing leaves, the mountain air, and the distinct lack of fourteen-lane stretches of Interstate. Ragged Gap was quiet, no one knew her, and of the two attorneys in town, one handled commercial real estate, while the other had a small-town catch-all practice of wills and closings and DUI defense. She could live with that.

On her third day there, she walked into Ragged Gap Mercantile, which was having a "going out of business" sale, and chatted with the elderly owner. By the end of her vacation, Bitsy was in negotiations to buy the place, and she found herself a cabin to go with it. In the two years since, Bitsy had been a blessing to local artisans, as she was almost always willing to give handmade products a try. She bought on consignment at first to see whether the new items would sell, but once she knew she had a winner, she put in steady orders. Even with the cabins I kitted out, no one bought more of my wares than Bitsy did.

And she *still* did calligraphy for every major event in town.

Bitsy wasn't necessarily my best buddy—I mean, it's not like I could spill my guts to her—but we'd moved past a mere business relationship. We might have been even better friends had she not fallen in with the Mystic Mountains crowd. Bitsy's parents scoffed, but she'd dabbled in the metaphysical since she was sixteen and could sneak off to shop alone. She knew the supposed properties of various crystals, she'd done tarot readings for me over drinks, and she'd learned to make her own sage bundles, just in case something popped up in need of smudging. She'd tried to get me to come to events down the street during the early days of our acquaintance, but she'd since learned. I was happy to talk about chakras and reiki and astral projection with Bitsy, but we managed to do so without bringing up Mystic Mountains.

I'd never told her about my abilities, and she'd never asked for a demonstration, or even confirmation of what I suspected were some *wild* tales. Someone in the woo-woo brigade had to have warned Bitsy that I was dangerous. To her credit, however, she didn't shun me, and the only difference I could tell was that the invitations to come hang out at the metaphysical shop ceased to be extended.

With my schlepping and unboxing complete in the stockroom, I slipped into the store and headed for the section with my products to look for anything that needed straightening or refilling. Bitsy did a good job of keeping my stuff on display, sandwiched between a rack of soy candles from a woman in Ellijay and a collection of bath bombs from a pair of ladies in Ragged Gap—business partners to anyone who asked, spouses to those in the know. I added a few of my cards to the holder, but other than that, my corner of the store looked to be in good shape.

"Jane!" Bitsy called from the counter. "Come over here, will you? This lady just *had* to have some of your honeysuckle lotion. This is Jane Fortune," she said to the customer as I hurried to join them. "She makes everything by hand. If you've got any questions, this is the woman to ask."

The customer did have some queries, but lucky for me, I had answers to the most common ones memorized. No dyes or unnatural perfumes, but there were plant oils in my products. My stuff obviously wasn't vegan—not with goat's milk items on offer—and I couldn't guarantee a complete lack of cross-contamination, but I sterilized thoroughly between batches. Common allergens were marked on the packaging as applicable. No animal testing, but then I didn't really use anything harsh. Yes, I shipped.

By the time the tourist finished grilling me, the rest of Bitsy's browsers had taken their leave. She waited for my inquisitor to depart, then locked the door behind her and flipped the wooden BACK SOON! sign. "Got a minute?" she asked, her voice low and her eyes sparkling. "There's something I need to show you."

"Sure." I stepped aside as she passed me, then followed her into the stockroom.

"Stand by the counter, okay?"

Bemused, I took up my assigned position. "What are you hiding back here?"

"You'll see," Bitsy replied in a singsong, then flipped off the lights.

The stockroom was a windowless space, and when she closed the door to the front, I could barely make out shapes a foot from my face. "Uh...Bitsy?"

"Stay there, I'm coming."

I felt more than saw her as she joined me, a darker blot against the shadows of the stockroom. "Just a minute," she muttered, "let me concentrate..."

Suddenly, a dim but rapidly brightening glow burst forth between us, and when I stepped closer, I realized it was Bitsy's fingertips. "What the *hell*..."

She wiggled them, laughing at my shock. "Crazy, isn't it?"

"Bitsy, what...what did you..." I tried to process what I was seeing, but no logical answer readily came to mind. "Did you paint your fingers?"

"Not like you're thinking." She leaned toward me, the glow of her hands casting her face into planes of light and shadow, giving me the impression of a kid with a flashlight telling ghost stories around the campfire. "There's a new girl in town, and she's *good*. Really talented. Stephanie's been hosting her at weekly sessions all summer."

Given my relationship with the Mystic Mountains crowd, I wasn't surprised to be the last to know of its events, but the fact that they'd led to real results with Bitsy left me stunned. Sure, Bitsy was charming, but she was as solidly human as one could ask for. Humans just didn't *have* magical talent. Dad told me that some scholars in the Pactlands theorized that the odd human might be born with talent, but these were the same bunch who theorized that sorcerers had started as humans with funky mutations—plausible to me, but apparently fighting words to other sorcerers. In any case, they had yet to find proof of a full-blooded human with any magical ability beyond sleight of hand. But here was Bitsy with her light-up fingers and triumphant grin, and if what she was saying was true…

"When did this start?" I asked, catching one of her hands for a closer look at the glowing area. "Is it just you, or have other people learned to do this?"

"About three weeks ago," she said, giggling as I puzzled over her party trick. "Isn't it neat? And it's so easy! I never imagined magic could be like this! There's about two dozen of us who come to the seminars, and they're *great*."

"How are you doing this?" I demanded.

Her expression shifted toward a teasing smile. "Ooh, are we jealous?"

"Confused and concerned."

"Well, don't be concerned," she said as she withdrew her hand from my grip. "It's perfectly safe. Katarina—"

"Who?"

"That's the new girl, Katarina. Super-gifted witch, and so sweet. She's worked out these blends of essential oils to help people tap into their innate abilities, right, and once you learn to focus, anything's possible. This is just the beginning," she added, flashing me her hands as if she were showing off French tips. "Jane, this is going to be life-changing."

Though my inner awkward teenager was miffed that Stephanie had apparently allowed this Katarina woman into her clique after I had been exiled, I pushed down my old hurt feelings to deal with the much larger problem of what had to be gross potion misuse. "I've never seen anything like this," I murmured.

Bitsy clasped my arm. "Which is why you should put aside whatever tiff you have with Stephanie and come to the seminars. It's not good to work alone," she said earnestly. "Those of us in the *community* need each other, and we should help each other learn and grow. You've been on your own for far too long."

"I really don't think Stephanie wants me around."

"Well, she can be a big girl—this is more important.

Now, there's going to be a seminar tonight at eight. You should come."

I made a face. "Probably going to have to pass. I told my dad I'd help him around the house tonight."

Bitsy huffed. "Come on, you know you want to be there. He'll understand!"

"Maybe," I allowed, and sighed. "Eight, you said?"

Her smile returned. "You're going to come?"

"I'll...see what I can do," I replied, and extricated myself. "Got to go pack orders. Mind turning the lights back on before I bump into a shelf?"

She obliged, and with a little frown of concentration, her fingers stopped glowing. "I want to see you there," Bitsy said with all the sincerity of the VBS recruiters years ago as she followed me out to my truck. "This is the start of something huge, Jane—you need to be with us."

"I'll try," I promised, and backed out before Bitsy could ramp up the proselytization. Fishing my phone from my bag, I tapped the screen and held it to my ear, hands-free laws be damned.

Three rings later, Dad picked up. "Hey, Janie. If you're calling about lunch, don't worry—"

"I'm on my way," I interrupted. "Got a problem."

Dad paused. "Another body?"

"Not today. But there's something squirrelly going on in town, and I need a potions expert."

"Janie, *what*—"

"I don't want to do this over the phone. Be there shortly, okay?"

"Of course," he replied, concerned. "You be safe, honey. Is anyone hurt?"

"Not yet. I hope," I said, and signed off.

Despite his end-stage brew, Dad met me at the door before I'd even cut the engine. "Talk to me," he said, holding the door open as I jumped out of my truck.

"What's happened?"

I waited until I was inside, then pointed toward the back of the house. "Your brew—"

"It's stable. What's got you bothered, girlie?"

Sighing, I leaned against the wall and folded my arms. "There's someone new in town, calls herself Katarina. She's doing classes or something at Mystic Mountains."

He cocked his head. "All right…"

"So I stopped in at the Mercantile, and Bitsy took me to the back and showed me how she can make her fingertips glow now," I continued. "Said this Katarina person has an essential oil blend that helps people find their abilities, or some bullshit like that."

"Potion," Dad muttered without hesitation. "Eucalyptus and bitter orange won't give you talent."

"Right? But Bitsy's fingers *were* glowing, and she seemed to have control over it. What could possibly give her that power?"

He frowned and shoved his hands into his pockets. "I've got a few ideas, but all I can give you without analyzing the stuff is educated guesses. Do you think you could get me a sample? Does Bitsy have any extra lying around?"

"I didn't ask her…but I think I can make this happen," I told him. "Katarina's giving another seminar tonight, and Bitsy invited me."

"Thought you have no truck with that crowd."

I smirked. "Who says I'm going?"

Dad's eyes narrowed. "Janie…"

"I'll be careful," I insisted. "And besides, if there's another sorcerer in town, operating in the open, wouldn't you like to know about it?"

"Of course, but if this Katarina *is* a sorcerer, I don't want you getting crossways with her." He held my stare, his mouth tight. "No fires."

I rolled my eyes. "Dad—"

"*No. Fires.* Is that understood?"

"Yes, sir," I mumbled, feeling like a disobedient child once more. Pushing myself off the wall, I said, "Going to make sandwiches. Do you have any cold cuts?"

"Ham and turkey," he said, following me toward the kitchen, "but you don't have to do that."

"I drove all this way," I replied, opening the fridge. "I'm not leaving until I'm sure you're not going to pass out from hunger."

When I turned around, arms laden with sandwich fixings, Dad was waiting to relieve me of my burden. "You're a good kid, Janie," he said, dumping the bags and bottles on the counter, then squeezed my shoulder and headed back to his work. "You're a damn good one."

CHAPTER 7

Around seven that evening, I stood in front of my bathroom mirror, deciding who I wanted to be.

My childhood lessons had included the art of masking. According to Dad, only sorcerers and elves, the two most magically gifted of the Pact races, could manage it unaided—all of the others required the use of masking jewelry to manage the trick. I hadn't noticed Liogh's, but I imagined that they kept a necklace beneath their shirt. While I'd never seen a nymph in the wild, even I knew that there was no way in hell the detective actually owned the face they'd worn to Ragged Gap.

I'd learned to make masking jewelry as a side project when I was sixteen, partly for the challenge, partly because I enjoyed playing with gemstones and beads, but mostly because Dad wouldn't let me get close to the explosive potions yet, and I needed something to do. But the jewelry was merely a hobby—I'd been able to mask since I was about ten, which had proven useful when teenage acne hit. Aside from covering up the odd pimple and hiding my hair when I'd gone too long between washes, I seldom had cause to mask, but it was one of those skills that I could do in my sleep. I knew the techniques from Dad's grimoire collection cold. Honestly, the hardest part of the process was figuring out my aesthetic for the night.

I considered my reflection in the bright bathroom lights. Tanned from a summer spent foraging for plants. Blonde hair falling to just below my shoulders, veering dangerously close to "oil slick" territory at the roots. Large brown eyes with thick lashes, probably my best feature. A pair of small acne scars on the right side of my forehead. Unremarkable nose, thin and slightly upturned at the tip…where another pimple was trying to break free, damn it. Stress was *never* kind to my skin. Chapped lips that no amount of balm ever seemed to fully protect. I liked my ears, which had detached lobes large enough to support the matching triple piercings that I'd had done in college, much to Dad's dismay. Apparently, sorcerers didn't go for ear jewelry.

Not that I gave a damn.

First things first. I lightened my skin to goth pale, then backtracked and colored in a healing sunburn, especially along my part. My hair darkened from blonde to black, and I added green streaks around my face—nothing professional, but rather something that I might have done with a box kit when I was a teenager. I turned my eyes icy blue and lengthened my lashes, then added dark eye makeup and deep plum lipstick. A few more piercings helped the look, including one on my eyebrow and a little silver ring on the other side of my nose. I smiled, thickened my lips to a pout, and whitened my teeth.

The girl I was designing was a walking cliché, but I thought she could pass the smell test.

I switched my T-shirt for a burgundy velvet corset top completely inappropriate for the season, let alone the century, which I paired with black pleather leggings and Doc Martens, scuffed for authenticity. A pentacle necklace seemed too easy, so I settled for a silver pendant with the triple goddess symbol, the waxing, full, and waning moons—a sign either that I was sufficiently well versed in neopaganism to understand the meaning behind the jewelry or that I was trying to get a rise out of my presumably conservative parents without being accused of turning into a full-on Satanist. To sell it, I took a few years off my face, making it a little fuller and removing even the first hints of lines around my eyes and mouth. Granted, I looked good for twenty-seven—Dad said my aging from this point would slow dramatically, and I would actually need to mask to look my age by human standards in a few years' time—but an older teenager, insecure and searching for guidance, seemed like my best bet.

"Hi, I'm Raven," I said, listening to my voice come from a stranger's mouth, then pitched it down a bit and added significant fry. "Is this, like, the magic group? My parents are at a cookout or something stupid, so I'm here."

There. Annoying but perfect.

I locked the house and turned my attention to my truck. Obviously, Raven couldn't show up in town driving my ride—she needed different wheels, something she'd borrowed from her family. I wasn't going to try to *transform* my truck, which would have taken hours and might have left me with a nonfunctional heap of metal, but rather to mask it, giving it the illusion of a Lexus SUV. Unfortunately, since masking anything other than myself took actual work, I called up a reference picture on my phone, focused on the image, then began muttering.

Fairy tales and such are replete with references to magic words, particular syllabic formulae, often in Latin, that make spells happen. In truth, there are no per se "magic" words; sorcerers tend to work best by speaking their intention into being, and since most are taught using the same books and methods, they tend to assign the same words to a desired outcome. The majority of these standard words were in Pactish, I gathered, having seen the penciled-in notes littering the margins of Dad's old books, but anything would work as long as it put the sorcerer in the proper frame of mind. While I did speak Pactish, I *thought* in English, and so all of my mutterings were in my mother tongue.

"Shift, damn you," worked as well as anything, really.

In one way, working on the truck was a relief. Elves were innately more comfortable working with living things, while sorcerers excelled with inanimate objects. Thus, while I could mask myself without any trouble, working the kind of heavy illusion necessary to mask someone else without using jewelry would be a headache. The truck, however, seemed to listen to my orders, albeit at a snail's pace.

At least I was sorcerer enough to cast without a wand. Dad had started me on one when I was a kid just learning the basics—pretty standard for baby sorcerers—but the goal is always to outgrow it. A wand is a crutch, like using a pencil grip when you're starting to write or putting training wheels on a bike, and can help a sorcerer focus if they lack the skill to do it on their own. I hadn't used mine since I was fourteen. Dad said that some spells were complex enough that even well-trained sorcerers needed the occasional focusing tool, but most adults in that position opted for a staff, which conveyed a certain degree of gravitas to the wielder and left no question as to their general competence.

I didn't have a staff of my own, but I didn't need it that night. Slowly, the illusion of the SUV came into focus and solidified, and after about five minutes' work, Raven hopped into the leather-covered driver's seat and started toward downtown.

There was little need for me to worry about the cops unless I ended up in a ditch or drove off a mountain. My truck had long been ensorcelled to avoid radar, and I'd spritzed the license plate with a mild memory potion that would make my tag impossible to recall for a few hours. As I drove through the quiet town, however, my precautions seemed like overkill—the tourists were still out enjoying the last of their evening, while the local police were surely waiting by the biggest of the lakes to catch drunks. Thus, spoiled for choice as to parking, I pulled into the public lot and walked two blocks to Mystic Mountains, mentally rehearsing my cover story in case anyone pried.

One problem I'd thought about that afternoon was

how to explain my presence at the shop that night. Bitsy had invited me, but how was *Raven* to know? I'd mulled over a few possibilities—a friend of a friend had mentioned the store, or she was just out late and saw lights, or perhaps she'd eavesdropped earlier and learned of the event—but to my relief, I spotted a flyer in the window as I neared, three lines of white text superimposed over a colorful chakra diagram:

MONDAY 8 PM
KATARINA WELLER
UNLOCK YOUR POTENTIAL!

That the poster designer had chosen a font in the Comic Sans family was an absolute travesty, but that wasn't my problem.

The bell over the door tinkled as I walked into the store on a pleasant breeze of incense-scented air conditioning. Getting into my role, I hung back near a display of polished agate pieces, studying the place as if it truly were my first visit.

Little had changed in the two or three years since I'd been by. The front of the store was what caught most window shoppers' attention, a space filled with tables and Plexiglas display units offering crystals of various sizes, small statuary, bits of jewelry, books, tarot cards, and ritual items. A unit next to a power strip showcased a handful of selenite and salt lamps, chunks of rock with a hole drilled into the base and a lightbulb shoved up inside—pretty enough, but nothing I'd deem particularly mystical. The incense bar on the far wall was perhaps half stocked, and I saw that no one had bought the footlong dragon burner with the garnet eyes that had been there since I was a kid.

Behind the primary retail area was the sales counter, which served as a dividing point between the realms of the casual browsers and the regulars. On the right-hand side of the back of the shop was the café—still Mystic Munchies, dear *God*, though the sign had been changed from "Vegan" to "Holistic." On the left side was an open area that could be modified as needed: café seating, lecture space, yoga studio. A door at the very back of the building led to the staircase, as the business office and the private session rooms were on the second floor.

That night, the seating area had been set up with two curving rows of maybe twenty chairs all told, with another chair at the focal point. Soft instrumental music heavy on the pipes flowed from the speakers at the back, and though the café's lights were out for the evening, two glass pitchers, a hot water carafe, and a bowl of what appeared to be teabags had been set out on a table for the attendees. But what piqued my interest was the *adjacent* table, which had been decorated with a few pieces of amethyst and rose quartz, some burlap, and three stacks of small, thin boxes, the sort that might hold cosmetics tubes. One stack were white, the next were blue, and the final boxes were black. From where I was standing, I couldn't see any sort of logo, but it didn't take a genius to deduce that these were Katarina's wares.

I took stock of the assembled. Stephanie, naturally, was holding court near the tea bar. Bitsy was chatting with one of the regulars, a brunette named Didi who never spoke to me in public but had sent a cousin to me for help with a revenge porn situation. About half the chairs had already filled, and to my surprise, *Jerry* was sitting with one of the old hippies, a guy who looked like he'd enjoyed a long career as a roadie for the Grateful Dead. Most of the others were folks I'd seen flit through the store's orbit over the years—merchants, artists, a quiet woman who was married to a Baptist deacon and kept her visits on the down-low. Several of them bought from me, something of which I was sure Stephanie wouldn't approve.

And then there was Tabitha Bradley with her customary gray-streaked box braids, who was browsing through the books while she waited.

Tabitha was one of my regular customers, both for her personal use and for the two rental cabins she'd bought as investment properties. She was a pharmacist—not just a drugstore employee, but a compounding pharmacist who had her own place in a strip mall near the grocery store. She also bought from Dad, which was how I'd made her acquaintance. When I'd started working out the kinks in my initial product line, I'd invited her to lunch to pick her brain for safety concerns, and she'd been gracious enough to chat with me. In the years since, we'd gotten together for the occasional meal or glass of wine. While we weren't precisely friends, I had nothing but respect for Tabitha as a sort of mentor—she, too, was a small business owner, and she'd been at it a lot longer than I had.

Given her profession, it might have seemed strange that Tabitha was a peripheral presence in the Mystic Mountains crowd. She'd be the first to warn starry-eyed newbies about the potential dangers of, say, keeping malachite in their water bottles, and considering her thoughts on mystery smoothie additive powders, I doubted she put much stock in the purported benefits of the beverages on offer in the café. But Tabitha was a Wiccan, she'd explained in our early acquaintance, when her pentacle had slipped from beneath her shirt. She'd been practicing since her college days, but she kept that side of herself somewhat private, as a good chunk of her churchgoing customer base would surely disapprove. Indeed, she'd laughingly told me one night, her grandmother, a pillar of the AME church back in Savannah, threatened to call the minister every time the subject arose. While she'd participated in a coven in her younger years, since moving to Ragged Gap, she'd become a solitary practitioner, observing the Sabbats as she could and performing the odd magical ritual. I wasn't an expert in her beliefs by any stretch of the imagination, but I appreciated that she was sincere about her faith and willing to answer questions without proselytizing—and she insisted that she only practiced white magic, which was more than I could say. Some of my work definitely had a gray cast.

Much as I would have liked to pull Tabitha aside and ask what she'd heard about this Katarina person, I played my role, by which I mean I stood awkwardly in the front of the shop, letting my attire and my overdone makeup tell my story for me: older teenager on her own, trying to figure things out, wanting to fit in with someone *cool*. After a few minutes, Stephanie took the bait.

"*Hi*, there," she drawled, beaming as she made a beeline for me. "Are you here for the seminar?"

I nodded.

"That's great!" Her smile widened, and she stuck out her hand. "I'm Stephanie. Welcome to Mystic Mountains. Don't believe I've seen you in here before, uh..."

"Raven," I mumbled.

"*Raven*. That's pretty. Are you visiting?"

I tried to convey the depth of Raven's suffering in her sigh. "My parents have a cabin. Got it last year. They insisted that I come on this *bonding* vacation before going back to Athens..."

Stephanie winced in sympathy. "Not going so well?"

"Ugh. They just want to go drink with their friends, and my little brother is glued to his Switch, so..." I shrugged. "Here I am, I guess. If that's okay."

"Of course." She put a hand on my bare shoulder and smiled again. "You're most welcome, sweetheart. Why don't you come with me and get something to drink, hmm? We're about to start."

I slunk along behind Stephanie, casting wary glances at the other participants and nibbling at my lip, which seemed to do the trick nicely. Soon enough, I had a glass of lavender iced tea and a seat in the front row between Stephanie and one of her staff, Penny, a matronly woman with long gray hair and a closet full of broom skirts. Before I had time to do more than lie to Penny about my nonexistent undeclared major, the door to the staircase opened, and out strode a stranger. She was unreservedly pretty, a tall, shapely woman with a golden-blonde C-cut, big blue eyes, and the sort of porcelain complexion that fries at the first hint of sunlight. Her ensemble, a flowy green blouse over jeans, spoke more of the suburbs than of the secrets of the universe, but she'd accessorized with gold hoops and about half a dozen thin gold necklaces studded with semiprecious focal pieces. She flashed a dazzling smile at us, and as the crowd applauded, I understood that this had to be the mysterious Katarina Weller.

She strode to a spot a few feet from the middle of our semicircles, standing close enough to convey a sense of intimacy and eschewing anything resembling notecards as she spoke. "Hi, y'all!" she said, and laughingly motioned for the clapping to cease. "Y'all are too much. It's great to see everyone tonight…and some new faces, too," she added, letting her gaze linger on Tabitha and me. "Wonderful! I'm glad you could all be here."

Her accent sounded genuine, I thought—maybe not north Georgian, but probably not from anywhere north of the Mason–Dixon Line. It didn't seem like an act.

"So," said Katarina, clasping her hands, "has anyone had any successes they'd like to share this week?"

Bitsy's hand shot into the air, and the others laughed as she did her best impression of an overeager schoolgirl. "Me! Let me show you!"

"Come on up, Bitsy," Katarina replied, beckoning her forward, and Bitsy hurried to join her. "Now, what did you want to demonstrate?"

Bitsy scrunched her face in concentration for only a few seconds before her fingertips illuminated, and she grinned triumphantly up at Katarina.

"That's *wonderful!*" Katarina purred. "You must have incredible focus. I'm so proud of you," she said, and pulled Bitsy in for a hug. "Looks like someone will be moving to the advanced level tonight."

Once blushing Bitsy had returned to her seat and dimmed her fingers, Katarina looked around at the assembled. "Anyone else? Has anyone who's had a breakthrough experienced any difficulty of late?"

"Not me!" said the old hippie, who happily wiggled his glowing fingers. A woman did likewise, then another, and when I glanced back toward the front, both Penny's and Stephanie's fingers were alight.

Katarina clapped for them. "*Y'all.* I'm speechless. You are *such* a talented group of people, and I'm so privileged to be here to help guide you through your awakening. Now," she said, taking her chair, "what I thought we could do tonight is some meditation—let's work on tricks to help you *really* solidify your focus. That way, once we move on to magical techniques, you'll be pulling them off in no time."

With that, Stephanie got up to dim the lights, and Katarina led us through a forty-five-minute guided meditation with a backing soundtrack of ocean waves and gentle strings. I played along, but the meditation was pretty mundane—a little drawn-out for my taste but inoffensive. It was only once the session ended and the sales began that my radar for hinky behavior pinged.

"For the benefit of our new friends," said Katarina, lifting a white box off the display table, "*this* is the secret that will help you become your most gifted self. I call it Oil of Life. It's all natural, non-GMO, nontoxic, vegan, and allergen-free. You can use it on yourself, your children, your pets…though once you try it for yourself, you might just hog it," she added with a stage whisper. When the laughter died away, she said, "I bet you've tried essential oils in the past—maybe you've had great experiences, maybe not so great. I *guarantee* that this is the last essential oil you will ever need…and it smells lovely, too!"

She opened the box and extracted a pink glass vial about the size of a fat tube of mascara. "This is the beginning dose, a full week's worth. You can dab it on your wrists and at the third eye," she explained, tapping her forehead with two fingers, "but if you really want to accelerate the effects, take a little sip before bed. What this oil does is help unblock your energetic flow so that as you meditate and practice focusing, your innate power will awaken."

I tried not to look dubious about *that* load of hooey.

"You see I've got three colors of boxes over there," said Katarina. "Beginner, intermediate, and advanced, if you like. The dosing changes as you acclimate to the oil. All of our friends here tonight who've begun to show that energetic flow in their fingers are going to be getting those black boxes, right?"

A few of the attendees cheered.

"*Finally!*" she said in mock frustration. "But for our newbies, I want you to be able to try Oil of Life without any great financial commitment. Ten dollars is all I ask to change your life."

At the end of my row, Tabitha raised her hand for Katarina's attention. "What's in this blend of yours?" she asked.

Katarina smiled. "Well, now, that's proprietary, but I assure you that it's all natural—"

"So is hemlock," she countered. "I appreciate your assurances, but without an ingredient list…"

"*Tabitha,*" Stephanie scolded, turning to stare at her, then flipped on her fingers. "Look at what it does! Stop being so picky—this is *magic!*"

"It's okay," Katarina insisted with a smile for both women. "I appreciate your enthusiasm, Stephanie, but…Tabitha, was it?"

She nodded.

"Believe me, I understand your reservation. If I were you, I'd have serious doubts. I mean, this must seem like snake oil, right?" she said, shaking the pink vial to a chorus of knowing chuckles. "Now, you've seen how Oil of Life has begun to work for your friends—the finger glow is just the first sign of success. Let me show you what it can do for you in the long term, eh?"

Gamely, Tabitha gestured for her to proceed.

Katarina's smile didn't falter as she tossed the vial into the air, taking advantage of the shop's high ceiling. Her lips parted ever so slightly before it began its downward trajectory, and though I couldn't hear whatever she whispered, I knew she'd cast a spell when the vial froze inches above her head and began to slowly flip over.

The surprise on my face wasn't just an act. I was in the presence of an apparent sorcerer, who was casually casting in front of a room full of humans with no more concern than if she were demonstrating techniques at the weekly knitters' meeting at the library. Tabitha gasped, but as she was the only one, I took it that this wasn't Katarina's first such display of talent.

I'd never been to the Pactlands, but even I was *pretty* sure there were rules about this.

With another whisper, the vial flew back to the display table, and one of the glass tea pitchers floated into Katarina's hands. "Refill?" she asked sweetly, and topped up stunned Tabitha's glass as the others clapped. "How about you, dear?" she offered, turning to me.

I held up my cup and tried to stay in character. "I'm, uh…I'm good…*whoa.*"

She laughed and sent the pitcher back to the beverage table. "Didn't mean to blow your mind. But this is why I'm so passionate about Oil of Life. I was just like y'all, looking for the secret to real power, the ability to tap into my own gifts. And if *I* have these abilities now, then *you* certainly do," she said, holding the stares of some of the most fervent attendees. "I want that for all of y'all. That's why I keep the price as low as I can—just a little more than what it costs me to make the oil. Let it be the key that unlocks your true potential."

I hung back as Katarina's customers lined up with cash

and cards in hand to pay for their week's supply of the seemingly miraculous elixir. Last to approach was Tabitha, who handed over a folded bill for one of the white boxes. Katarina grinned and shook her hand, promising her that she wouldn't regret taking the first step on her new journey. As Tabitha moved aside, Katarina noticed me and beckoned me closer. "Hi, sweetie. Do you want to give it a try?"

"I, uh…" I feigned a brief struggle, then blurted, "I'm going back to college in a few days, and I *want* to try it, I really do, but I'm not going to be able to drive up here next week for a refill."

Katarina's expression warmed. "Oh, no problem! You can buy a couple boxes at once. Most folks here just get one at a time because we see each other so frequently, and you'll want to move up to the next level once you see progress…but tell you what. Let me do this." She plucked two white boxes from the stack, then added a blue one. "Three weeks' supply. I've got a good feeling about you, and I'm almost *positive* that you'll be ready to advance after two weeks. Switch to this one," she explained, wiggling the blue box, "once you notice a faint light around your fingertips. Don't wait for a full glow like you've seen here tonight—just a little change is all you need. For you, student discount. Twenty bucks?"

I smiled and thanked her with as much effusiveness as I could muster, then clutched my little boxes like I'd won a prize.

"If you can get away, I'll be back on Friday night for another seminar," said Katarina as she slipped my cash into a pleather zip pouch. "Think about it." Reaching across the table, she clasped my free hand and stared into my eyes. "This can be *life-changing* for you. Trust me."

The night quickly wound down after that. With the last of her sales made, Katarina started packing her wares, and Stephanie walked me to the door, encouraging me to visit. "You're in Athens, right? That's only about an hour and a half with good traffic. Come join us when you can. Visit our website," she said, pressing one of her business cards into my hand. "There's a mailing list you can join that will tell you when Katarina's holding seminars. Or if you need other supplies, books, anything, just let me know. We've got a great community here, and I'd love for you to be part of it, Raven."

I plastered on a smile for her. The last time Stephanie had spoken to me with such kindness, I'd been that gawky girl on her bike, looking for friends and eager to learn, not yet a threat to Stephanie's dominance. Part of me was shocked that she allowed Katarina to work from her store, but then again, Katarina was promising Stephanie actual power. All I'd had to offer her was a challenge.

Walking toward my disguised truck, I tried not to dwell on what could have been and the lonely teenager who'd only wanted friends. This was no time for melancholy and a pity party for my past self.

I dropped my vocal mask as I turned out of the parking lot and dialed. "Hey, Dad," I said when he picked up. "Got the goods. I'm on my way."

CHAPTER 8

Though he was visibly exhausted from the long weekend brew, Dad was waiting up for me with a fresh pot of coffee and a pack of Oreos when I arrived.

As I removed the illusion from my truck, Dad stepped out of the house and burst into a deep belly laugh. "What the *hell* are you wearing, Janie?"

I struck my best "disaffected teenager" pose, then flipped my green-streaked hair from my face. "Oh, my God, it's *fashion*. Why are you so lame?'

He snorted and stepped aside. "Get in here. And what do you call that look, 'goth brothel'?"

"You can't possibly understand the depths of my tormented soul," I deadpanned, but hugged him as I headed inside. "How's the brew?"

"Cooling. I'll decant and pack in the morning." He closed the door and locked it. "Get comfortable, girlie."

I removed my mask, resisting the urge to shake like a wet dog as it fell away, then followed Dad back to his hidden brew room, where he kept a long lab bench stocked with bowls, beakers, a mortar and pestle, and racks of potion bottles. "Here's what she sold me," I said, handing over the three boxes. "Calls it Oil of Life. Those two are the beginner's dose, and the blue box is presumably more concentrated. She said you can rub it on but also encourages people to drink it."

He grunted and began unpacking the pink vials as I pulled up a wooden stool. "Did she tell you anything about the ingredients?"

"Proprietary, she said. Also vegan, if that makes a difference."

Dad snorted. "Seeing as the vast majority of potions are…" He opened one of the vials and gave the liquid a test sniff. "And what does this supposedly do?"

"Unblock energetic flow and release power."

He arched a brow. "In practical terms?"

"Glowing fingertips. Katarina demonstrated some obvious spellcraft tonight, but everyone else—"

"Hold on. *What?*"

I nodded. "Basic object levitation. Nothing incredibly exotic, but—"

"She did it out in the open?"

"For an audience. It's a great marketing schtick—'I've been using this oil, and look at what I can do!'"

"Except for the fact that she's likely a sorcerer," he muttered.

"That was my impression."

He held my stare. "Did she notice anything odd about you?"

"I don't think so. She was perfectly nice to me. The mask fooled people who've actually met me, so…"

Dad seemed to relax. "Good," he said, then pulled a small glass bowl from the nesting set and dumped out the vial's contents—a purple liquid, I noticed, but far paler than the potion Liogh had used to reveal the murder scene.

"Any guesses what that is?" I asked.

He gave me a reproving look as he reached for an open box of disposable gloves. "What have I said about confirmation bias, Janie?"

I sighed and propped my chin in my palms. "All I'm suggesting is that it might speed things along."

"If you try to speed along the identification of an unknown potion, you make mistakes, and then it takes even longer to fix your errors," he replied, snapping his gloves into place. "Do I have guesses as to this potion's primary components? Yes. Am I still going to use the standard identification battery? Also yes."

There was no point in trying to rush him, and so I made myself as comfortable as I could while Dad methodically pipetted the potion into about three dozen test tubes and added a variety of magical reagents. Some of the tubes remained unchanged. Several shifted color. Two began to smoke, and one emitted a sulfurous stench like rotten eggs. One fizzed, while another turned to foam and spilled onto the counter. Working with a hand-drawn chart, Dad noted the details of each reaction, saying little but making the occasional grunt as he went through his analysis.

I must have dozed off, as I became conscious that my head was on the cool countertop at one point. Hastily sitting up, I glanced at Dad, who was too engrossed with the tube that had turned green to tease me for falling asleep. But he must have noticed that I'd awakened, as before I could ask for an update, he said, "I've got the major component. Still working on the minor ones, but I was right about the major."

"And?"

"Patience. Maybe you could get me a refill, hmm?" he suggested, nodding toward his empty mug.

I could take a hint. The microwave clock said it was close to midnight, and I zapped Dad's drink, as the coffee in the pot had long since gone lukewarm. Munching Oreos while I waited, I looked out the kitchen window at the night, listening to the calls of the frogs around the pond in the backyard pasture. An owl hooted in the distance, the sound piercing even through the glass. I took comfort in the familiarity of my childhood home, though I couldn't fully relax. Between the murderer on the loose and Katarina the scamming sorcerer, my town was in danger. My *people* were in danger.

And even if they didn't like me, they were my responsibility to protect. A good old boy with a shotgun is useful in many circumstances, but not against sorcerers making trouble. For all its flaws, Ragged Gap was home, and I'd be damned if I let some assholes out of the Pactlands run roughshod over my turf.

When I finished my snack and returned to the brew room, Dad had finally landed on the other stool, and he flashed a satisfied little smile. "Thanks," he said, taking his mug from me, and closed his eyes as he drank deeply. "Oh, yeah, that hits the spot."

"Any luck?" I asked, resuming my seat with my own microwaved coffee.

He nodded. "Your new buddy wasn't entirely fibbing. Two of the minor ingredients are bergamot oil and mandarin oil. That's where the citrus portion of the profile comes from."

"What about the rest?"

"You tell me," he said, and slid the half-emptied bowl across the counter.

I lifted it to my face and inhaled deeply, trying to pick apart the scent profile. Dad had told me that there were trolls at DPP who could smell minute quantities of potions in a blood sample, but my senses were nowhere near that keen.

"The citrus is strong," I said. "Uh…am I smelling mint?"

"Yep. Peppermint. Which, with the citrus, is helping to mask the alcohol being used to dilute this. Those are the minor components—what's the major?"

I sniffed again but gleaned nothing new. "Beats me."

"I guess I'm not being very sporting, as you've never seen this one," said Dad. "I've had no reason to brew it. In its unadulterated form, it's darker than that," he continued, pointing to the bowl, "but seeing how much this Katarina person cut the potion, I'm not surprised that the color is wrong."

"What *is* it?" I asked.

He smiled. "Fingerflash."

"Fingerflash," I echoed. "Sure, that makes sense. There's a damn potion called Fingerflash, because of *course* there is. And you couldn't have deduced this from the get-go, when I told you about people with glowing fingers?"

"Oh, I did," he said smugly, "but when dealing with an unknown substance, it pays to follow protocol. Trust me, girlie, I saw *far* too many accidents in my DPP days from people who got careless and lazy with potions and such they *thought* they had identified."

I raised my mug in brief salute before sipping again. "So what does this potion do?"

"Basically, what you're seeing. It's the magical equivalent of Silly Putty or the Post-It Note."

"Huh?"

"Developed by accident while the researcher was working on another problem, then marketed in a radically different direction. Fingerflash is useful if you're working in small spaces or with tiny mechanics, say. Most of it is sold to hospitals—healers use it in surgery. If you drink it in its concentrated form, you can generate *very* bright lights from your fingertips...and from your toes, oddly enough, which might be useful if you have to go to the bathroom in the middle of the night."

"Do you have to have actual talent to trigger the glow?"

Dad shook his head. "Nah. If you can focus at all, you can make it work. Trolls, gnomes, centaurs...I don't see any reason why humans shouldn't be able to manage it. But this is definitely not something humans could *make*," he continued, tapping the rim of the potion bowl. "That's got to be brewed. They wouldn't have the ingredients, the knowhow, or the ability to manipulate the energies during the process. So where did this woman find a supply of Fingerflash?"

"Bigger question: what's her game?" I replied. "She gets her hands on a potion that's a glorified party trick, dilutes it, and sells it to unsuspecting humans."

He shrugged. "Profit?"

"Not much of one. I listened in while she was ringing up purchases. The high-end stuff was only going for fifteen bucks a bottle. If she's having to buy her own packaging, plus the essential oils and alcohol, plus however much it's costing her to get the potion, she can't be making much of a profit at all."

He mulled that over for a moment, then opened the blue box and pulled out the intermediate dose of Oil of Life. Giving the liquid a quick sniff, he said, "Same scent profile, but fainter. Hand me another bowl, will you?"

I did as he asked, then watched him pour out the potion. Unlike the beginner dose, this one was a rich purple.

"I'll analyze this in the morning," said Dad, "but based on color alone, I'd say this is almost purely Fingerflash."

"You take that, you see stronger results, and you think Katarina's not full of bullshit," I said. "But what's her endgame? She's up there showing off actual spellcasting—if her flock keeps buying her crap for months and never manages more than glowing fingers, they're going to rebel."

"Possibly. You didn't get a sample of the third-tier oil, did you?"

"No," I muttered. "She was only selling that to the people who'd graduated from the second tier."

"Pity. Well, maybe you could dose yourself with real Fingerflash, come back in a few weeks, and convince her to sell you the good stuff. I'd be curious to see what else is in the bottle. Maybe it's nothing more than pure potion. Weird," he muttered, and reached for a roll of plastic wrap. "I'll cover the bowls tonight and get back to this tomorrow. Need to sleep, you know?"

"Sorry to add more work to a brew weekend…"

He smiled. "It's no trouble, baby. Want to help me clean the tubes?"

I carried the rack to the deep, scuffed sink and started

washing them. "Hey, Dad?"

"Yep?" he said, bringing over additional glassware to be rinsed.

"Is there a potion that could give someone power?"

"No," he said without hesitation, but leaned against the counter with his arms folded and watched me work. "There *is* a potion that can enhance talent," he murmured, "but it's difficult to make, not to mention highly illegal."

I glanced up from my washing and smirked. "Sorcerer 'roids?"

"Wish it were that simple."

"Okay, so what is it?" I asked, wearily chuckling as I did the dishes.

"Oleum Vitae."

I frowned, parsing the words. Contrary to the common human conception, very few spells or potions had Latin names. "Oil of Life? Another one?"

"Yeah, but the real deal." He met my gaze, then turned and stared into the recesses of the brew room, where his weekend's potion was cooling. "Developed by a sorcerer in the thirteenth century. Somewhere in present Germany, I think. Maybe Austria. It doesn't really matter. Wherever he was, the guy was a psychopath."

"What was wrong with him?"

"Well, I can't speak to him directly," Dad admitted, "but his work speaks for itself. Oleum Vitae is blood magic of the first order."

I'd heard of such in my lessons and deep in the back of Dad's grimoires, but I'd never experimented with blood magic, and when I'd broached the topic as a teenager, Dad had forbidden me to play with it. Blood magic was dangerous, he'd explained, not to mention unsanitary if you didn't treat your wounds properly.

"How does it operate?" I asked, setting a tube back in the rack upside-down to dry.

Dad stood quietly for a moment, and I let him gather his thoughts while I continued to scrub and rinse. When he spoke again, his voice was low and lacked any shred of the evening's earlier teasing. "It's slow murder. When you brew it, one of the crucial ingredients is the blood of a family member with talent, the closer, the better. A parent, a child, a sibling. Not a spouse," he clarified. "It's the bloodline that you have to work with. When you drink the potion, your talent increases, but in so doing, you drain the life force of the person whose blood you used. Make a few batches, and you'll need a new blood source because you'll have killed the previous one."

"Shit," I muttered.

"It's dark stuff," said Dad. "The good news is that Oleum Vitae isn't at work here—not unless Katarina is secretly kin to half this town. Plus, if memory serves, the potion is brown. It would be difficult to disguise that as Fingerflash."

I cut my eyes to him as I picked up yet another soiled tube. "They actually taught you to brew that crap?"

"Heh. *No*," he replied. "I learned of it in school, and then I saw the formula during my agency days. It's not widely disseminated, and as I said, it's illegal to brew or possess without strict authorization."

"Good," I muttered. "Who the hell would make that? I mean, I understand familial problems, but to kill your own kin…"

Dad's arm landed on my shoulders, and I briefly leaned into his side hug. "The more you study magic, girlie, the better you come to understand that there have been far too many talented people throughout the ages who have decided to grow and build and brew without stopping to ask whether they *should*. It's a time-honored tradition for us. I've told you about Miri, haven't I?"

I frowned as he released me. "Uh…maybe?"

"Miri Afanuru," he said with a soft chuckle. "Wood nymph, one of the best botanists I've ever known. He was in the greenhouse when I took over, and he'd probably still be there if I hadn't had to fire his ass."

"Dare I ask?"

"He had a bad habit of cultivating strains of various plants that went in unhelpful directions. There's a poppy cultivar known as Blue Fire that he crossbred. Pretty flower, and its sap is about a hundred times more potent than that of the average heroin poppy. We might have been able to control it had one of the trainees not sneaked out a few plants to start a side gig." He snorted. "And then there's Miri Special, which he swears was an accident."

I arched a brow.

"Marijuana with *extremely* high THC levels. See the pattern? Anyway, I had to let him go in 1989. Director's orders. I hated it, but Miri was a loose cannon. That said, what I'm trying to tell you is that sometimes, people get excited about the possibility of a new potion or plant and don't stop to wonder whether they *really* need to pursue it."

"Is that what happened to the guy who came up with Oleum Vitae?" I asked.

Dad's mouth tightened. "Not according to what I've read. He really was just a sick son of a bitch who wanted more power and didn't care who he had to hurt to get it. If the accounts are accurate, his cousin killed him in his sleep."

"Lovely." Going to town on one particularly stubborn tube with the bottle brush, I said, "It seems like a bad idea to even keep the recipe for that potion around."

"Yes and no. I mean, smallpox hasn't been a problem in years, but there's a supply of it kept in Atlanta, just in case it's needed for research."

"Yeah, but that's a *disease*. You're talking about a deadly potion with a highly specific list of potential targets—"

"And it's far too late tonight to debate Pact policy," Dad interrupted, kissing my head. "Thanks for washing up. I'm going to get a few hours of sleep. You're welcome to stay…"

"Appreciate it, but my bed's calling me," I replied. "I'll

sneak out in a few minutes."

But as Dad turned to go, I couldn't help asking, "Has anyone actually attempted Oleum Vitae besides that one guy in the history books? Like, in recent memory?"

He rubbed the back of his neck as he glanced at the ceiling. "Just one that I know of, and it didn't go well. See, what the casual brewer may not understand is that the potion doesn't just drain the life force of the people whose blood is used, but also that of the drinker. Records suggest that it can be crippling. So once you start, it's not enough to get a little boost from your three-hundred-year-old great-aunt who's already on her way out. If you don't keep taking the potion, you'll end up in a worse position than where you started."

"Yikes."

"And on that lovely note, sleep well, Janie," he said, then shuffled toward the door. "Don't worry about the Fingerflash tonight—your friends aren't going to spontaneously combust by morning."

Calling most of the users of Katarina's adulterated potion my friends was definitely too generous, but still, the fact that they were being duped in that fashion left me uneasy. I stewed all the way back to my cabin, and though I changed clothes and tried to get comfortable in bed, sleep played hard to get.

Well, I thought, if I was going to be staring at the ceiling until dawn, at least I could do something useful.

Unplugging my phone from the cord on the nightstand, I scrolled through my contacts until I found Liogh's information, which I'd stored under "Leo Beard," just in case. The phone number was unlike any I knew, sixteen digits long, and I wondered how the people responsible for setting up mobile communication in an artificial world had managed to make their tech work with the systems on the outside. As I was in no state to contemplate the complicated spells behind *that*, I settled for sending Liogh a text message: *Hi, it's Jane. Could you give me a call in the morning, please? Got a situation.*

I tapped the screen to send it, musing that I had no idea what time it was for them and whether their phone would automatically translate my English text into something approximating Pactish. Since it was quarter past one for me, I plugged the phone in and rolled over, resolving to close my eyes until my body submitted out of sheer boredom.

Not two minutes later, my phone rang.

I yanked it from its charger again, saw the caller, and opened the line. "Sorry, I don't know your time zone—"

"Are you safe?" Liogh demanded. "Are you in harm's way at this moment?"

"Uh...no. I'm home in bed."

The detective released a soft exhalation on their end. "Good. I was worried you'd started playing amateur investigator in my absence."

"Not quite. Look, if it's not morning there, this can wait."

They chuckled. "For future reference, Beukal is a little west of Richmond. We're close."

"Shit. Sorry."

"Eh, I'm awake. What's on your mind, Jane?"

I sat up in bed and pushed back the rumpled covers, as something didn't feel right about having this conversation all snuggled up. "In brief, there's a sorcerer in town, she's doing magic in the open, and she's conning a bunch of would-be witches into buying watered-down Fingerflash."

The line was silent for a second, and then Liogh said, "I'm sorry, *what?*"

"More details?"

"*Yes.*"

"Okay." I rubbed my forehead in the darkness as I quickly compiled my thoughts. "So...I went to see a friend today, and she told me she had to show me something, and she was able to make her fingers glow. Said she'd bought this essential oil blend from a gifted witch, Katarina Weller. Anyone you know?"

"That's not a typical name you'd hear in the Pactlands," they replied.

"Maybe it's her local alias, then. My friend said Katarina was doing a seminar tonight...or last night, whatever. She invited me, but I don't get along well with the Mystic Mountains crowd—"

"Who?"

"The would-be witches. Remember I told you I fucked up and displayed talent? It was to the owner of Mystic Mountains, and she hasn't wanted me to come around ever since. She has to be the one who's spread the word about me. Anyway, I didn't want to cause a scene, so I masked up and went to the seminar."

"You're proficient at masking?"

"Uh, *yeah*," I retorted, slightly miffed. "Katarina, whoever she is, did a basic meditation session, and then she made her sales pitch for the other newcomer and me. When that didn't immediately work, she levitated items in the room. Given the reactions from the rest of the crowd, that wasn't her first time showing off for them."

Liogh softly swore. "And you think she was selling Fingerflash?"

"A blend. She has three levels of products—calls it 'Oil of Life.' I was able to buy samples of the first two levels, and Dad analyzed the beginner one tonight. Fingerflash, alcohol, and some essential oils for scent."

"And the other?"

"He thinks it's more concentrated Fingerflash, but he's put it off until tomorrow. Katarina's scheme is that as you get 'better' at unblocking your energies, bullshit, bullshit, your finger glow intensifies, and then you get to buy the next product." When the detective had no response, I told them, "Dad doesn't think anyone is in immediate danger, and it's not like Katarina is making a huge profit off of this—"

"That's immaterial. If there's a sorcerer acting in the open and selling potions outside the Pactlands, then we've got problems." They groaned, and a faint rustling and squealing told me they'd climbed out of bed. "Technically, this would be DPP's purview—Interdiction often leads investigations into unauthorized potion distribution. Lucky for us, I've liaised with DPP for several decades, so I think I can assemble a cross-agency team on short notice."

"How short?" I asked.

"Plan to see us in the morning."

My stomach clenched. I'd confessed way too much with only Liogh asking questions—how the hell was I going to fare in front of more government agents? Since Liogh was Dad's friend, I thought I could trust them, but add in a bunch of strangers…

As if reading my racing thoughts, Liogh said, "The people I have in mind to bring in can keep their mouths shut. I'm going to alert a *very* select group, all right? This is my case, and no one joins up without my say-so. And I won't tell them about you," they promised. "Not the *interesting* details, at least."

I took a deep breath, then slowly exhaled. "If you're sure."

"Trust me," they replied. "And stay where you are until I arrive, yes? No more sleuthing tonight. Get some sleep."

"Yeah," I said with a weary laugh, "about that…"

"Try, then. Tomorrow may be a long day."

We said our awkward goodnights, and I stretched out, hoping sleep would come. It did, eventually, but all night, I dreamed of glowing fingers fluttering through the darkness around me, barely visible hands always just out of reach.

CHAPTER 9

It wasn't sunlight through the gap in my curtains that awoke me at dawn, but rather the rumble and crunch of vehicles pulling into my gravel driveway, then the flash of the security light by the front door. "The hell?" I muttered, pulling on my threadbare blue summer bathrobe, and hurried to the window to see what awaited me outside.

I recognized Liogh's black agency Jeep off the bat. Obviously the lead vehicle, it was parked close to the cabin, and the detective was walking around the hood as I peeked out the window. A young woman closed the passenger-side door and nodded at them. By my best guess, Liogh stood a few inches above six feet, more than a solid head taller than I was. The woman with him, a green-eyed brunette sporting a black T-shirt over jeans, was close to my height. Like the detective, she'd pulled her dark hair back into a simple ponytail, a wash-and-wear style appropriate for the early hour, and she'd slung a black messenger-style bag over her chest. She was pretty, I thought—not a stunning beauty, but possessing ample girl-next-door charm—and while she looked perfectly human, I knew better than to trust appearances.

The second vehicle was another Jeep, this one brown, and I studied the occupants as they emerged. First, from the front passenger seat, stepped a man with short, golden-blond hair, brown eyes, and a pair of disarming dimples, which he revealed when the brunette from Liogh's Jeep waved at him. He was shorter than Liogh, maybe six feet, and slender in build—not scrawny, I thought, but not a bodybuilder by any means. While Liogh and the woman had opted for casual attire, he'd rolled up in a crisp white button-down shirt and chinos, and adding in his scuffed brown leather satchel, he looked a bit like a graduate student on his way to TA a class. Obviously, *someone* hadn't read the dress code memo.

From the back seat emerged a redheaded woman, yet another person who seemed about my age. She was sunburned—and that *had* to have hurt, I mused, comparing the color of her cheeks to that of her French braided hair—but if she was in pain that morning, she didn't let on. From where I was standing, her eyes appeared to be gray, maybe blue, though it was hard to tell; in any case, she'd obviously been wearing sunglasses when she got fried, considering the paler area around her eyes. She'd chosen a loose-fitting beige tunic over black leggings and flats, and I saw the top of a sketchpad peeking from the canvas tote slung over her shoulder.

But it was the driver of the second Jeep who really caught my attention, simply for the sheer *size* of him. He had to be seven feet tall and looked like he lived in the gym—the guy was built like a Bigfoot with a bad case of alopecia. Blessed with the sort of olive complexion that always tans, he wore his dark hair in a crewcut, to which he'd added a trim mustache and chinstrap beard. His black T-shirt and pants seemed pretty standard for the group, as did the black duffel he carried. As he drew near, I noticed that his nose was twisted—an old, bad break, I surmised—and to my surprise, his fingernails were bright turquoise.

Tightening my robe belt, I opened the door before they could ring the bell and glanced at Liogh. "This is your crew, I take it," I said in Pactish.

The detective nodded. "May we come in?" they asked, their voice froggy with the hour.

I stepped aside, and Liogh led the way. "Make yourselves comfortable," I said, heading for the kitchen. "Coffee?"

"That would be *great*," said a curiously accented female voice, and I turned to see the brunette flashing a hopeful smile. "You need some help? Did we wake you?"

I grinned. "Going to give me crap for it if I say yes to both?"

She snorted and shook her head. "Point me to the grounds. Or beans. I can work with whatever you've got in here, but if you want something fancier than a latte, I make no promises."

"How about a Mr. Coffee?" I replied, gesturing toward the old black pot on the counter.

"Perfect. And hi," she said, sticking out her hand, "Annie Humphries. You must be Jane."

Though my brain wasn't yet firing on all cylinders that morning, I realized then what was so odd about Annie's accent: it wasn't Pactish, or at least nothing like what I'd heard from Dad and Liogh. Instead, it seemed almost…southern? Yes, that was what I was hearing, a slight drawl.

I shook her hand. "You're a sorcerer?" I guessed.

"Not in the slightest," she answered cheerily. "Why don't you go get dressed, eh? I'll handle things here."

A few minutes later, having thrown on jeans and brushed my teeth and hair, I emerged from my room to find the five of them clustered close to the coffeepot. "Unless one of you knows a spell to speed up the brew cycle that I've missed…"

"No, just hopeful," said Liogh as the group turned toward me. "Let me make the introductions. You've met Annie"—the brunette waved—"who's an Interdiction trainee at DPP. Pars Mera is her supervisor, yes?" they asked, looking up at the giant standing by my sink.

He wiggled a hand the size of a catcher's mitt. "*One* of her supervisors," he replied in a rumbling bass. "The kid gets around."

Annie smiled smugly at him, and Pars winked.

Liogh nodded to the remaining two. "This is Yven

ti'Ansha," they continued, gesturing toward the blond man, "from DPP's Regulatory side—"

"We're still trying to poach him," Pars interrupted, to which Yven looked at me, grimaced, and quickly shook his head.

"And this," said Liogh, ignoring them, "is the farseer I told you about—"

"Hey, there," she interjected in English—and like Annie, she had a slight drawl. "I'm Rose. Sorry to bust down your door like this, but Liogh wanted to make an early start..."

"Don't worry about it," I said, switching languages, then stifled a yawn and stepped past them to get to the cabinet of cups and glasses. "Just let me wake up." After counting out half a dozen mismatched mugs, I turned back to Rose and said, "You, uh...you're quasi-human, right?"

She chuckled. "And my reputation precedes me. Yeah, 'quasi' is a good way to describe it. I'm from Richmond. So is Annie," she said, and Annie nodded vigorously.

I frowned. "Seriously?"

"Born and raised," Annie replied, slipping into English as well. "So when Liogh said there was a *Georgian* sorcerer out here with a problem, I mean, that was a no-brainer."

"And you're *not* a sorcerer?" I hinted, fishing.

Annie spread her hands. "Guilty. Human until three months ago."

"Come again?"

She peered through the kitchen window at the woods beyond my cabin. "Safe to unmask here?"

"Safe enough, I should think," I said.

"Great." With that, she reached under her shirt and extracted a silver pendant, which she gripped for only a second before her mask fell away. It wasn't much of a mask—her eyes switched from green to amber, and her ears suddenly rose to points—but I could see why she'd covered up before coming out. "Long story short, I joined the Wild Hunt back in June," she told me, "but before then, I was pretty solidly human otherwise."

"Crazy little badass human," Pars said fondly, giving her a pat on the back strong enough to dislodge food.

It clicked for me, then, what Liogh had done. If I'd learned anything about the Pactlands from Dad, it was that by design, there was virtually no one with a human tie within its borders. Liogh had specifically recruited the agents least likely to freak out if they learned the truth of my pedigree—well, the women, at least. Pars seemed to like Annie well enough, and while I didn't know much of Yven, he appeared to be relatively at ease in my kitchen.

"*You're* not masked, are you?" Pars asked me.

"Uh…nope. This is all natural," I said, running a hand down my front to encompass my long-sleeved shirt—stained, I suddenly noted—and well-worn jeans. "I mean, if greasy hair offends, I can hide it—"

"No, no," he insisted, softly laughing. "I was just wondering…" He stepped closer and peered down at me. "You're *young*."

"You don't look so old yourself," I countered.

"Old enough to have an agency gig. How old are you?"

Annie elbowed him in the gut. "Rude."

"It's okay," I said, "not a massive secret. Twenty seven…and a *half*," I added, raising my eyebrows at Pars in mock challenge.

To my surprise, he and Yven traded glances. "Shit," Pars muttered in Pactish, "*another* one?"

"Another one what?" I demanded.

Before he could answer me, Rose stepped in. "Has anyone ever told you that school lasts until you're thirty-five in the Pactlands?"

I nodded. "Sure. But I was homeschooled, and I got my bachelor's five years ago—"

"Oh, no, I'm not criticizing," she hastily interrupted before my hackles could rise. "I'm twenty-eight. Went to normal schools, but otherwise, it sounds like we were on the same educational path. Liogh said you run your own business?"

"Yeah." Pointing to the pump bottle of hand soap beside the sink, I said, "Lotions, soaps, salves, candles, bath soaks…"

"Huh. Nice," she replied, and picked up the bottle to give it a sniff. "Ooh, *very* nice. Annie, smell this."

"I can smell it from here. If you like that, you're going to love the building out back." Seeing my bemusement, Annie explained, "Heightened sense of smell. I figured you were up to something like that the moment I got out of the car."

"Anyway," Rose continued, putting the soap back, "I had my own business out here, too…as did Annie."

"Private investigator," she offered, raising a finger.

"Painter," said Rose. "Far fewer fun war stories. What the guys are bothered about is that I didn't have any magical training until I was twenty-six, and since I'm decently talented, that's kind of a scary proposition."

"You're better than decent," Yven quipped.

She grinned at him, then looked back at me. "Liogh told us you were a sorcerer. If you're twenty-seven and haven't had an education…"

Rose fell silent as I conjured fire, which licked up and down my arms without burning my shirt. "Don't worry," I assured the goggling agents, "my dad taught me what I need to know. Maybe I don't have all the advanced fancy bits down, but I—"

"You're a pyro," said wide-eyed Annie, and turned to Liogh. "Did you know she's a pyro?"

"Yes, I was aware," they replied calmly.

"Well, damn, we should have brought Fell. Is your dad a pyro, too?" she asked me.

"Uh…no, he's a floramancer—"

Pars groaned. "A half-educated sorcerer without the specialized training for pyromancy…what's the director *thinking*?"

Seeing that my flames had been far less reassuring than

I'd intended, I extinguished them and folded my arms. "Maybe Liogh wasn't clear, but I don't work for DPP."

"No, but your father has DPP licensure, correct?" asked Yven. "It's one thing to keep a greenhouse outside, but to raise a child here…I've only been in Regulatory for fifteen years, but I've never heard of an arrangement like that. Nor of a sorcerer named *Fortune*, incidentally."

The agents traded uneasy looks, and I sighed to myself as I caught Liogh's eyes. "You're positive that you trust them?" I murmured.

The nymph nodded. "I've said little."

"And I appreciate it. But if we're going to be working together…" Steeling my nerve, I looked at the rest of the crowd, waiting for the sudden popping and hissing of the brew cycle to end, then cleared my throat. "Uh…my dad's not a Fortune. He's Coby Hewt. Yacovi, I mean," I amended. "He used to work in the greenhouse—"

"He *ran* the greenhouse," Yven interrupted. "They speak of him fondly in there. I'd heard he'd retired, but I didn't know he'd come out here."

"How'd you miss *that?*" Pars teased.

Yven scowled at him. "Do you honestly think they'd give a junior agent *Yacovi Hewt's* file? I wouldn't be shocked if the chief deputy handles him herself."

"Can't say," I cut in. "I'm never around during inspections. I don't, uh…that is…I don't officially exist, okay?" I blurted. "My bio-dad is dead, my mom dumped me here, and Dad's raised me off the books, if you know what I mean." Slipping past them, I started pouring out the coffee. "Sugar's in the cannister, and there's milk in the fridge."

A brief silence descended over the kitchen, interrupted only by the splashing of coffee against ceramic.

"I'm not sure that I follow," said Pars. "What do you mean, off the books?"

But Rose seemed to have caught on. When I put the carafe atop its base, she gently gripped my shoulder until I met her eyes—gray, not blue, I saw in the warm yellow light. "How human are you? A quarter?"

"Half," I muttered.

"How—" Pars began, but Rose cut him off with an upraised hand.

"And obviously talented," she continued. "I'm so sorry you're in this position, Jane. It *sucks.*"

I cracked a little smile.

"Been there, gone through this mess. *I get it,*" she said, leaning almost close enough that our foreheads bumped. "And I promise you that no one here is going to say a damn word to the Powers that Be until you're ready."

Looking past her shoulder, I saw the other three newcomers nod. "I just don't want to get Dad in trouble."

"You won't," she assured me. "That said, we do know a pyromancer who could be looped in if needed. Elven techniques are different than the ones sorcerers use, but there's enough overlap with wild talents that she might be able to guide you...if you need guidance, that is."

"Thanks, but I'm pretty much in control of the fire," I replied. "It's stuff like brewing that I don't know well yet."

Rose grunted and rolled her eyes. "Join the club. But why don't we divvy those up, and you can fill us in, hmm?" she suggested, pointing to the line of mugs.

It might have been barely dawn, but the rules of hospitality don't set firm time limits. While my guests doctored their drinks, I rummaged through the fridge and found two tubes of biscuits and a pack of turkey sausage patties—not great fare, but *something.* By the time they'd situated themselves around the mismatched furniture in my den and the conversation had segued back into Pactish, I'd put the biscuits in to cook and set the sausage aside, intending to zap it once the other half of the spread was out of the oven.

"That's sweet of you," said Annie when I poked my head into the room, "but you don't have to make us breakfast."

"Too late," I replied, shrugging, and sat on the couch beside her. "So, what has Liogh told you about the murder?"

Apparently, the answer to that was *nothing*, as the detective and I had to fill the others in about the dead faun and the likely sorcerer who'd shot him in the woods before I turned to Katarina and her adulterated potions. I paused for a moment when the oven timer beeped, then returned with sausage biscuits on a plate and a stack of paper towels. "Hope this is edible…"

Pars started with two, which I took as a good sign, and spoke between bites. "Wonder what happened to Mouse. I mean, the two of them were pieces of work, but I kind of feel bad for Daniot."

"I don't," Yven snapped. "Remember that part where we were ambushed?"

"That's why I only *kind of* feel bad. But for him to have taken the draught, only for her to die a year later…"

"He got to spend it with her. Maybe that was worth it. In any case, he won't have to live through the end stages of the draught, so perhaps a quick death was a mercy."

"Forget him for now," said Rose. "He's not our problem any more. We're looking at two rogue sorcerers in the area, at *least*, and one of them isn't even trying to be subtle." Pivoting to Liogh, she said, "This is your show. What's the plan?"

In turn, they asked me, "The potions you bought last night are still with Yacovi, yes?"

"Yeah. Dad's supposed to analyze the second one this morning, but I wasn't going to call for an update for a few more hours. It's *kind* of early."

"He'll forgive the intrusion," they replied, and grabbed a sausage biscuit as they stood. "Let's pay him a visit. Jane, would you be opposed to wrapping those up for the road?"

"No problem," I said, rising, and soon returned with the package. "Uh…hey, Liogh?"

"Yes?"

"Dad told me most nymphs were vegetarians."

They laughed deep in their throat. "Let me just say that if you find yourself on long stakeouts with a troll for a partner, you learn to eat whatever's available, and that may well be half a ham."

Pars nudged Yven in the shoulder. "I don't think Chief ever leaves ham behind."

"I don't think I'd say that too loudly around her," Yven replied.

"The woman has a healthy appetite. Leave her alone," Annie cut in.

Pars grinned. "Your standards are skewed, Humphries."

"You've never seen my brothers-in-law two hours into a big dinner. Trust me," she said, lifting her mug to shoot back the last of her coffee, "Gentle Breeze is *dainty* compared to the boys."

"How many guys are we talking about?" I asked her.

Annie wiped her lip. "My husband is one of forty-seven still living—"

"Forty-*seven*?" I cried.

"Let's just say it gets a little rowdy once the ale flows. Sorry to ask, but is there any chance of getting a refill to go?"

"Uh...yeah, there's enough left in the pot," I managed, still stunned by the size of her in-laws' family. "I think I might get a car cup, too—"

"Actually," Rose interrupted, "would you mind terribly staying behind with me? I'd like to get to work, and the fewer distractions, the better." Thumbing one hand at the other agents, she explained, "As soon as the potions come out, they're going to be busy. If you need to get your own work done around here and I'll be a bother, I'll certainly go, but—"

"Nah, you're fine," I replied. "Liogh, do you remember the way to Dad's?"

"Not a problem," they said. "Come on, then, load up. Annie, if you're getting more coffee, grab it, and let's go."

She darted past me into the kitchen, and as I handed over the wrapped sausage biscuits to Pars, I said, "I'll give Dad a call and make sure he's awake by the time you get there."

While Liogh shepherded the others out the door, Yven lingered in the den, regarding Rose with concern. "I can stay—" he began.

"*You* need to go play with potions," she insisted. "I'm a big girl. Jane and I will be fine, right?" she said, glancing my way.

I flashed a thumbs-up, and Yven, with evident reluctance, headed for Pars's Jeep.

Once Liogh had closed the door and the engines had started, Rose sighed and shook her head, albeit fondly. "He's a tad overprotective," she said, falling into English once more. "A sweetheart, but he worries about me too much."

"Is he your supervisor?" I asked, refilling the brew basket. Annie had taken the dregs of the pot, and given my brief sleep, I needed more chemical assistance to start my day.

"Fiancé."

"Oh." I turned and sneaked a glance at Rose's bare left hand.

Obviously, I hadn't been quick enough, as she lifted it and wiggled her naked fingers. "Engagements rings aren't common for elves. He offered, but I'm not about to ask him to blow his salary on jewelry, especially since my great-uncle controls one of the best jewelry stores in the Pactlands."

"Sounds convenient."

"Since he's one of the handful of my grandfather's siblings who like me, yeah, it's pretty sweet." Catching my frown, she explained before I could ask, "I helped send their parents and three of their siblings to prison. It's still a sore spot for some of the family. Anyway, Yven's my fiancé, and he gets a little twitchy when he's not around in case of emergency."

It struck me that Rose had dropped *quite* a bit of information with practiced nonchalance, but since she'd breezed past it, I didn't pry. "And what were you planning to do, exactly?" I asked. "I can offer fire extinguishers, but that's really about it."

"God, if I end up needing a fire extinguisher, I'll have done something *horribly* wrong," Rose replied with a laugh. "Liogh told you that I'm a farseer, right?"

"He mentioned it…"

"Ever been around one?"

I grinned.

"Dumb question," she said, smacking the heel of her hand against her forehead. "Okay…typically, farseers can look into the past or the future. We get random flashes, but we can also put ourselves into a more focused, trancelike state to look for specific information. I'm the weirdo of the bunch…for multiple reasons," she mumbled, "but pertinent here, I see present events. Useful when you're trying to find missing people or, say, random sorcerers skulking around north Georgia."

"Cool." As the coffee started to percolate, I asked, "What can I do?"

"If I could borrow a quiet room, that would be excellent," said Rose. "Also, if you have any pictures of the shooter or Katarina that I could use…"

"Nothing of Katarina, I'm afraid, but I've got some trail cam photos of the killer from behind."

"I'll take it."

A few minutes later, as the brew cycle finished, Rose and I stood over my laptop at the kitchen counter, flipping through the pictures of the faun's murder. She said little as she studied them, and I thought she was just focusing until she murmured, "I watched him take the draught."

"Who, Frim?"

She nodded. "Liogh gave it to him, but I was spying from elsewhere in the hotel. Saw the whole thing. It was…fucking horrifying."

"What happened?" I asked, readying our mugs.

"I mean, the potion hits hard. He was a mess when we let him go that night. But more than that…fauns can live *long* lives, fifteen hundred years or better. Once you take the draught, you're lucky if you see another thirty. So more or less, I watched him start his suicide."

"For Kii," I said softly.

"Yeah, Mouse. I hoped it might actually work out. She wasn't in great shape when we ran into her—hard life, almost certainly on drugs. Probably in her forties, but she looked older. I'd have been shocked if she'd lasted much more than another thirty years, so while what Frim did to himself was awful, at least they'd go together. But judging by his tat, she didn't even make it a full year."

"Stupid waste."

"The alternative was DOL hauling Frim back to the Pactlands to face trial, and given the evidence on him, she'd have been dead by the time he got out. Guess he preferred to take his chances with the draught, but damn." Catching herself, she shook her head and faintly smiled. "Sorry, I've got some *feelings* about the draught. Your dad's told you about it, right?"

"He's told me enough," I replied, and thought of what Liogh had said in the woods. "Your grandfathers took it, didn't they?"

"Yep. I've got pictures of both, and the farsighted one left me a bunch of audio recordings, but my grandparents are long gone. You know," she said as I slid her a hot mug, "the stupid thing is that by all accounts, my grandmothers were smart women. They both knew *what* they were marrying. I can't imagine that they'd have gone blabbing the existence of the Pactlands to the world—they loved their husbands. But there's a decent contingent over there that thinks the only good human is a dead one, so here we are."

"Cheers," I said, lifting my coffee.

She smirked and tapped her mug against mine, then took a long sip. "Well, this isn't getting it done. Would you mind if I stretched out somewhere?"

CHAPTER 10

Around ten, as I was packing lavender shea butter bath bomb components into their molds, Rose knocked and poked her head into my workshop. "Hey," she croaked. "Got something I need you to see. Can you step away?"

"Sure." I covered my materials and stripped off my gloves, then followed her back to the house. "Are you okay?"

"Oh, I'm fine," she replied, though she sounded groggy. "I always look like I've had a rough night after a couple hours of trance, but give me a minute to clear my head."

"Hydrate," I suggested, and sat her down at the kitchen table, where she'd left her sketchpad, while I poured water from the filter pitcher. She drank greedily, then accepted a refill, and I suspected I knew why Yven had been so hesitant to leave her.

"So," said Rose once her eyes no longer seemed glazed, "tell me if you can ID either of these people." As I watched over her shoulder, she opened the pad, flipped past a series of half-finished drawings and one prairie landscape with colored pencils, then stopped on a page with two figures facing each other. Their expressions suggested they were in the middle of a heated discussion, edging toward a full-blown fight, and part of me noted that whatever else she might be, Rose was an artist with a true knack for portraiture.

A much larger part of me was too shocked at the faces I was seeing to worry about such minutiae as artistic merit.

"That's Katarina," I said, pointing to the woman on the right. Rose had captured her likeness well—the blonde C-cut, the large blue eyes, the stack of thin gold necklaces—but her cheeks were flushed, her brow furrowed in anger.

Facing her was a brown-haired man with hooded brown eyes, whose face had colored to match Katarina's. His mouth was partly open, exposing a short incisor on the left side, a tooth about half as long as the front tooth and canine flanking it. He had thick eyebrows like bunched-up caterpillars, which almost met over his nose, and several days' stubbled growth on his chin and upper lip.

"I don't recognize him," I told Rose, "but she's *definitely* Katarina from last night. You're good."

Rose smiled wearily. "You're kind. And if I'm not mistaken, your problems here have a common source." Tapping the sketchpad, she said, "I focused on the shooter. That's him, I'm positive. So if he's hanging around with Snake Oil Girl…"

"They're working together," I muttered.

"That's what it sounded like to me." She leaned back in her chair and stretched. "Now for the important question: what's their grift?"

"And how the hell does that faun figure into it?" I started to reach for my phone to call Dad and pass on the news, then paused as something Rose had said hit me. "Wait—it *sounded* like they were working together?"

"Yeah…" She regarded me, perplexed by my confusion, but her face relaxed as the realization hit. "*Ah.* I don't just see events—I hear them. Experience them. It's like I'm a ghost, I guess, but without the weird footsteps and flickering lights."

"Huh. Slightly freaky."

"Oh, totally," Rose concurred, "but it's an eavesdropper's dream talent. I was in your room so long this morning because I was watching the two of them yap at each other. And making some sketches," she added, flipping to the next page of her pad, which revealed a full-color scene of a cabin set along a gravel path, flanked by leafy hardwoods and a bear-proof dumpster. "That's where they seem to be staying."

I grunted as I looked it over. The cabin wasn't immediately recognizable—frankly, it looked like any number of rentals in the area. "What were they arguing about?" I asked.

Rose smiled, but there was no warmth in it. "Sounds like Dirk is in trouble."

"Dirk?"

"Him." She turned back to the page of the arguing pair. "She kept calling him Dirk."

"Is that a normal sorcerer name?"

"Not that I've heard. He called her Katin, which I *have* heard in the Pactlands, so maybe he prefers his alias. It was odd, though," she continued, frowning in thought as she considered the drawing. "They argued in English. I wouldn't expect that from a pair of sorcerers, even if they'd lived here for a while."

"Dad and I use English at home all the time," I countered.

"Yeah, but this is your mother tongue, is it not? I suspect he wanted to make sure you could speak it like a native. Your Pactish is really good, though," she added. "Much better accent than mine."

I made a face. "Dad forced me to study it."

"Count yourself lucky. I learned it via potion, and I'm going to be getting weird looks due to my pronunciation for the foreseeable future. Ditto for Low Elvish. But I digress. To put it mildly, Dirk done fucked up."

"How so?" I asked, taking the chair beside hers.

"Well"—Rose leaned across the sketchpad as if conveying a choice morsel of gossip—"bear in mind that I'm having to extrapolate a little, but from what I can gather, he wasn't supposed to kill Frim, and Katin's *pissed*."

"Did Dirk say why he killed him?"

"Blackmail. Frim found them here a while back and asked for a job. They turned him down, but he cornered Dirk at a bar and asked again. Said he'd rat them out to DPP if they didn't play nice. Dirk got scared and took matters into his own hands. Got Frim tipsy enough to be suggestible and said he'd show him their facility. I think you know what happened next."

"Unfortunately," I muttered, thinking of that wide purple stain on the forest floor where Dirk had tried to hide the evidence. "But why'd he unmask the faun? That seems like an idiotic move."

Rose nodded. "Katin would back you there. Dirk told her that once he knew that Frim had been a producer for Silver and cut a deal to save his own skin, he thought he could pass off the murder as a revenge killing by unmasking him. From what Dirk was saying, I think Frim told him that he's got a handler, and he's playing both sides. Dirk thought that leaving him unmasked for his handler to find would point suspicion toward his old gang."

I mulled that over. "Still sounds weak to me."

"Agreed, but something tells me Dirk isn't the brains of this operation—Katin's the one in charge." With a half-smile, she added, "Even if Frim had a handler, Dirk would still be screwed, since everyone Frim used to run with is either dead or incarcerated. We caught that whole group, and DPP and Laws have been ferreting out the other producers in hiding over the last year, ever since the old family business fell apart."

"Huh?"

Her smile sharpened. "The great-grandfather I helped prosecute used to work as a jeweler. He pivoted to drugs and illegal potions in the last century, calling himself Silver. Now he's locked up, and we don't talk." She spread her hands. "Family's messy. But back to Dirk—Katin yelled at him for killing Frim without running the plan by her first. She's panicking, afraid that DPP is going to come snooping around. Told him to go back and mask the corpse."

I grimaced. "You mean the one he left by the creek down there? The one that Liogh carted off?"

"Don't freak out just yet," she said as my heartbeat accelerated. "Dirk confessed to Katin that he doesn't remember where he put the body."

"*Seriously?*"

"He says he doesn't know the woods, and he was a little drunk, too. Not so drunk that he didn't clean up his mess, but drunk enough to forget exactly where he dumped Frim. This factoid isn't making Katin any happier, which is just too damn bad, I'd say."

"So what do we do now?"

"Now?" Rose smiled in triumph and turned to the cabin drawing again. "I couldn't get an address, but this is their cabin. We could get a strike team together and take them down."

"Oof."

Her smile faltered. "Something wrong?"

"Slight problem," I said. "I have no idea where that cabin is."

"Well…this seems like a small town, right? How many cabins in the woods can there be?"

I regarded her incredulously. "You do realize this is a vacation destination, don't you? Like, tourism keeps the lights on. I don't even want to think about how many cabins are hiding in northeast Georgia."

Rose's face fell in earnest. "Ballpark?"

"Not as bad as Gatlinburg, but…"

She groaned and buried her head in her arms atop the open sketchpad.

"Want me to call Dad?" I offered. "Let the others know?"

"They'll reach out once they're finished playing with the potions," she mumbled into the table. "Should we go cabin hunting while we wait?"

When I'd just come back to Ragged Gap and was looking for a place to make my own, I spent days on real estate websites. Browsing neighborhoods via aerial maps, comparing houses far out of budget, rejecting homes I'd never be able to afford for the color of their kitchen granite or their overabundance of carpet—it was a game, really, about as practical as trading Monopoly properties.

Rose, I gathered, had never played the "What will half a million bucks get me?" game. Almost apologetically, she explained that she had inherited her parents' house in her early twenties, a four-bedroom, two-story place in a nice, quiet part of Richmond, and hadn't felt the urge to look elsewhere until she'd moved to the Pactlands. "I haven't sold it yet," she said as she browsed through one of the many cabin rental sites to which I'd directed her. "It's a money suck right now, but there's something so *final* about handing over the keys to your childhood home, and…"

"Memories," I suggested.

She nodded. "If my parents were still around, I don't think it'd be such a problem to sell, but the house is one of the last pieces of them I still have, you know? And they're buried in Richmond, so it's not like I'll never come back to town…" Her voice faded again, and she flipped around her laptop, a remarkably ordinary human-made computer, considering her line of work. "What do we think?"

I looked from the listing photos to Rose's sketch, then zeroed in on the address. "Nope, not that one. You said their cabin is pretty remote?"

"From what I could see."

"Well, I've got some customers in this neighborhood. The cabins are cute, but they're way too close together. It's a new development designed to look older."

She muttered and tabbed back to the aerial map. "Okay, let's see if we can set better parameters. Where *won't* this cabin be?"

I considered the satellite view, a green swath of undulating terrain with lighter patches of civilization, towns and tiny hamlets that had carved out space for themselves along the highways that snaked through the mountains. "Stay north of Atlanta. I wouldn't look anywhere farther south than Dahlonega, really. Ellijay, Blue Ridge, Helen, Clayton…and that's just Georgia. We're close enough to the Carolinas that they might well be over the border, but I kind of doubt it," I said, thinking out loud. "Katin's working here, and Dirk was comfortable enough in the area to take Frim into the woods. Even if he can't remember exactly where he went, he must have some idea of the general terrain."

"So let's narrow it to…what, areas half an hour from here?"

"Sure." I zoomed in and started pointing to neighborhoods and landmarks as they popped up. "That's a good possibility, and that one"—Rose started making notes—"and there's a bunch of rental cabins here…"

"What about there?" she asked, tapping a marked spot about twenty miles from me.

"East Branch? No. It's a weird little commune in a holler. They keep to themselves—Dad says they're not even on the power grid. Rumor has it the gene pool's kind of shallow around there, if you get me, and the residents go armed against trespassers."

She winced. "Banjos. Noted."

"Now, *Whitford* might be an option," I continued, pointing to the town nearest to East Branch. "It's a cute little place—not really touristy, but there are a few rentals. I've got a customer who owns three cabins around town."

Rose arched a brow. "Three?"

"And she lives in Atlanta, so I deal with her *people*," I said drawing out the word. "Nice enough crew, just not locals. Why don't you start looking around there? That way, if you don't find the cabin, we can cross it off and move on. I'll keep tackling Ragged Gap."

We settled into a comfortable near-silence, for a time broken only by the tapping of keys or the shuffling of the sketchpad between us to compare the view to the photos. But after a while, my curiosity got the best of me.

"If it's not too personal, how'd you lose your parents?" I asked. "I thought elves were basically immortal."

She was quick to reply. "More or less, yeah, barring accidents. The pyromancer Annie mentioned earlier, Fellora? Her grandfather died while climbing a mountain. Splatting will do the trick."

"Ouch."

"I doubt he suffered." She squinted at her computer for a moment, then dismissed a cabin with a frustrated snort. "To answer your question, my parents died in a car wreck. Black ice, telephone pole. It's been about five and a half years, so it's not exactly fresh," she reassured me, "but you see why I hold on to the house?"

"I'm so sorry."

Her smile was brief and polite, but there was a warmth to it. "What about you? As long as we're asking personal questions…"

"Fair, I guess. Wait, hold that thought…ah, crap, nope," I said, and tabbed to the next rental. "My bio-dad was a convenience store clerk, and he died in an overnight robbery gone bad. Well, gone *worse*, I guess," I amended.

Rose hissed. "Shit, Jane—"

"It's okay. I don't remember him. I was two weeks old when he died, so it's not like I knew him to miss him."

"Still…"

"I appreciate it," I said, reaching over to grip her wrist. "But really, the only parent I've ever known is Dad. I'm fine."

She spoke cautiously. "Your bio-dad…he was human?"

I nodded. "Average guy, Dad says."

"No family to claim you?"

"Not that my mother ever mentioned. I don't know if he was estranged or a foster kid who aged out of the system, or what. Guess I could go searching for them," I allowed, "but I've never felt the urge. Whatever Fortunes may be lurking in Virginia, they wouldn't know what to do with me, and no one's ever come looking."

"So your mother's the sorcerer, then?" Rose asked.

"Evidently." Scrolling through the next page of cabin offerings, I said, "She was working in the greenhouse under Dad, met my bio-dad in town, and ran off with him. They married, they had me, he died, and then she dumped me with Dad and split. I haven't seen her since I was, oh, about a month old."

I tried to sound casual, hoping Rose would accept the information and move on, but when I glanced up, she was staring at me over her laptop like she'd seen a ghost. "What?" I asked.

"Your mother was working in the *greenhouse*," she said urgently. "The DPP greenhouse?"

"Yeah. That was at the end of Dad's tenure."

"Where is she now?"

I grunted and made myself stare at my screen. "Hell if I know. She skipped right on out of my life. Didn't want to be a single mom, I guess. Maybe she sneaked back into the Pactlands, started a new family. Could be having a grand time over there—"

"Probably not. If she took the draught before you were born…"

Rose didn't finish that thought, and I fixed her with a long stare. "See," I murmured, "you assume she took the draught."

"Oh. *Oh*," she said more vehemently as the pieces slotted into place, "that explains your talent. I was wondering…"

"Dad said my mother was a pretty solid sorcerer—"

"Yeah, but if she'd taken the draught, that would have nullified your talent as well. Shortened your life, too. That's what happened to both of my parents. But she didn't, so here you are, a fully talented albeit half-human sorcerer— and with a *wild* talent, I should say."

"You can't tell on Dad," I insisted, grabbing her arm.

"Please. All he did was let my mother live. That can't be so bad, right?"

"Jane, relax. You're preaching to the choir," said Rose. "I hate the fucking draught. But..." She hesitated as I released my grip, then said, "A while back, Pars's wife told me about her cousin, who worked in the greenhouse and fell for a human guy. She said her cousin's chief gave her the usual choice: leave him and come back to the Pactlands, or take the draught. The cousin opted to stay with him and gave her chief a letter to send to her parents, and they never saw her again." Rose paused, then murmured, "That would have been about the time you were born."

Despite my attempts at nonchalance, my heart started hammering. "You think..."

"What's your mother's name?"

"Essa," I replied. "Essa Nerin."

Rose covered her mouth. "Pars's wife...she's *Canna* Nerin. Oh, my God..."

I'd imagined, from time to time, what reaction my long-absent mother's family would have, should they learn of my existence. The older I got, the more I became convinced that the response wouldn't be a seat at the table. Dad had always been gentle when breaking difficult truths, but I was mature enough to understand that in the Pactlands, having human blood wasn't anything to be proud of, and I'd be a dirty secret at best.

But Rose seemed to have missed that memo. "Let me tell her," she pressed. "Canna's a healer at DOL—she knows how to keep a secret."

"What good would that do? I don't have any information on Essa's whereabouts."

Her brow wrinkled. "You're her *daughter*. I know Canna pretty well, and trust me, she'd want to hear this."

I waffled—the last thing I wanted was to expose Dad to even more risk than I already had—but Rose sounded sincere, and after a moment, temptation won out. "If you're sure…"

She beamed and pulled her phone from her bag, then found the contact, turned on speaker mode, and put it on the table between us, atop the open sketchpad. It rang three times, and a woman's voice answered in Pactish: "Hi, Rose. What's up?"

As I scrambled to discern meaning from those few syllables—was she busy? Annoyed? Bored?—Rose replied, "Hey, there. Can you talk?"

"Sure."

"Privately?"

"Uh…if you'll hang on for a minute."

I listened to the faint sounds of footsteps on tile and the indecipherable babble of background voices, and then I heard the firm click of a closing door. "We had a group of trainees go out to the Edolis over the weekend, and they came back last night with a few broken bones. It's been a *time*. Is Pars behaving himself?"

"Last I checked," she said. "What happened to the trainees?"

The woman—Canna, I assumed—groaned. "Troll in the group brought along a bottle of some troll-only liquor, and his idiotic non-troll buddies thought they could cut their shots in half and be fine. They waited until their supervisors went to bed, and then they got raging drunk. Some of them came to us with alcohol poisoning, but a few of them managed to walk off the freaking mountain. They're lucky they didn't crack their skulls."

Rose hissed. "They still have their jobs?"

"That's a question for the director, and she hasn't told me anything. Between you and me, though, it's the rare trainee class that doesn't engage in the occasional shenanigans, so I'm not overly concerned for their careers. But enough about our crazies. What's on your mind?"

She met my stare for a second, then said, "I know this is out of the blue, but that cousin of yours who worked in the greenhouse and took the draught—what was her name?"

Canna hesitated briefly, perhaps parsing that question out of left field, then said, "Essa. My mother's older brother's daughter. Why—" she began, then softly gasped. "Have you found some trace of her? Out there?"

"Essa *Nerin?*"

"Yes, exactly. All of my uncle's children were given his surname, I don't know why. Have you seen her with farsight or something? Is she okay?"

Rose waited for a break in Canna's rapid questions, then said, "I haven't seen her, no. But I'm sitting here with her daughter right now."

Silence filled the line.

"Canna?" Rose asked. "Are you there?"

When Canna spoke again, her voice wavered on the edge of tears. "You're serious?"

"You're on speaker. She's listening."

"Can she understand us? I haven't been given a potion for—"

"She's fluent."

"Um…hi," I said—awkward, yes, but nothing had quite prepared me for an introduction like this. "I'm Jane."

"Jane," Canna repeated, and sniffled hard. "Hello. It's…it's so nice to meet you…"

By the sound of it, Canna was barely holding herself together, and so I took the lead. "I don't know where Essa is. Sorry. She, um…she dropped me with my dad when I was a baby and split. My adopted dad, I mean. Bio-dad's dead. Essa's never tried to contact me, so I don't know if she has a new family or sneaked back into the Pactlands, or what."

"Oh, sweetheart," said Canna in a wobbly tone, "it's been nearly thirty years since she took the draught. I don't know what you may have been told about it, but she's almost certainly…um…that is…"

"Dead?" I finished, saving her from the unpleasantness of having to break the news to me that I was an orphan.

"I'm so sorry." Before I could explain, she asked, "How did Rose find you? *Where* are you?"

"Northeast Georgia," I replied.

"About an hour west of the Central portal," Rose offered. "Do you know it?"

Canna laughed weakly. "Never been out, remember?"

"Southwest of my hometown, then. In the mountains. Now, before I say anything further, this is *absolutely* confidential, yes? We've got an active investigation here—"

"Not a word," Canna promised. "Not without truth serum."

I glanced sharply at Rose in query, but she shook her head. "That's almost never used, especially not on an agency employee," she whispered. "Nasty potion, from what I've heard."

"Yeah," I muttered, "I was going to say…"

She smiled reassurance and turned her attention back to Canna. "Your cousin left Jane with Yacovi Hewt. He—"

"Why him?" she demanded, the sudden warmth of anger drying her tears. "He's the one who gave her the damn draught!"

"He didn't," I cut in. "Dad just said he did. He faked whatever he needed to and let Essa go with her boyfriend."

Again, the line fell quiet, but only for a few seconds. "You mean—"

"Essa never took the draught," said Rose. "She could very well be alive. And Jane here…well, she's a full-fledged pyromancer."

"Are you certain?" Canna asked, shocked.

"Dad is," I replied. "Fire's always come easily to me."

"But…but I don't know of any pyros in the family…"

"It's a wild talent," Rose reminded her. "These things can pop up, right?"

"Yes, but…" She sucked in a quick breath. "*Training.*

Pyros are supposed to have safety training, are they not?"

"That's my understanding," said Rose, "but Jane seems to be decently in control."

Given the little I'd displayed, I decided that Rose was going on what she'd seen and hoping for the best.

"Dad's trained me," I told Canna. "Homeschooled me in magic and everything else...except college, I mean. I did that in person. He hasn't taught me much about brewing yet, but I've got enough basics down that he'll let me out of the house," I joked.

"And I suspect he's done as well as he can for you, but you should be *here*. In school, or at least being tutored," Canna pressed. "With your family."

I bristled. "*Dad* is my family."

"Oh, I didn't...oh..." Canna swore. "I'm sorry, that came out all wrong. What I'm trying to say is that there's a Nerin cousin outside the Pactlands with evident talent, and you should be allowed in. You've got family here, cousins, aunts and uncles, grandparents...you can cast?"

"Pretty well."

"Then we should push for citizenship for you. Bring you in, let you continue your education. If you can cast, there's no reason you should be denied."

"Except for the part where I'm half human," I murmured.

Canna paused. "Well, *yes*, there's that...but I'll vouch for you," she offered, ramping up. "We'd just need to bring the case to our Forum representatives. It's not as complicated as it is for elves," she added. "Ask Rose if you want the details of *that* mess. But come on, your mother's a sorcerer, and you're a *pyromancer*—they'd have to let you in."

"That's...really nice of you, and I appreciate it," I said slowly, "but if I come forward, Dad will be exposed."

"What do you mean?"

"My existence is proof that Essa didn't take the draught. Won't Dad get in trouble if the truth about that comes out?"

"Oh…" She groaned. "Shit. Hence the silence?"

"Exactly," said Rose.

"And I've got problems here to work out before I do anything else," I said. "Couple sorcerers on the loose."

Canna's tone sharpened. "Do they know about you? Are you in danger?"

"I think I'm all right for now," I assured her, "and since I've got a detective and four DPP agents here, I've got backup."

"No offense, but Rose isn't a full agent yet."

"Pars and Yven are," Rose reminded her. "We're fine, and we'll take care of Jane."

She sighed, a sound that didn't suggest approval of the current arrangement. "Be careful. *All* of you. I can tell Pars, yes?"

"Sure," I said. "He's heard the rest of it already."

"Good. Rose, give Jane my number, please. You stay in touch, little cousin," Canna ordered. "I mean it. We're going to work this out."

"Appreciate it," I replied. "I, um…thanks."

"Call me anytime. Rose, any other explosions you'd care to set off today?"

"I think we're set for now," she said, grinning at the phone as she lifted it from the table. "And I'll keep the boys in line. See you."

Once she'd hung up, she pushed back her chair and set about refilling her coffee. "Canna's got four kids. She lives in 'mom mode,' and I get the full force of it, too, sometimes. Don't take it personally."

"Noted." Joining her, I eyed the inch left in the pot and took it from Rose before she could pour. "Let me freshen this."

Rose allowed me to work in peace as I rinsed the pot and prepared the brew basket, but I could feel her watching me. Once I'd started the cycle, she said, "I'm guessing you've got mixed feelings about the Pactlands, huh?"

I smirked as I leaned against the counter. "Is it that obvious?"

"It's logical."

"Look, I'm sure it's great for y'all, and it must be nice to practice magic without looking over your shoulder, but if Dad had followed your laws, my mother would be dead, and I wouldn't be talented at all. The death draught…that's fucked up, you know?"

"Oh, I'm right there with you," she said emphatically. "My dad's father died when he was little, and my mom's only lasted until she was in her teens. As for my parents, even if they were still here, the draught left them functionally human. Lucky for me," she said with a wry smile, "it's an unstable potion, and I'm, like, ninety percent elven. Got all the genes I needed. But if my parents had married anyone else, I'd probably be just like them and none the wiser about the Pactlands." Picking a spot along the counter beside me, she folded her arms and stared at the wall as the coffeemaker gurgled. "Don't get me wrong, I don't regret moving over there, but I do still have *issues* with the place."

I glanced at Rose, and when she looked my way, I saw the understanding there.

"Canna's excited, but she'll keep mum," said Rose. "As will the rest of us. Until you're ready to go public—*if* you get to that point—I don't know nothing about nothing."

A wild thought popped into my mind, and before I could overanalyze it, I asked, "Can you help me find Essa? With farsight, I mean."

"I could try, if that's what you want. After we find the damn cabin, that is," she muttered, glaring at our abandoned laptops.

"Just putting this out there, but I've got an old computer in the closet, and Dad has one or two of his own. If the rest of your posse know enough English to poke around online…"

"They do."

I tossed my head toward the coffeemaker. "Want to take this to go and draft them?"

The smile that greeted my suggestion wasn't entirely nice or friendly, but since my eyes were practically crossing, I felt it in my soul.

CHAPTER 11

It was Annie who stumbled upon the cabin around three that afternoon, and she screamed like she'd just won the lottery.

In fairness, the six of us had been clustered around the computers perusing real estate websites all day, taking shifts...and occasionally a nip of Dad's latest batch of aged 'shine to ease the pain. Though Dad certainly hadn't expected to be invaded by Pact agents that day, he made a generous host, even driving into town to pick up sandwiches while we worked. I didn't know what Liogh had told him, but Dad squeezed my shoulder and flashed a familiar smile on his way out the door, and I trusted that the detective had been able to allay whatever fears he had of agency company.

They'd been busy while Rose and I stayed behind, watching and assisting as needed while Dad ran his tests on the remaining two bottles of Oil of Life, repeating his analysis of the beginner dose and starting fresh with the intermediate. Liogh reported that it was as Dad had suspected the night before: the intermediate bottle was similar in composition to the beginner but with a more concentrated dose of Fingerflash. And, they confided in me with a little grin, Dad hadn't minded the audience. "Yacovi used to give educational presentations when he was at DPP," they told me once Dad had driven off. "Exotic plants, preservation techniques, any number of subjects. He was a frequent speaker during annual training sessions—Laws even used him on occasion."

Apparently, Yven could talk to a rock about horticulture, and though I got the feeling that Pars would rather be breaking down a door than babysitting test tubes, Annie was a trainee—fresh meat, in other words, and green enough to find Dad's work intriguing. Per Liogh, he'd lectured while he'd analyzed the potion, and Annie had sat nearby and taken notes. I'd found that odd at first—even I, though no potion expert, understood the steps of analysis—but Pars had quietly explained that the entirety of Annie's magical education had been on-the-job training. Sure, mine had been less than perfect, but she was starting from scratch. "She can't brew, of course," he told me while we took a stretching break on the front porch. "Can't cast, either. But she's been pushing herself to understand the process, and I can't fault her for that. She's one of the best trainees I've seen yet."

"Not to be rude, but what *is* she?" I asked. "What happened to her?"

He chuckled to himself as he braced his hands on his lower back and swiveled, working out the kinks. "Born human—*fully* human," he added, staring down at me. "About two years ago, she was exposed to an experimental potion. This asshole in Richmond with an illegal greenhouse was using locals as test subjects. She survived, but she ended up with an impressive rack of antlers for a while, until our lab worked out an antidote."

"*Dang.*"

"Yeah, we had to keep her in the Pactlands for everyone's protection. She ended up coming on as a trainee, and once she was cleared to stay, she decided she liked the job."

"And she's...*not* human anymore? Because of this potion?"

"Oh, no, the potion had nothing to do with it. Ever heard of the Wild Hunt?"

I racked my brain, searching for the term. Annie had mentioned it... "Maybe once or twice."

"Big group of burly guys on flying horses. They go hunting once a year or so—it's part of this ancient, foundational magic, or some such. I'm no expert there," he confessed. "But they've all got antlers, if you see where I'm going with this."

"So...what," I said, grinning, "they adopted her?"

"In a manner of speaking. She and the guy who's now their leader fell in love, and since he's more or less this primal sink of magic, he...well, made the necessary alterations to let her legally stay in the Pactlands. Canna swears that if you run Annie's blood now, you don't find *any* human markers." He paused, then said, "She called me about an hour ago to give me the update. Don't worry, Yacovi doesn't know."

"Thanks."

I jumped as his meaty arm fell around my shoulders and pulled me in for a brief hug. "Welcome to the family, eh?" he said.

He patted my back with enough force to make me brace myself against a support pillar, and I wondered if there wasn't secretly a troll in Pars's ancestry. "You don't mind?"

"Mind what?"

"You know...Essa didn't exactly elope with a sorcerer."

Pars grunted and waved it off. "Don't worry about it. You've seen my posse in there, yeah? Besides," he added, giving me a long look, "my wife is *very* fond of your mother. Looked up to her like a big sister. Wherever Essa is, whatever she's done...you've got Canna in your corner now, kid, and trust me, that woman can be a force of nature."

Coming from Pars, who looked like he might smash rocks out of boredom on occasion, that wasn't entirely reassuring, but I smiled back at him and held it close, all the same.

Our break on the porch had been far too brief, and

we'd both returned to the house to take our turns on the computer, comparing likely cabins to Rose's drawings. I'd feared that Annie's shout had been yet another false bingo, but all seven of us concurred once we saw the details in the rental photos—the blue flowerboxes on the front windows, the welcome mat of bright green plastic grass, the leftmost shutter hanging slightly askew.

"You're *good*," I marveled, glancing at Rose.

She accepted the compliment with a little smile. "It's a living."

Quickly, I scanned the property details. The cabin was deep in the woods, down in a valley surrounded by hunting tracts. The nearest town was indeed Whitford, but the drive from there to the cabin was a solid fifteen minutes of winding roads, some of them gravel. From what I could tell, the place wasn't huge—four bedrooms and a furnished basement, according to the webpage—and when I checked the listing, I saw that it was fully booked for the next six months. Katin and Dirk had found themselves a cozy hideout, I mused…but what were they up to out there?

"So, what's our next move?" I asked the others.

"*You* are not doing anything," Dad immediately replied. "This is nothing for you to get wrapped up in, Janie."

I snorted as I crossed my arms. "*Bullshit*, first, and second, it's way too late for that. I've been involved in everything to this point."

"Which, while certainly appreciated, is not ideal," said Liogh in a placatory tone. "We try not to make a habit of drafting civilians into investigations…"

Their voice faded as Rose broke out in incredulous laughter. "Oh, *really*?" she managed after a moment. "News to me."

The detective's face scrunched like they'd tasted something bitter. "You're a special case—"

"And me?" Annie interjected.

"Yes, and you," they grudgingly allowed. "But—"

"Third time's the charm, right?" I said, flashing my most winning smile.

Liogh and Dad shared a long, pained look. "Is she always like this?" Liogh asked.

Dad nodded and gave me a familiar stare…which, unfortunately for him, had lost its efficacy once I hit my late teens.

"Come on, I'm in this now. Let me help," I wheedled. "You don't know this area—*I* do. And you're busy," I said to Dad before he could interrupt me. "How many shoeing appointments do you have this week, six? And that's including Mr. Morrison's crazy stallion, yeah? Plus bottling up the weekend brew and the next batch of moonshine?"

Much as he might have wanted to argue with me, Dad knew I was right.

"Annie and Rose might be able to get around without attracting too much attention," I continued, turning to the agents, "but you guys have weird accents. Sorry, I'm not trying to be rude—"

"No offense taken," said Pars. "You're correct."

Spreading my arms, I said, "I can be useful. I know the terrain, I actually have reasons to go to Whitford, and lest we forget, I have a *personal* interest in this case. So how about it? A stakeout?"

"What's in Whitford for you?" asked Annie, frowning.

"Couple of customers. I make deliveries to some of the cabins on Wednesdays. If I just *happened* to get turned around near Katin and Dirk, well, that would be too bad, wouldn't it?"

"Points for attitude," said Pars, "but we have a safer option." Nodding to Rose, he asked, "Any big plans in the next few days, or can you spare the time to spy for us?"

She made a show of cracking her knuckles. "Cleared my calendar before I came this morning. Is there any chance that one of you might be willing to put me up for a bit?"

The best option was for her to stay with Dad, as I only

had my bed, a couch, and a spare room full of junk to offer company. He put Rose and Yven in my old room, then gave Liogh the guest bedroom. I'd assumed that Pars and Annie would bunk in the den—Dad's sectionals were worn in all the right places—but the agents were reluctant to leave me unattended, seeing as a flash of memory from Dirk might send a killer snooping around my yard. With many apologies for the state of my accommodations, I let the two of them decide who wanted the couch and who would take the floor, and was unsurprised to see Pars's bedroll on the thin rug.

"What now?" I asked as they made the most of my den.

Plugging his computer in through an adaptor, Pars looked up from his task and grinned. "Now we wait and let Rose work. I've got some reports in the meantime—"

Annie groaned.

"—as does the trainee here, so we'll keep ourselves busy until Rose has enough intel."

"And me?"

"Your job," said Annie, "is to maintain appearances. Do what you would normally do around town and be our eyes and ears for now."

My brow furrowed. "But if Rose is already spying—"

Pars shook his head to cut me off. "She can't see everything. Certainly useful, don't mistake me, but she has her limits."

"Besides," Annie added, "as you said, you're the local. Right now, you're the canary in the mine—if something seems off, you might pick up on it before we do. There's no need to start playing Nancy Drew, I mean, but if you could keep your eyes peeled and your ears open…"

"You've got it," I replied, and glanced at the clock on the mantel. "Pizza for dinner?"

"Ooh. *Yes*, please," said Annie, and Pars pulled a stack of familiar green bills from his wallet.

I had no idea whether the money the agents carried was

genuine or some sort of magical forgery, but since Annie insisted that her supervisor could eat a large pie all by himself, I didn't ask too many questions.

Wednesday morning, I rose early and jumped in the shower, trying to be a decent hostess by freeing up the bathroom by the time my guests awoke. When I emerged in pajamas and a towel turban to start on breakfast, however, I found the agents already at work, the coffee hot, and a road atlas spread across the kitchen table. As I watched, Annie flipped the page and placed a small black marker down, and a bright blue line began to glow.

"Uh...good morning?" I ventured, my insufficiently caffeinated brain defaulting into English.

She looked up, brushed her dark hair from her eyes, and smiled. "Morning," she rasped in a froggy contralto. "Don't mind us. Need to get in here?"

"Not really. Did y'all want breakfast?"

Pars, who'd spread a notebook across the counter, lifted a piece of cold pizza in salute. "Under control, thanks."

I hesitated, reluctant to bother them, but my curiosity quickly won out. "What's going on?"

"Just a little hiccup," said Annie, leafing back through the atlas. I noticed a blue line glowing on another page, then saw that she'd stopped on Georgia. "Seems our friends left town overnight. Rose has been tracking them." Tapping the atlas, she explained, "We're just plotting their positions in case we need to send teams after them."

As I joined her at the table, I saw that two lines left Ragged Gap, the blue one headed south and a green one veering north. "Where did they go?"

"Dirk"—she pointed to the blue line—"is actually still moving. He just passed Gainesville on 75, so he's probably bound for Tampa."

"*Tampa?*"

She nodded. "One of Florida's two portals is outside the city."

"Liogh's put in a monitoring request for inbound Tampa traffic," Pars added, "but that's a crapshoot." Smirking at my bemusement, he said, "The best and the brightest don't become portal attendants, and a *remarkably* high percentage of them can be convinced to look the other way for sufficient compensation."

"You think Dirk's trying to run?" I asked.

He shook his head. "Nah. Buying or selling, I would imagine. It's a common pattern: if illegal producers out here don't directly import into the Pactlands, they'll set up camp near a portal for, say, a few days a month. Sell to middlemen, buy what they need. We bust whole pop-up markets once or twice a year. Assuming Dirk's headed to one, I'm curious to see who else is lurking."

"What about Katin?"

"Katin," he said, glancing at his papers, "overnighted in...uh..."

"Chattanooga," Annie finished, turning to the Tennessee page to show me.

"Can't read my own notes," Pars muttered.

Attempting to be diplomatic, I offered, "I guess some of our place names can be strange if you're not from around here."

"No, that's not the problem." He pulled a small brown plug from his ear. "The reading aid works well for Pactish, but it's not so helpful when I write foreign terms phonetically."

As he popped it back in, I squinted at him, trying to deal with far too much unfamiliar magic in my kitchen before coffee. "What—"

"I'm severely dyslexic. The earpiece works with my contacts to convert text to speech. Our in-house tech folks have done a decent job of adding English characters to its capabilities, but this language is so damn *irregular* that half the time, I'm left making my best guess."

"Huh," I said. "Probably doesn't help that 'Chattanooga' is a corruption of a Native American name."

"Not in the slightest," he cheerily concurred. "Anyway, Katin is currently in a hotel somewhere in that city. Rose says she hasn't moved yet, but it's early."

"Another portal?"

"Probably not," said Annie. "The only Tennessee portal is near Crossville. I think she's spooked," she continued, looking at Pars. "Maybe she's looking for a new hideout. Chattanooga's less than two hours from here— whatever she's got going on, she could either commute or move her base of operations pretty easily."

"But for now, what's going on at their cabin in Whitford?" I asked, glancing back and forth between the agents. "If they're gone, couldn't we, you know...poke around?"

Sure, I was hanging out with law enforcement, but these folks were well outside their jurisdiction. As long as we weren't trespassing...

But what if we needed to get on the property? Obviously, we couldn't go to the local cops for help. What grounds could we possibly give to support a search warrant?

And did one even *need* a search warrant in the Pactlands? Was that going to be a consideration for this crew?

Annie made a face. "*I* wouldn't mind casing the joint, but—"

"This is still Liogh's show, and they want to stand back," said Pars. "Frankly, I don't blame them. Rose doesn't have a good idea of who else might be at that cabin, and until we get a sense of what we're up against, prudence suggests we wait."

"Okay, then," I said, planting my hands on my hips in exasperation, "so can *Rose* look into it?"

"Not without someone to focus on," said Annie. "And since both of her focus targets are out of the state, we're momentarily blind. I mean, there's a silver lining—like Pars was saying, we might get information we can use from Tampa, and if they're planning to move, Rose will see where they end up."

"But what do we do while she's watching them?"

Pars shrugged and bit into his pizza. "We wait."

Though disappointed, I could do nothing to speed along the investigation, so I went about my business. Grabbing a granola bar and a travel mug of coffee, I slipped out to my workshop for an hour to finish packing the day's deliveries and double-checked my list, then loaded the cardboard cartons into the back of my truck and returned to the kitchen to find the agents hunched over their computers. "Going to drive around and drop off boxes," I announced. "Any update?"

"Dirk is at a Waffle House near the portal," said Pars, not looking up from his screen, "and Katin is sitting in the hotel lobby, breakfasting and looking at rental listings. Or so said Yven twenty minutes ago. About what we anticipated—"

"Hi!" an annoying voice chirped in Pactish from Pars's computer. "It's been a while. Do you want to save your report?"

"For God's sake, man, *mute* that thing," Annie muttered, and closed her computer as she stood. "Jane, could you use a hand?"

The look Annie was shooting me spoke of a desperate need for a change of scenery, and I played along. "Sure. We'll pick up lunch, Pars," I said, and pulled her toward the door before he could object.

"I've got seven deliveries to make," I told Annie as we wound down the hill toward town. "Three B&Bs, four rental cabins. They're all clustered around Ragged Gap, but if you *wanted* to swing over to Whitford…"

"Bad idea." She clung to the door while I rounded a

sharp corner. "For all the reasons heretofore enumerated, and because Pars will have my hide if I let you go investigate on your own."

"I don't know, he seems to like you."

"Yeah, well, he likes Canna a whole lot more, and she's already laid down the law concerning you." Catching my surprise, Annie said, "The five of us know about your Nerin connection, but it's not going any further. Liogh knew what they were doing when they asked for us specifically."

I quirked a brow.

"Rose lost her grandfathers to the draught," she said, counting on her fingers. "Yven knows what it can do, but he was contemplating taking it to be with Rose. I almost got a mind wipe via potion, and as for Pars, he and Canna have been mixed up with the human and quasi-human craziness for the last couple of years. Don't worry," she said, reaching over to squeeze my shoulder when I came to a four-way stop. "We're on your side, Jane."

Softly exhaling as I started forward again, I said, "I appreciate that, but right now, other than the murderer on the loose and whatever the hell it is that Katin's doing, my biggest concern is keeping Dad out of trouble."

"Understood, so we're going to play this by ear. Let's see what we can do to get you into the Pactlands without dragging your dad in front of a tribunal."

I nodded and drove for a moment in silence, deep in my own troubled thoughts.

At the next stop, as I paused to let a pair of vultures hop away from the raccoon they were eating in the middle of the road, I asked, "What's it like?"

"What's what like?" Annie replied.

"The Pactlands. Dad's told me a little, and Liogh gave me their take on Beukal, but what do you think?"

"Well…" She hesitated, frowning in contemplation while I eased around the roadkill. "DPP is headquartered in Beukal. It's nice, as cities go. Maybe a little smaller than

Richmond, but ridiculously clean. I don't know what sort of magic keeps the place spotless, but you can almost eat off the sidewalk. The best arts and nightlife are there in the capital," she said, warming to the subject. "There are decent restaurants and little local theaters and stuff elsewhere, but if it's trendy or avant-garde, it's in Beukal. Plenty of people live in the city—Yven and I used to, and Pars and Canna have a house on the outskirts—but lots of us commute."

"Too expensive?"

"Not really. You see the usual dynamic: people in the city think everyone else is provincial, and people outside can't imagine living in tiny apartments and being happy about it. I had a nice place near DPP while they were working on me," she said, "and I do miss it sometimes, but living with my husband's family has its perks. Better scenery, room to sprawl, *privacy*..."

"Out in the 'burbs?" I asked.

Annie chuckled. "Not exactly. The lodge is sort of a hidden pocket within the Pactlands—you can't get in unless you're part of the Hunt or someone brings you. I'd be happy to show you sometime, if you'd like," she offered with a grin.

"Assuming I could get through the portal."

"See, that's one of the perks of joining the Hunt. Portals are optional for me." Her smile widened as my head whipped toward her. "Guess Rose didn't mention that I can, for lack of a better term, teleport."

"*Seriously?*"

"Yup. If I've been somewhere and remember it, I can return there...which means that if a certain someone lacking credentials wanted to pop over to the Pactlands and take a peek around, I could make that happen."

"And you wouldn't get in trouble?" I pressed, my heart racing.

"Not if we weren't caught. Anyway, my Wylan's a Forum rep now, so I'm not overly concerned about the potential repercussions. Just file that away for later," she told me as I turned to detour around our so-called downtown. "Once this mess is more manageable, if you want to see what you've been missing...let me know, okay?"

"Thanks," I said, fighting the urge to slam on the brakes and hug her.

"Sure. I mean, for heaven's sake, you're a freaking pyromancer. You'd think they'd want you *inside* the Pactlands so that you don't do something crazy out here," she groused.

"I'm responsible," I protested, then reconsidered my answer. "Mostly. Within reason."

Annie's mouth twitched. "Do I want to know?"

"Sometimes, things need burning."

"Like...trash piles?"

I sucked my teeth. "More like 'enough of the house to make the abusive partner run for the hills.'"

She stared at me.

I shrugged and smiled. "Someone's got to take care of this town, right?"

"Cops, usually."

"Ah, but no one suspects the lotion lady," I replied, and started up the next hill toward my first delivery.

We returned to my place around one, my truck bed emptied and a bag of takeout from Mama Hen's on Annie's lap. While I had no idea what Pars liked, Annie seemed to think the most important quality of the food we chose for him was sheer quantity, so we'd brought back a selection of sandwiches and enough sides for six.

"He's absolutely not part troll," she laughingly assured me during the drive. "Have you ever seen a troll?"

"If so, they were masked."

"*Right*," she muttered. "Well, I work with several. The Interdiction chief—that's my chief's boss—is a troll, and she's got more than a foot on Pars."

"Whoa," I mumbled.

"Muscular and green. Tusks, too. She's a nice lady when she's off the clock, but she's a damn good agent, and you don't want to see her pissed. You also don't want to get between her and her dinner, incidentally," she added, smiling to herself. "Talk about big eaters. She favors buffets on date nights."

"You keep track of your boss's dates?" I asked, perplexed.

"Not directly, but she's seeing one of my brothers-in-law, so word gets around." Catching my deepening look of confusion, she explained, "He's basically an adopted troll. It's complicated. But they seem happy, and if it's working for them, I'm not one to judge."

As I opened the front door for Annie, Pars called to us from his makeshift kitchen office, "Anything amiss?"

"All quiet," I said. "Anything from Rose?"

He unfolded himself from his chair and unkinked his back. "Katin is driving around the outskirts of…*Chattanooga*," he said slowly, "and Dirk has gone to market. Hope he gets what he needs, since I'm pretty sure DPP will be raiding it in a few weeks' time, but Rose is giving us names and faces. I'm trying not to bother her," he said, and perked as Annie started unpacking the food. "Something for me in there?"

"The chicken salad is Jane's, and this is mine," Annie replied, snatching up a Reuben, "but you can have your pick of the rest."

He hurried over, scanned the wrapped sandwiches and cartons of sides, then fondly ruffled her hair. "What did I tell you, Jane?" he said, grabbing a club and a bag of chips. "Best trainee, right here."

CHAPTER 12

I loitered around the house as long as I could Thursday, hoping for a game plan, or at least an update. At ten that morning, Yven called Pars to pass on the latest from Rose: Dirk was on his way north again, while Katin remained in Chattanooga, scoping out rental properties with few neighbors. With no direction forthcoming in the immediate future and the agents in my house busy with their paperwork, I slipped off alone to make home deliveries.

I was proud of my monthly subscription service. Sure, I had yet to work out all the issues, and I wasn't yet taking orders outside of about a twenty-mile radius because I was still studying my shipping options, but in the year I'd offered the program, I had yet to screw up an order, and that was saying something. My local customers could order any of my products for monthly or quarterly delivery, and I kept careful notes in a spreadsheet, which I triple-checked before sealing my custom-printed cardboard boxes. I always threw in a little something extra, and for the September orders, that meant votive-sized pumpkin spice candles, which I'd only poured the week before. Granted, the warm weather didn't inspire thoughts of festive gourd season, but at least I was *trying*.

With the truck loaded, I made my way down the mountain, relying on the delivery route I'd plotted to minimize the trip. My first two customers actually lived within a couple miles of me, and both ladies were at home when I drove up and rang the bell. We chatted briefly about their kids going back to school and how we'd spent our respective Labor Day weekends—for obvious reasons, I didn't mention the murder—and then I pressed on.

My third stop was in a midcentury neighborhood behind the downtown area at the home of Hazel Paulson, a retiree who swore by my bath soak. She was a friendly woman, the sort who could talk your ear off, though frankly, I was surprised she bought from me because she was a frequent presence at Mystic Mountains' events. Perhaps her love of dried lavender overcame whatever reservations she had about me, as she'd been one of my first subscribers and remained a loyal customer.

I parked behind her Subaru and climbed the porch steps, box tucked under my arm, then rang the bell and waited. A minute later, with no sign of life, I rang again, thinking perhaps I'd caught Hazel in the bathroom or running the vacuum cleaner. Still, the house remained quiet—odd, especially as she hadn't driven anywhere.

I tried a third time with no success, then left the carton on her welcome mat and started off. Before I reached my truck, however, I heard the screen door squeal open, and I turned to see the lady of the house standing on the threshold, staring blankly at me.

"Ms. Paulson? Are you okay?" I asked, returning to the porch. "Just dropping off your subscription box…"

She squinted at me as if trying to recall who I was.

"It's Jane Fortune," I said, forcing a smile and hoping she hadn't just had a stroke. "Bringing by your September items…is everything all right?"

"Jane?" she mumbled dazedly. "Um…yes. Yes, I'm fine." Slowly crouching, she retrieved the carton and hugged it to her thin chest. "I'm fine."

To my eyes, she was anything but. "Are you sure? I can call a doctor," I offered. "Or do you want to go to the hospital? I'll drive you if something's wrong."

"I'm fine," she repeated, her mouth curling into an approximation of a smile. "Tired. Going to lie down."

By then, I'd come close enough to get a good look at her eyes, and while they seemed a little glazed, they *were* focusing on me. "If you're sure," I said, retreating a step. "My phone number's on the packing slip in the box. If something changes and you need a ride, you give me a call, okay?"

"Okay," she replied, and backed up into the house, letting the screen door close between us. "Thank you."

"Yes, ma'am." I waited until she closed the main door as well, then climbed back into my truck, puzzling over Hazel's reaction. Maybe she'd slept poorly the night before, I thought, trying to rationalize her demeanor. Maybe she'd just received some bad news. Maybe she really was having a medical emergency, and I'd kick myself for not taking her to a doctor...but by then, the house was locked tight again and quiet, and hoping for the best, I backed out of her driveway.

Annie was waiting with leftovers from Mama Hen's when I got home. "Hey, didn't know if you'd eaten," she said, gesturing to the three sandwiches left on the counter. "Got a few extra, just in case..." She paused and frowned as I dropped my purse on the counter. "What's up?"

"I don't know," I said, heading for the sandwiches. "Folks are weird today."

"How so?" she asked, and Pars looked up from his computer.

"Kind of hard to say. Some of my customers seemed out of sorts. Disoriented." The first sandwich I found was a ham and Swiss—good enough. "I was afraid that one of them might have had a stroke, she seemed so dazed, but a couple more were acting just like her. Two didn't come to the door at all." Taking a bite—my stomach was begging for food—I continued with my mouth full. "Don't know whether they're under the weather, too, or just out of the house, but the other three bother me."

"Any commonalities?" Pars pressed.

I thought as I chewed. "Hazel Paulson is in her seventies, retired. I have no idea about her medical history, but she seems to get by on her own. Juniper Fenwick is…thirty-five, I'd guess. Married, no kids. She's a quilter. And the third was Denise Contri. Maybe fifty? I know she had breast cancer two years ago, but she's in remission."

"They live around here?"

"Within ten miles of me—"

"You seem to be stuck," Pars's computer chirped in Pactish. "Would you like for me to—"

Annie slammed the laptop shut with a grunt, and Pars rolled his eyes at me. "The software assistant can be slightly aggravating. You were saying?"

"Why not disable it?" I asked the agents.

"Because," said Annie, folding her arms, "the geniuses who made DPP's software didn't include a way to turn it off. Honest to God," she grumbled, "we've got people over there who can see the freaking future, and no one foresaw that this could be obnoxious."

Pars turned to her and smirked. "Going to take it up with Lord ti'Dana?"

"Don't tempt me," she replied, lifting her cell phone off the table.

"Sorry," I began, "who—"

"One of Rose's great-grandfathers is a future farseer," Pars explained. "Maybe the best out there. Also the director of the Division of Intelligence, so we don't ask too many questions…except Annie here, who somehow has him in her contact list."

"Don't be jealous that Diriem likes me," she said primly, and stuck out her tongue. "Right, where were we?"

"My customers who seemed off," I said, putting my sandwich aside for the moment. "Three locals, all female, all use my products, but I *know* my stuff's unaltered…" The answer hit me like a bolt between the eyes, and I groaned at my own stupidity. "Mystic Mountains. *Fuck.*"

"That's the New Age shop where Katin's been selling her potions, right?" said Annie.

"Yeah. Hazel hangs around there, Denise always stops by their tent on Market Day, and Juniper goes in for tarot readings—she invited me a couple months back. Juniper was at the Monday event with Katin," I said, searching my memory of that night for a glimpse of the other two faces. "I…I can't recall if Denise and Hazel were there, but if all three of them are on the Oil of Life plan…"

"There's nothing in the vials Yacovi tested that would make someone disoriented," Pars told me, shaking his head. "Glowing fingers, yes, but not fuzzy minds."

"Dad only tested two of Katin's products," I reminded him. "She didn't sell me the advanced stuff. If the three of them are on that, and they're having a weird reaction…" I paused as Annie marched out of the kitchen. "Where are you going?"

"To get my kit!" she called over her shoulder.

Pars sighed. "*Humphries…*"

"Don't start that, Mera!"

"Annie," he tried again, raising his voice as she rummaged through her gear in the den, "I know what you're thinking, and no. We can't just bust in on them."

"Like hell we can't." She stormed back into the room, zipped black nylon bag in hand. "I've got a broad-spectrum neutralizer in here. Let's go."

"Annie—"

"You've never been on the receiving end of an experimental potion," she snapped. "*I* have. And if this bitch has been making guinea pigs out of humans, then I take that *personally*."

"We don't know whether they were exposed to whatever is in the third of Katin's products," Pars said, his tone low but calm. "This might be…I don't know, the flu or something."

She fixed him with a withering stare. "I've had the flu. Jane, what about you?"

"Yup."

"Did that look like the flu to you?"

"Not at all."

"Then that's settled. You're driving," she told me, and turned to leave.

"Humphries, *wait*—" Pars tried again, but Annie wasn't having any of it.

"If Chief has a problem with this, she can chew me out later," she said, throwing open the front door. "Jane, let's go."

Torn between the agents but sharing Annie's concerns, I mumbled, "Back in a bit," then grabbed my sandwich and purse, and bolted before Pars could stop me.

As I pulled into Hazel's driveway for the second time that day, I asked, "What's our cover story?"

"Our story," said Annie, double-checking the contents of her kit, "is that you are a concerned Good Samaritan, and I'm your visiting cousin, the EMT. Does that work for you?"

"Sure." I cut the ignition and hopped out, and Annie followed, bag in hand. "Should we have grabbed a blood pressure cuff or something to sell this?"

"If she's that disoriented, she might not even notice."

Crossing my fingers, I led Annie up the porch steps and rang the bell. After the fourth ring, I heard shuffling footsteps approaching, and then Hazel opened the inner door. She looked no better than she had that morning—if anything, she seemed less certain of how to respond to people on her doorstep—and I spoke slowly. "Hi, Ms. Paulson. I'm sorry to bother you again, but I'm concerned about you. This is my cousin Annie. She's an EMT. Would you mind if she checked you out real quick?"

Hazel's brow furrowed as her eyes tried to focus on me. "You..."

"It's Jane," I said, and opened the screen door. "May

we come in, please?"

She didn't nod, but she did retreat far enough to admit us, and she didn't resist when Annie took her elbow and steered her into the recliner. "Hello, there," Annie said with feigned brightness. "My name's Annie. What's yours?"

It took the patient a moment to mull over the question. "Hazel?"

"Hazel. Nice to meet you." Pulling a penlight from her bag, she flicked it on and held it in front of Hazel's face. "Could you do something for me, please? Could you follow this little light with your eyes? Not your whole head," she said gently as Hazel started to move, "just your eyes. That's it, good."

As Annie moved the penlight in various directions, she asked, "Miss Hazel, have you fallen lately?"

A long pause. "No?"

"Okay. Have you had anything weird to eat or drink? Any allergies?"

Again, Hazel took far too long to contemplate the answer. "No?"

"Glad to hear it." She turned off the light and put it away. "Now, this may sound like a strange question, but can you make your fingers glow for me?"

When Hazel didn't immediately react, I wondered if my intuition had been mistaken, but then she faintly smiled and raised her hands. As her fingertips lit up, Annie nodded. "That's *great*, thank you so much. You can stop now."

By the time the light had died, she'd pulled a small vial of thick, dark green liquid from her pouch and was drawing the potion into a syringe. "This may make your tummy a little upset," she said in the tones of a mother trying to coax medicine down a cranky toddler, "but you're going to feel *so* much better in a bit. Let me see your arm, now..."

She didn't bother with consent or an alcohol swab

before plunging the needle into Hazel's deltoid.

While Hazel stared blankly at the injection site, Annie repacked her gear, then beckoned me into the next room and lowered her voice. "Neutralizer. It works fastest when it's drunk, but she'll get the full effect. Also, that shit tastes *foul*, so a shot's kinder, really."

"You think a potion did this to her?"

"Absolutely. Now, where is the...*ah*." She hurried through another door and found the kitchen, then hastily dug through the cabinets until she found a bright pink plastic bowl. "Hope this isn't her favorite."

Five minutes later, as poor Hazel violently threw up into the makeshift basin, I understood what Annie was afraid of. "It's okay," I said lamely, holding back her gray hair as she bent forward and emptied her stomach. "Almost over..."

"That's the other disadvantage to the injection route," Annie muttered from behind me. "The nausea tends to be worse. At least she doesn't have to drink it again..."

"You've been through this?"

"Training protocol, unfortunately. You're doing great, Hazel," she said, patting the patient's shoulder while she heaved again. "Just let it all out."

By the time Hazel's stomach had calmed, Annie had brought a Sprite from her fridge, which Hazel drank without much coaxing. "Why don't you stretch out, hmm?" Annie suggested, popping up the footrest on the recliner. "Jane, could you grab a blanket? I'm going to go...dump this," she said, holding the puke bowl well away from her as she went in search of the bathroom.

Soon, Hazel was asleep in her chair, pale but breathing normally, and Annie whispered, "Come on, while she's out. Let's check her trash."

The bathroom can was a bust, but halfway down her kitchen can, I found a thin black box. "Oil of Life," I said, holding it up for Annie's inspection. "This is the advanced stuff."

"Bingo. So where's the bottle? It's pink, right?"

"If it's like the others," I said, grimacing at the mess of garbage through which I had yet to dig.

"It shouldn't be below the carton in the trash strata," Annie pointed out, to my great relief. "So she hasn't thrown it away yet."

We found it in her nightstand table, sandwiched between a well-thumbed KJV New Testament and an alarmingly large adult toy, the precise function of which I didn't want to think about in conjunction with my senior customer. But when Annie held the vial to the light, we saw that it was empty—slightly dotted with faint traces of purple but dry.

"She used the whole thing," said Annie, and huffed a sigh. "Well, that's not helpful."

"Maybe Dad can analyze what's left," I suggested.

She made a face. "Unlikely. He'll need *something* to work with, and this is barely stained. Still, let's get it out of here."

We packed up and checked on Hazel, who moaned and stirred as we started for the door. "Jane?" she croaked.

I slipped back to her side and patted her arm through the blanket. "It's going to be okay, Ms. Paulson. You rest."

"Wha...what happened?"

Her eyes were focusing again, I noticed, and decided not to completely lie. "Oil of Life. You had a bad reaction."

"But...it works..."

"Kind of. I think you might be allergic to something in it. Do you even remember when I came by this morning?"

She regarded me blankly, then shook her head.

"I thought you might be sick, so I came back. You're going to be fine now," I said, hoping my confidence in the neutralizer wasn't misplaced. "But stay away from that stuff, all right?"

Her eyebrows furrowed. "I've never had trouble before," she protested. "It's good stuff. Everyone says so."

"I know, but sometimes, allergies just pop up," I ad-libbed. "Hey, how long have you been using the advanced-level oil?"

"About two weeks, I guess." She started to sit up, then thought better of it and sank back into the chair. "Oh, I feel *awful.*"

"I'm so sorry. It'll pass, I promise. You, um…you just take it easy for the rest of the afternoon. Want your TV remote?"

Soon, I'd found a rerun of a game show for Hazel, and I left her to doze while Annie sneaked out ahead of me. Climbing into my truck, I asked, "How much of that neutralizer do you have left?"

Annie checked her pouch. "One dose."

"Who else has it?"

"Probably not Yven or Rose. Liogh might."

"Great," I said, and threw the truck into reverse. "We'll stop by Dad's on the way."

I wasn't surprised to learn that the detective shared Pars's sentiments about Annie and me running around town as a two-woman potion detox squad. "This is the sort of decision that needs approval from a supervisor," Liogh protested while Dad stood by, hands in the pockets of his potion-stained jeans. "Jane, I appreciate that you're concerned, and you as well, Annie, but let's be sensible—"

"Excuse me," she interrupted, "but did *you* get dosed with Roulette?"

"No—"

"And did *your* friends and neighbors die from that shit?"

Their mouth tightened. "No, but—"

"Then I don't want to hear any complaints from you about Jane and me checking up on a handful of misguided idiots who've been conned into taking God-knows-what! That poor woman was messed up," she said, staring them down. "Barely knew her own name. Now, look, I get that they're just humans and beneath Laws' notice," she continued, her voice thick with sarcasm, "but this is *personal*, bub. So give it," she demanded, extending her hand.

"Annie," they tried, "that's precisely the problem. This is too personal for you. I shouldn't have asked you to come in on this one—"

"How much do you need, kid?"

Liogh's head whipped toward Dad, who'd straightened and focused on Annie. "Yacovi—"

"How much?" he repeated, keeping his gaze locked on her. "If it's just neutralizer you want, I brew the stuff. Got a barrel sitting around for emergencies. Take what you need."

"This needs to be approved," Liogh insisted. "Maybe not the director, but *someone*—"

"You don't live here," Dad said firmly. "I do. And if people are as affected as the girls say, then we don't have time to deal with bureaucratic bullshit. Go fill up," he said to Annie. "There are plenty of clean vials in the brew room. Take extra, eh? Make an old man feel better."

Once Annie had left, Liogh glared at Dad. "We have rules and regulations for a reason. You know that."

"Sure," Dad said simply. "And I also know that sometimes, they do more harm than good. As do you, old friend. Else," he said, cocking his head, "you wouldn't be standing here with me right now, would you?"

Their shoulders slumped. "Yacovi…"

"What? I should have my license stripped at the *very* least, should I not?"

Rubbing their forehead, Liogh said, "This is different. We can hide Jane easily enough, but you're talking about using potions on humans without proper protective measures. There should be memory potions administered, if nothing else!"

"Ordinarily, I'd agree with you, but for two wrinkles

here. First, we don't know what they've been given, and I'm loath to dose with anything unnecessary without knowing what sort of cocktail we've got as a baseline. And second," said Dad, glancing my way, "you've got Jane in the mix."

Liogh followed his stare. "Meaning?"

"My daughter's got something of a reputation around here. If people believe they've witnessed true magic and connect it to Jane, there shouldn't be a great outcry." Catching my surprise, Dad smirked. "I'm not stupid, girlie. You think I haven't heard about Jane Fortune, possible witch and definite firebug?"

My face heated as I flushed. "I don't advertise or anything—"

"You don't have to. Word is that you fix problems. I can't tell you how many of my clients and customers have asked whether the rumors are true."

"And what do you tell them?"

"That I have no idea what they're talking about. But between you and me...well, let's just say that I know enough about your arson hobby."

"It's always for a good cause," I muttered.

"Uh-huh," said Dad, but when Liogh looked away, he winked.

As the agitated detective stepped outside to collect themself, Dad drew close to me and quietly said, "You do the right thing, Janie, okay? Liogh's going to do what they think is best, and I like where Annie's heart is, but you listen to your own gut. DPP and DOL can do as they like. You know this place a hell of a lot better than they do, and I trust you, kid."

I smiled weakly. "They're the ones with badges, remember."

"Which don't mean a damn thing to anyone outside the Pactlands. They're visitors here. This is *our* town. Yeah?"

"Yeah," I said, and hugged him.

"Love you, girlie," he whispered, and kissed the top of

my head before releasing me. "Go with Annie and do what you need to do. I'll handle Liogh."

"They're not happy," I said, glancing out the front window to see the detective pacing the scrubby lawn.

He snorted. "Believe me, they've seen worse."

Annie and I caught Denise home alone, sitting on her porch and staring into space, and coaxed her inside for a dose of neutralizer. She reacted much as Hazel had— copious vomiting, followed by lethargy—which gave us a chance to search her house. I found the telltale pink vial in her bathroom, standing up in an empty slot in the ceramic toothbrush holder, but like Hazel's, it was too empty to be of any help. Still, we bagged it and waited for Denise to come around, and then I questioned her about her use of the miraculous oil.

"Katarina said I should drink it," she mumbled, clutching a jelly jar of water. "It would work best that way. Make sure the cancer doesn't come back."

I pitied Denise—her flat chest and short gray curls were proof of how rough her illness had been—so I tried to be gentle. "How many medicines are you on right now?"

She thought briefly. "Five."

"Uh-huh. And you know how doctors want you to tell them about any supplements you're on so you don't get a bad interaction?"

She nodded, then sipped her water with shaking hands.

"Ms. Contri, what's in Oil of Life?"

Guilt flashed across her thin face. "It's all natural…"

"That doesn't mean it can't hurt you. Think about that little boy who accidentally ate peanut butter at the Fourth of July party downtown and almost *died*. Peanuts are natural, right?"

"You don't understand," she said plaintively. "It's *working*, Jane. It'll keep me safe, make me stronger—"

"It's a scam," I murmured, taking her hand, "and it's making you sick. No more mystery potions, okay?" I said as I released her and stood. "At least get the ingredient list."

I'd almost reached the door when she called my name.

"Yes, ma'am?" I replied, poking my head back into the living room where she'd landed.

Denise seemed wounded as she stared up at me. "Stephanie says you know secret types of magic, but you won't share. You keep it all to yourself."

"Does she, now?" I folded my arms. "Stephanie says a lot of things."

"Is it true?"

There was, I thought, a very thin path here across the abyss, and I chose my words carefully. "I have some talents. They can't be taught," I said, holding her gaze. "Least of all to someone like Stephanie. Now, I don't know who this Katarina woman is, but I'm telling you that Stephanie's playing with fire, and she's dragging you and everyone else who trusts her straight into the flames. For your own safety, no more Oil of Life."

"Can *you* keep me healthy?"

Could I? Was there something in one of Dad's grimoires that would fight disease and prolong life?

"I don't think so. Get some rest, Ms. Contri," I said, and hurried out before she could ask for details.

I'd hoped our third stop would be easier, but when we got there, Juniper's husband, Alan, was home. "I stopped by earlier to make a delivery, and Juniper seemed a little out of it," I said to him when he came to the door. "Just checking up on her. This is my cousin, an EMT—"

His eyes widened, and he practically pulled us into the house. "Thank *God*. I've been trying to convince her to go to a doctor for the last half hour..."

"Let me see the patient," said Annie. "Alan, was it? Maybe you and Jane could make a list of anything Juniper's been taking in case she needs to go to the hospital."

Annie worked quickly while Alan and I tabulated the bottles in his wife's medicine cabinet. I wasn't at all surprised to see an empty pink vial in there, but I played dumb. "What's that one?"

"That?" He pulled it out and frowned as he turned over the unmarked bottle. "I don't know. Something about a nail strengthener. One of her friends is into this new MLM or something," he said dismissively, "you know, like Avon? Juniper's been going to her parties to be supportive."

A likely story. Juniper got her cards read, but Alan, who ran a successful lawn business, was of a less spiritual bent.

"May I take that?" I asked, pointing to the vial. "I don't recognize the brand, but maybe she's having a bad reaction."

He shrugged and handed it over, and I pocketed it without a fuss.

By the time we finished, Juniper was throwing up in a kitchen trash bag, and Annie met her alarmed husband with a professional smile. "Mild emetic," she explained. "This is the third case we've seen today. I suspect there's something she's eaten…has she bought any locally made bread, by chance?"

Alan stammered, thrown by the question. "Uh…I…I don't know, I've been out…"

"Ergot poisoning, I suspect. I've seen it before. Listen, she's going to be tired once she gets that mess out of her system," she said over the sound of poor Juniper's heaving, "so put her to bed and let her sleep it off. Clear fluids, broth tonight if she can stomach it. She should be fine in the morning."

As Alan thanked Annie and walked her to the door, I leaned close to Juniper's bent head and whispered, "No more Oil of Life. It's poison."

Her glazed eyes couldn't quite focus on me, but I left her in her husband's hands and climbed into the truck.

Annie leaned back against the seat and sighed as I backtracked toward home. "How many people in this town have been buying that shit, do you suppose?"

"Too many," I muttered.

"My thought exactly. So," she said, turning my way, "how do we get a list?"

CHAPTER 13

The one person who would be able to tell us how many of my neighbors were endangering themselves with Katin's mystery potion was Katin, and she remained annoyingly out of pocket.

Dirk, who'd left Tampa on Thursday morning after only a single night in town, failed to make an easterly turn toward home once he passed Atlanta, instead pushing on for Chattanooga. Rose called that evening to inform us that he and Katin had just grabbed a late dinner and talked about her ideas for potential relocation. "She seems more relaxed today," said Rose, her voice distorted by the speaker of Pars's phone. "Apparently, word from Ragged Gap is that no one has found a faun in the woods."

"They have another associate here?" Pars replied.

"Seems like it. I wasn't able to get any details from their conversation, and I missed the call earlier today, but they're not working alone. Someone's probably at that cabin."

"Any idea how many someones?" Annie pressed.

"Sorry, no. And I likely won't know for a couple days. Based on what I'm hearing from these two clowns, they won't be back in town until Saturday."

"*Saturday?*" Annie echoed, and groaned in frustration. "We can't afford to wait that long!"

"And maybe you've got bad intel," I interjected, "but we should expect Katin back by Friday night. She's got another seminar scheduled at Mystic Mountains."

Rose grunted. "I could be mistaken, but everything I've

heard in the last few hours suggests a Saturday departure. Plans may have changed after Dirk told her what he's been up to."

"Just putting this out there," Annie began, "but since we know they're going to be gone for at least another day, we could take our chances with the cabin—"

"*No*, Humphries," Pars snapped, scowling at her across the kitchen table. "And that is *not* negotiable."

"Absolutely not," came Liogh's voice in the background. "This isn't enough of an emergency to warrant that sort of risk."

"You didn't see those women today," Annie retorted. "We don't know how many others may be affected—"

"And I regret that," said Liogh. "I sincerely do. But I've walked into more than my share of ambushes and unfair fights in my career, and I'm not adding this one to the tally. We wait, we let Rose work, and we do this sensibly and *safely*."

"But—"

"Your life and the lives of everyone else on this team are worth no less than those of the potentially afflicted." Their tone, low and firm, invited no debate. "We will help them as we can. I promise you that, Annie. And you, Jane," they added. "I know this is difficult, and considering what Yacovi has been telling me of your...*exploits*, shall we say, I can only imagine that inaction is an unfamiliar mode for you. But we need to wait and use our best information before jumping into a fight."

As Annie glowered at the phone, I said, "Idea."

"Oh?" asked Pars.

"Stephanie Love. She wasn't handling Katin's sales, but she'd have a good idea of who's been buying. What if I went to Mystic Mountains tomorrow and tried to talk to her? I could bring Annie as backup," I suggested. "She could give me cover to walk in the store, at any rate."

I heard nothing but silence on the other end of the line for a few seconds, and then Rose said, "That's not a bad idea. And maybe Katin left some of her products there—if they could get a sample tomorrow, we could analyze it and know what we're dealing with before our masterminds return."

"Glad you agree. I'm going anyway, but I'm happy that you're on board with it."

Annie glanced my way and waggled her brows, and Pars, witnessing all, simply sighed.

Our espionage plan kicked off at ten Friday morning, as we needed to ensure that enough stores were actually open downtown to make our subterfuge convincing. I masked myself in the bathroom, going for an older appearance—mid-thirties, I thought, with unremarkable brown shoulder-length hair, brown eyes, and a diamond nose stud—and when I emerged, Annie was likewise unrecognizable, platinum blonde, well endowed, and tanned like she'd spent the summer baking in the tropics.

"Subtle," I said, giving her a once-over as she ran her now pink-tipped fingers through her hair.

She grinned, then answered me in a drawl far more pronounced than her usual accent: "Honey, if you've got masking jewelry, you may as well *employ* it."

"You don't want to go with something a bit more, I don't know...toned down?"

"Nope. Let them notice me," she said, posing with her hand on her shapely hip. "You're the one being sneaky."

Though Pars still wasn't entirely keen on the plan, he waved goodbye with his coffee mug as we climbed into my masked truck, now disguised as a white Camry.

"You do good work," Annie remarked, inspecting the interior of the vehicle as I drove down the mountain. "This is impressive, especially for someone missing a few classes."

"Dad's a good teacher," I protested.

"Oh, no offense to him. I just notice how twitchy the

guys get every time your homeschooling comes up." She rapped her knuckles against the newly beige glove compartment, then sat back, satisfied. "Don't get me wrong, Pars and Yven are great, but they grew up in a system with decades of mandatory education, especially for those with potentially destructive abilities. Now you've got Rose running around with no formal training—she's got private tutors these days, but she's still playing catch-up. I'm less worrying because it's not like I have actual talent to develop."

I gave her my best side-eye. "Says the woman who can teleport."

"Eh, that's mostly been intuited. And then there's you, the baby *pyro* with questionable credentials."

"Believe me, it's under control."

"I don't doubt that," said Annie, "but having come to know a pyro, and having witnessing what she can do when provoked...I mean, I get where the guys are coming from."

I slowed as a jacked-up truck swerved out of a hidden driveway and onto the main road. "What did she do?"

"Killed a dude."

"*Shit.*"

"He was a piece of work," she said. "And it was very much self-defense. But she didn't just fry him—she threw him into a wall with a fire jet, and the impact actually did him in." She paused, then asked, "Can you do fire jets?"

"Uh...maybe," I mumbled, absorbing *that* charming story. "And this pyro, she's...trained?"

"Somewhat. DOL's giving her better training on the job. I should really introduce you two," she said, propping her elbow on the door. "Fell's good people. Also hilarious at karaoke night," she added, smiling to herself, "but you didn't hear that from me."

"Huh," I managed, still hung up on the possibility of death by pyromancy, and focused on the road.

I knew my wild talent could kill. Dad had made that

abundantly clear when I was a kid, stressing over and over how crucial it was that I develop self-control and master my temper. While I'd done a fair bit of property damage with my abilities, I'd made it a point never to kill. To release that sort of fatally destructive power, then have to live with the aftermath...

I wondered what Annie's friend's nightmares were like.

That was, however, a matter for another time, as my focus shifted to the task at hand as soon as we neared the outskirts of the downtown district. Pulling into the public lot, which was only about a third full that morning, I found a space near the back and cut the engine. "Ready?"

"Ready," Annie confirmed, slipping on a pair of large sunglasses. "Where to first?"

Ordinarily, I'd have popped by the Mercantile, but I didn't want to play-act in front of Bitsy. "There's a shop called The Robin's Nest about two blocks away. Home goods and knickknacks. Let's start there, poke around, and make our way to Mystic Mountains."

We strolled through the lot and up the sidewalk, skirting the weekend tourists with their to-go cups from the overpriced coffeeshop who kept pausing to examine menus and window displays, and slipped into the store. I decided not to buy anything, lest someone recognize the name on my credit card and realize my face didn't match, but Annie had come with cash, and she carried a floral, summer-weight throw blanket to the register with a satisfied smile. "I live with *men*," she said once we were back on the street. "*So* many men. My home office is maybe a tad too feminine just to counteract the gallons of testosterone around me, but whatever. On occasion, I like pretty things."

"You don't have to justify yourself," I assured her.

"Thanks—*ooh*," she said, pulling me to a halt outside the window of the candy store. "Look at those!"

Featured atop the table in the window was a rose-printed porcelain plate covered with oversized pink sugar cubes, some dusted with gold, others dotted with lilac or violets. "Fancy," I said. "Not sure what you'd do with them…"

"My horse would *inhale* that plate."

"You've got a horse?"

She turned to me and grinned. "Hunt, remember? She's a gentle girl with a massive sweet tooth. Easily bribed, and since I like to stay on her good side, let's just pop in here for a second…"

Twenty-five dollars later, Annie left the store with the goods for her mare—Jimbo, she told me with a pained sigh, and the name was *not* her choice.

Slowly but steadily, we pushed on for Mystic Mountains. By the time we arrived, Annie had accumulated enough bags to pass as a well-heeled tourist, the sort who attracted the attention of clerks eager for a sale. I let her walk in first, following a few steps behind and immediately veering toward a different area of the shop to observe.

To her credit, Annie played the role she'd given herself with aplomb, picking up expensive semiprecious carvings and peering into the jewelry cases. I'd have expected at least two of the staff to move in for the easy pickings, but no one came. Digging through a bowl of smooth palm stones, I looked around the store, searching for the problem…and then it hit me.

The place was *dead*.

On an ordinary Friday, with the influx of weekenders, Mystic Mountains did a healthy business. The groupies came around for the yoga sessions or for tarot appointments, or just to hang out. Even people who didn't believe in the healing powers of crystals liked shiny baubles, and I couldn't fault Stephanie's jewelry selection—whatever else could be said for the woman, she had decent taste. But aside from the two of us and a trio of women in yoga pants camping in the café, the store was nearly empty. A guy I didn't know manned the café counter, but Penny, Stephanie's longtime associate, was sitting at the main register, staring into the distance like she was miles away.

Five minutes later, when the only thing that had changed was the addition of a young couple browsing the agate bookends, I took action. "Uh, hi," I said to Penny, putting a polished green chunk on the counter. "I'm kind of new to crystals, and I think I'm *drawn* to this one, but I didn't see any information cards, and, uh…could you tell me about it?"

My question was a gimmie. The rock was aventurine, allegedly good for enhancing prosperity, and if even I knew that, then Penny should have had volumes more to reveal about the palm stone's origin and uses. I'd seen her at work during my rare trips to the store, guiding neophytes to various rocks that might cure their ills and suggesting pendants and bracelets to keep the necessary stones on the buyer's body. She was a master of the up-sale, and the persona I employed—curious, friendly, a little unsure—should have sent her into "educational retail" mode.

Instead, Penny slowly turned to look at me, then blinked a few times as if trying to clear her vision. "Uh…"

"This stone," I said, nudging it closer to her with two fingers. "Could you tell me about it, please? What is it?"

"Um…" Her eyes drifted from my face to the rock on the wooden counter, and she continued to blink in silence as her head tilted downward. Her gray hair fell forward, curtaining off her peripheral vision, but she paid it no mind. Positioned in front of her as I was, I saw her forehead barely furrow as she stared…well, in the vicinity of the stone, at least. I wasn't sure her eyes were actually focusing.

"Are you okay, ma'am?" I asked. "Is something wrong?"

It took a solid twenty seconds for her face to lift again, and her expression seemed only slightly puzzled, as if she were trying to work out a calculus problem in a deep dream.

Annie walked up as Penny continued to gaze blankly at me. "She looks stoned," I muttered.

"I've seen stoned," Annie quietly replied. "She's past that."

"Got the goods on you?"

"Yeah. Is there somewhere private around here?"

"See the door in the back wall between the open space and the café? That leads to the business office and the session rooms upstairs. We should treat her in private."

"Is there a bathroom up there?" she asked.

"Let's hope so."

Leaving the aventurine where it lay, I came around the counter and coaxed Penny from her stool. She cooperated slowly but without any resistance, and with Annie's help, we half-carried her to the rear door. The women in the café didn't pay us any mind, and judging by the barista's face, he was nearly as far gone as his colleague. Working together, we tugged Penny upstairs, and I checked the rooms for witnesses.

"All clear," I told Annie. "Bathroom is halfway down."

As I shepherded Penny into a stall, Annie pulled her black case from her purse and readied the injection. "Get her to kneel, if you can," she said, drawing up the green potion. By the time I'd positioned Penny in front of the porcelain throne, Annie was ready to jab her in the arm, and I held the patient still.

"How long before—" I began, then swore and grabbed Penny's hair as she violently heaved. "That was fast."

"Your dad makes good product. *Fresh*," said Annie, who stepped out of the stall to clean up while I attended to Penny.

"Guard the door, okay?" I called over the noise, wishing I had something to block the smell.

When Penny's stomach calmed, I flushed and dragged her to the counter. Someone had stocked the bathroom with a sleeve of little plastic cups beside a communal bottle of bright blue mouthwash, and I urged sips of water down Penny's throat as she tried to collapse on me. While she wasn't a large woman, she was nearly dead weight, and Annie and I struggled to get her out of the bathroom and onto the couch in one of the session rooms before she fell asleep.

"We can't just leave her," I said, turning on a curtain of soft twinkle lights in case Penny awoke with a headache.

"She should be fine once she wakes," Annie replied, considering the sleeping woman. "That potion's miserable in the moment, but it'll clear whatever's affecting her."

"Not that. We need information." Before Annie could object, I asked, "Did you notice any of Katin's boxes downstairs? Any stock sitting around? Because I didn't. If there's anything here, it's not out in public."

"We could look for the stockroom while she's resting…"

"Or we could push for real information." I concentrated for a few seconds, and my mask fell away. "She knows me," I explained. "Let's see if I can get anything out of her."

"You want to blow your cover?"

"*You* don't need to," I said. "She's not going to talk to a rando, but she might give me answers."

A long ten minutes later, Penny began to stir, and I knelt beside the couch as her eyelids fluttered. "Penny?" I murmured. "It's Jane Fortune. Look at me."

To my relief, her gaze locked on my face. "Jane?" she rasped. "What…where…"

"You're at work, but we took you upstairs to rest. You've had a nasty reaction to Oil of Life."

"I…I what?"

Drawing upon whatever reserves of patience I possessed, I said, "That crap you've been using from Katarina. What's the last thing you remember?"

Though she was obviously confused by her situation, she answered my question. "Um…I drove in around seven. To defrost stuff for the café. Parked in the back…"

"Do you recall unlocking the store? Turning on the lights? Opening the register? Anything?"

She shook her head against the throw pillow.

"You're not the first," I said. "People who've been using Oil of Life have had bad reactions. My, uh…cousin's an EMT," I said, gesturing toward Annie, who lurked by the door. "She gave you a shot to counteract it." I got to my feet and helped Penny sit up, though she flopped back against the cushions, exhausted. "Do me a favor. Make your fingers light up."

That got her attention, but she tried to play dumb. "What do you mean?"

I folded my arms and stared down at her. "That stuff you've been taking makes your fingers glow. Show me."

Her mouth opened and closed twice before she formulated a response. "How do you know about Oil of Life? You haven't been to the seminars…"

"I have my ways," I replied, deciding not to throw Bitsy under the bus. "Y'all should expect *that* much from me. Now light 'em up."

Penny held her hands in front of her face and stared at them. When nothing changed after a few seconds, she brought them closer, then scowled at them in frustration. "Why…why are they not…"

"Good. That means the neutralizer worked."

Anger flashed in her eyes, but she was too weak to push herself from the couch. "You…you…*bitch*!" she sputtered. "What did you do to me?"

"Saved your life, quite possibly," said Annie, shifting her laden purse on her shoulder. "It's hard to tell without a sample of the stuff you took, but you *definitely* weren't in a good state half an hour ago."

Penny looked her up and down. "Who the heck are—"

"I'm maybe the best friend you have today besides Jane, since she's the one who insisted on dragging your sorry ass up here and treating you." Annie wasn't an enormous woman, perhaps five-foot-eight, but when she loomed over the couch, Penny shrank back. "You're playing with fucking fire. What's in Oil of Life?"

In fairness, Penny did a remarkable impression of a landed fish.

"I...I don't know," she admitted in a rapid babble, "but it works, it's giving us real power—"

"So you're using something you can't identify? Dabbing it on? Drinking it?" When Penny nodded, Annie leaned closer. "Do you realize how *stupid* that is?" Giving Penny another glance, she said, "Let me guess, you're a clean eater, right? No ingredients you can't pronounce?"

"Uh...well, yes," said Penny. "I try. It's better for your body," she said defensively, climbing atop what was surely a familiar soapbox. "Helps avoid the buildup of toxins you get in the typical Western diet—"

"So you won't eat MSG or Wonder Bread, but you've been knocking back shots of a mystery liquid that makes your fingers light up? Tell me, does that make any goddamn sense?"

"It's *magic*!" she protested. "I don't expect you to understand—"

At that, Annie flipped her sunglasses from the top of her head down to the tip of her nose, the better to glare at Penny over the lenses. "I have done things with magic you can't imagine," she snapped. "*Real* magic, not this shit you're playing with. And I know *very* well how the wrong potion can wreck you."

With that, she turned around and pulled up her shirt, and I stifled a gasp.

Annie had masked her whole body—her skin tone was uniform—but she hadn't covered *everything*. Crisscrossing her back, above and below the band of her bra, were white lines of scar tissue, some barely wider than a papercut, others the thickness of a pinkie.

"Most of those are from last year," she said, keeping her back on display. "Bad potion reaction did a number on me. I'm lucky that's healed as well as it has." Pulling her shirt back down, she turned to goggling Penny and murmured, "Just because someone tells you it's magic doesn't mean it's harmless. No one's sprinkling fairy dust on you. Potions can have side effects like any drug, and for you to blindly drink what some charlatan gave you—"

"*She* has power," said Penny. "Real power! More than you," she added with a spiteful glance my way. "And unlike *some* people, she's willing to share and teach."

I cut my eyes to Annie, who nodded.

"Katarina is taking you for a ride," I said, and let my arms ignite. I smiled to myself as Penny shrieked and tried to push herself into the back of the couch, but I retreated a step before she could start screaming in earnest. "What she can do...what *I* can do...that's not something just anyone can learn. It's inborn." I made a point of lifting and studying my arms, then drew the fire down my limbs and into a ball, which I held hovering between my palms. "She's robbing you blind. The stuff in the beginner and intermediate bottles of Oil of Life is no more than a party trick—yeah, your fingers light up, but that stops. You're not developing wondrous powers," I said with all due sarcasm. "But from what we've seen in the last two days, there's something different in the advanced bottle. I need a sample, and I need a list of *everyone* who's bought that stuff from her."

I wasn't playing fair. Penny was just a slightly deluded salesclerk who surely felt like crap after her neutralizer dose, and I was standing feet away from her with a basketball-sized globe of flames in my hands. There wasn't any way she could have perceived that but as a threat.

Still, she was made of tougher stuff than I'd imagined. "We don't have any here," she said, the barest wobble in her chin. "Katarina takes it all with her when she leaves. And I don't have a customer list."

"Could you *make* one?" Annie suggested. "Surely you could give us some names."

"We respect our customers' privacy. I won't do it."

I extinguished my fireball with a sigh. "Your customers are in danger, Penny," I said, moving closer to the couch. "I'm not trying to add them to mailing lists! We're really concerned, here!"

She shook her head.

"Where's Stephanie? I think *she* might be interested—"

"In how you took my power away?" Penny interrupted. "How you...you...I don't even know what you did, but you erased my memory—"

"We absolutely did not," said Annie. "You were off in la-la land, and I gave you a neutralizer to bring you out of it."

"You drugged me against my will!"

"Think of it as magical naloxone. You weren't in any condition to consent."

But by then, Penny had her dander up. Pushing herself as far as she could off the couch, she said, "If y'all aren't out of here in *one minute*, I'll call the cops! This is assault!"

"We're going," said Annie, and pulled me to the door by my arm. "And you're welcome," she added before nudging me down the stairs.

The store was empty when we returned but for the guy at the café counter, who stared at the far wall with his mouth hanging slack. "She won't make it down the stairs in time," Annie muttered, then quickly filled a clean syringe with neutralizer and jabbed it in the barista's arm. "Sorry, buddy," she said, and put an empty blender jar in his lap. "You're going to want that."

We made our exit as the poor man started puking. I turned the sign to CLOSED before shutting the door, and when I glanced to the left, I noticed the flyer in the window, which advertised Katin's next seminar. Friday 8 PM had been struck through with a red marker, and a handwritten note advised, *Will be rescheduled.*

"Great," I said, pointing to the sign. "Looks like Rose was right."

"That's the annoying part of hanging around farseers," Annie replied, leading the way back to my disguised truck. "They're often right…when they're willing to give you any information."

I smirked. "Speaking from experience?"

"Spend enough time with Diriem ti'Dana, and you'll both come to appreciate their abilities and find yourself fighting the urge to try to throttle answers from them. Oh, he's great when he's not in 'inscrutable oracle' mode," she added, "but when he is…" She shook her head.

"Annoying?"

"Frustrating. And what's our plan?"

"I'm thinking."

Once we were safely back in the vehicle, I said, "Part of me wants to go to Stephanie's house. She might have extra supplies or a list or something. On the other hand…"

"Penny's probably warning her," Annie finished. "And since Penny doesn't remember anything about her condition this morning, all she knows is that we took her power away." She frowned. "Does Stephanie keep guns?"

"Wouldn't be surprised. This is bear country."

Annie grimaced.

"Yeah. So if we show up on her doorstep, she might be dazed, but if she's not, then she might greet us with a rifle or call the police." I leaned back against my seat and groaned. "The only seminar I attended was last Monday's, and I didn't know everyone in the room. I can give you that partial list, but I didn't see which level of product they bought, so for all we know, they're fine…"

I doubted that even as I said it, and Annie's expression suggested that she concurred.

The women we'd treated on Thursday had been too disoriented to complain, but what did they think now that the fog had cleared? There went Jane Fortune again, the most selfish practitioner in the region, not only refusing to teach her tricks but now actively stymying others? I thought of old, crabby Jerry—what level of potion had he been buying? If I went to his house, gave him neutralizer, and took away his imagined power, the best outcome would be me running off his property at gunpoint.

"I think we need to wait," I said to Annie. "Not ideal, but I don't want to get shot or end up in a cell."

"Agreed." She buckled in while I backed out of the space. "You know, if we *did* get locked up, I could get us out."

"I appreciate that, but I live here, and fugitives don't pay their mortgages."

"Point," she said, and dropped her mask as we sped out of town.

CHAPTER 14

Rose's timetable didn't shift overnight. With Katin and Dirk not due to come home until later Saturday, I slept in a little, made a pancake breakfast—it didn't hurt to stay on Pars's good side—then left him and Annie to watch TV while I returned to the shops. "I just want to take a look around," I explained. "See who's on duty at Mystic Mountains. I'm not going to do anything stupid," I stressed before Pars could interrupt. "Not even taking neutralizer with me. If I see something weird, I'll call for backup, okay?"

Reasonably satisfied, they let me go alone, and I cranked the radio as I drove, enjoying the time away. While my houseguests were tidy and pretty quiet, they were still guests, and I hadn't had roommates in years. As unsettled as I was with the Oil of Life situation and Katin's continued absence, I needed a solo breather.

That morning, I didn't bother masking. I parked in the public lot and made a beeline for Mystic Mountains, but to my shock, the place was locked and dark.

Closed. On a *Saturday*.

Stephanie never closed on the weekends. Even when the big neopagan festivals fell on the weekends, she'd still keep the store running with a skeleton crew and flyers inviting the curious out to the woods. There was no note of explanation on the door, no sign of life within, and when I called the store's phone, I could hear it ringing through the glass—no one had bothered to forward it.

Troubled, I walked the streets for a time, trying to

distract myself with window shopping, then settled in at Mama Hen's for an early lunch while I put my thoughts in order. I'd just asked for a glass of tea when I detected motion coming up the aisle and spotted Tabitha Bradley approaching.

"Hey, there," I said when the waitress departed. "How's it going?"

"Honestly?" She glanced around, then nodded toward the empty seat in my booth. "Are you expecting anyone, or may I join you?"

"Please." I waited while she slid in and dropped her purse, then passed her my menu. "I think I've memorized this. Want to take a peek?"

"No need, thanks..." She smiled as the waitress returned with my drink, then ordered a glass of water. "This is going to sound crazy, Jane, but I think there's something strange going on around here," she murmured.

My heart raced, but I feigned ignorance. "What do you mean?"

Tabitha hesitated, and before she could answer, the waitress came back. We ordered our meal, and once we were alone, she leaned across the table toward me. "Okay, I know you don't have much to do with Mystic Mountains, but there's some weirdness with that place."

"You're just now noticing?" I asked, bringing the straw to my lips.

"*New* weirdness," Tabitha allowed. "I went to a seminar thing on Monday night, and this woman was selling an oil that she swears gives you magic powers. Don't laugh."

I shook my head. "Go on."

"Well, *I* wouldn't have believed it, but all these folks who'd been using it could make their fingertips light up like fucking E.T., and then *she*, like, levitated items across the room," she said, dropping her voice to a near whisper. "Goddess knows I'm not lying to you. If I hadn't seen it myself, I'd think this was bullshit, but Jane, I swear, stuff *flew*."

"I believe you," I murmured, and took her hand. "What happened next?"

"I bought some of her stuff. She wouldn't say what was in it, and I was curious…"

Leave it to the compounding pharmacist to try to analyze a potion. "So what was it?"

"Still haven't quite figured it out. Alcohol, some essential oils. The rest…I don't know. Organic compounds."

"Did you try it?"

Her dark eyes widened, and she shook her head so hard that her braids bounced. "Hell, no. I don't care if it gives you power—I'm not getting that near me until I know what's in it and how it works."

"Smart." I took a sip of tea. "What are you going to do, call the FDA or something?"

"I don't know. See, in the last couple of days, I've noticed people…missing. A couple of my customers were at that seminar, and from the looks of it, they'd been using for a while. They had prescriptions to pick up on Thursday and Friday, but neither showed—no call, no nothing. I've tried to reach them, even went by their houses, but no answer." She squeezed my hand, then released me. "I don't want to call the police over nothing, but I'm about *this* close to asking for welfare checks."

"That's probably not a bad idea," I replied, though I wondered what doctors would make of the potion-disoriented victims. "Do you, uh…you want some help?"

Tabitha held my gaze, absently nibbling at her lip, then quietly said, "I got a call yesterday from Ernie Flores. He's a longtime customer, and he tends to reach out with medical questions. Works at Mystic Mountains."

My stomach clenched. "Oh?"

"Yeah. Told me this weird story about how he lost a few hours yesterday morning—he remembered coming to work, and the next thing he knew, he was throwing up in the smoothie blender and felt like he'd been hit with the worst flu of his life. Passed out on the floor behind the counter for a bit, and when he came to, Penny Oglethorpe was standing over him. She told him this crazy story about you and another woman coming in and giving her some sort of drug, and all her power went away. Same thing happened to Ernie, he said—his fingers won't glow anymore."

I held my tongue.

"So I told Ernie he was an idiot for using that stuff and said to go hydrate, buy some Dramamine, and sleep it off. He asked if I had any Oil of Life—that's what the woman called it, Oil of Life—and I lied and said I didn't. He told me that Penny was going home to take whatever was left of hers to get her power back, but she didn't have enough to share with him."

"Good for Ernie," I muttered.

"That's what I thought. But what I want to know is what the hell you did to them."

"Tabitha—"

"All I've heard since moving here and getting in with the Mystic Mountains crowd is that you've got power. *Real* power. They say they're upset that you won't share it, but when I suggested to Stephanie that she invite you to give a talk, she balked. Frankly, I think she's afraid of you."

I nodded.

"I consider myself a fairly reasonable person," said Tabitha, "and I'll be the first to tell you I'm a practitioner, but I've never met anyone with half the abilities they attribute to you. Maybe it's all exaggeration, but I can't help but think there might be a grain of truth there."

Glancing around the quiet restaurant, I saw that the wait staff were nowhere close, and I whispered. The salt and pepper shakers slid across the table toward me, and as I caught them, I arched a brow at Tabitha in silent query.

While her face registered her shock, she didn't freak out. "Whoa."

"I fix problems," I murmured, manually putting the

shakers back in their holder. "Whatever they've been saying about me, that's what I do."

"And you can do…more than that?" she asked, eyeing the condiment basket.

"Yeah." Keeping my voice low, I said, "I know about Oil of Life. The beginner and intermediate bottles are pretty harmless, but I think there's something dangerous in the advanced stuff. Penny and Ernie were having bad reactions yesterday when I found them, and my…*colleague* and I treated another three on Thursday. I was hoping Penny would give me a list of buyers, but no dice."

Tabitha grunted. "From what Ernie was telling me, she thinks you assaulted her."

"We didn't hurt her. She got a shot of neutralizer to counteract whatever she's been drinking."

She cocked her head. "Neutralizer?"

Shit. "I…really shouldn't talk about that."

Smirking, she asked, "Going to tell me it's organic and all natural?"

"Organic in a carbon-based sense, I think…look," I said, "there are some things I'm not at liberty to talk about. I want to help, but if I start blabbing about everything I know…"

"You'll upset the wrong people?"

"Honestly, I'm not sure what would happen to me, but folks I care about"—Dad, specifically—"might get in big trouble. Do you trust me that I'm not trying to hurt anyone?"

She considered that briefly, and her gaze darted toward the salt and pepper again. "*Real* magic? Not parlor tricks?"

"The real deal."

A soft whistle greeted that pronouncement. "Can you teach me?"

"No."

"Can't or won't?"

"Can't."

Again, she leaned across the table, the better to stare

me down. "Who are you?"

"Just Jane," I said with a shrug. "For now, at least, can that be enough?"

Tabitha's mouth twitched, but she sat back and drummed her fingers on her folded arms. "Okay. For now."

"That'll do," I said, reaching for my drink. "And I've got an idea. Bitsy Prescott was at the last seminar, right?"

"How did you…you know, never mind," she muttered. "Yeah, Bitsy was there. She's been using Oil of Life."

"She got upgraded to the advanced level on Monday. I bet Penny and Ernie and the others we treated have been topped out longer. Whatever it is that's in that potion—"

"*Potion?*"

I gave Tabitha a long look, and she raised her hands in surrender.

"Whatever is in the *oil* might take time to build up," I said. "Like, I don't know—"

"Mercury?"

"Sure. Like mercury. If Bitsy just started it, then maybe she'll be in good enough shape to give us answers. Maybe a sample…or a list," I said, picking up speed as the thought hit. "She's been going to those seminars, she told me as much. Maybe she'll remember who was there."

"It's a plan," Tabitha began, but fell silent and smiled as our food arrived. Once the waitress stepped away, she gave her burger a longing look and said, "I guess we get this to go, huh?"

"Nah, eat up. I want to call in reinforcements," I said, pulling my phone from my bag. A few taps later, Annie answered, and I said, "Hey, I'm down at Mama Hen's. Want to come to lunch? Bring your bag of tricks?"

Annie cleared her throat. "Are you in trouble?"

"No, but there's someone I need to check on, and just in case…"

"On my way."

When I hung up, Tabitha asked, "Your, uh, *colleague?*"

"Just play it cool, okay?" I said, and bit into my chicken salad sandwich.

Annie arrived as we were wrapping up, and she eyed Tabitha with curiosity as she slid into the booth beside me. "Guess I'm just getting dessert, then…"

"I ordered you a sandwich as takeout," I said, and nodded to Tabitha. "Annie, this is Tabitha. Maybe the one person in this town who bought Oil of Life and didn't immediately drink it."

"Huh." Annie stuck her hand across the table to shake Tabitha's. "Congratulations?"

"She's a pharmacist—"

"Ah."

"—and a Wiccan who's heard a few things about me," I added in a rapid mumble, "so she wants to help."

"*Ah*," Annie said more pointedly, and gave Tabitha a careful stare. "And, uh…what have we heard, exactly?"

Tabitha smirked. "I've seen nothing, I know nothing, but I understand that you're carrying something effective against whatever's in the oil."

Annie nodded. "Works for me, but I think this is something we need to keep to ourselves," she said, circling a finger to encompass the three of us, "and not mention to the rest of the crew. Agreed?"

"Oh, definitely," I said, and nudged my plate toward her. "Fry?"

"Don't mind if I do."

I filled her in as we waited for her takeout bag and the checks, and then we gathered our things and headed out. "Bitsy's a friend of mine," I assured Annie once I was on the sidewalk, iced tea in hand. "She might be confused, but I think she'll cooperate."

"Let's hope so," she muttered. "Where's her shop?"

"The big one on the corner," Tabitha offered. "Ragged Gap Mercantile. She's got a bit of everything in there. This is probably not the time for it, but if you like old-fashioned candy—"

The door to the Mercantile flew open, banging against its frame, and an older woman I didn't know ran onto the sidewalk. "We need a doctor!" she cried, scanning the area for help. "Anybody! Is there a doctor here? A nurse?"

Despite the fact that none of us satisfied those criteria, we sprinted toward the store and past the woman to find a small crowd clustered by the counter. "Move," I barked, and a gawking tourist stepped aside to reveal Bitsy, who was lying on the warped wooden floor, jerking in what appeared to my layman's eyes to be a seizure. "Oh, *shit*," I said, stopping in my tracks. "Uh…"

Tabitha stepped into the breach. "Move aside, please," she said in a no-nonsense voice, and the crowd dispersed. Kneeling by Bitsy, she gently lifted and cradled her head as Bitsy continued to stare blankly at the ceiling and spasm. "Is she epileptic?" she asked me.

"Not to my knowledge. She's never mentioned it…"

While we waited for the seizure to end, Annie ushered the shoppers out and locked the door. Joining Tabitha on the floor, she pulled her black pouch from her purse and extracted a syringe and a vial of neutralizer.

"What's that?" Tabitha asked.

"You said she's not epileptic?" Annie murmured, glancing up at me. "If she's not, then I know of a few *oils* that might trigger a seizure. Uncommon side effect but something to look out for all the same. Let's hit her and see what happens."

"If she starts throwing up, she'll choke," I protested.

"We can handle it. Hold her as still as you can, okay?" she asked Tabitha, who did the best she could from her awkward position.

Gripping Bitsy's arm, Annie quickly gave her the shot of neutralizer. Almost as soon as the green liquid was out of the syringe, Bitsy's spasms began to subside to weak jerks. With Annie's help, Tabitha rolled her onto her side.

"Recovery position," Tabitha explained, adjusting Bitsy's legs. "This should keep her airway clear…"

A new sort of spasm shook Bitsy's torso and head, and she began vomiting onto the floor.

"I'll get the mop," I offered, running for the supply closet in the stockroom.

The other two kept watch, sliding Bitsy around as needed while I cleaned up after her. After a few minutes, her sickness calmed, and she lay curled up where she'd landed, exhausted and unconscious.

"What do we do?" Tabitha asked. "Get her to a doctor or let her sleep it off?"

"She should wake on her own in a few minutes," said Annie, repacking her gear, "but in light of her seizure, I don't know how much help she's going to be today. She may be too scrambled."

Pushing herself to her feet, Tabitha looked down at Bitsy, who was breathing more easily. "What would have happened to her if you hadn't given her that stuff?"

"I'm no expert, but based on what I've read, the seizure would have been prolonged, and she still would have had that crap acting on her system." Glancing around the store, she asked, "Is there something we could cover her with that isn't, like, that homemade quilt? I'm sure that's not cheap."

"Let me check the back," I said, and returned to the stockroom to hunt around. Flipping on the lights, I headed for the section of the counter that served as Bitsy's office and spotted a plaid blanket folded on the back of her chair—a little something to keep on hand for working in the drafty corners of the store during the winter months, I supposed. As I grabbed it, I noticed her purse in the seat of the chair, partly hidden beneath the counter.

Worth a look.

I unzipped the top and rummaged through the contents: wallet, keys, hand sanitizer, pepper spray, tissues, pocket-sized first aid kit…and then my fingers touched glass.

"Gotcha," I whispered, pulling a pink vial from the bottom of Bitsy's purse. There wasn't much liquid inside, but it was a start.

I quickly repacked her purse and returned to the store with the blanket and the vial. "Take this," I said to Annie. "Get it to the experts. I'm going to stay with Bitsy."

"Good work," she said, and tucked the vial into her bag. "Are you sure you don't want to come with?"

"That's my friend on the floor."

"*Right*. I'll keep you posted," she offered, and let herself out the front.

Tabitha locked the door behind her and flipped the sign to keep the window shoppers at bay. "These experts you mentioned...they can figure out what's in the oil?"

"That's what we're banking on," I replied, tucking the blanket around Bitsy. "Look, you don't have to stay. I'm sure you've got better things to do on a Saturday than hang out here."

"Are you a medical professional?"

"No..."

"Then I'm sticking around. Besides," she said, leaning against the counter, "someone's going to have to help you load her into a car once she wakes."

Bitsy dozed for nearly an hour. Once she began to stir, it took time just to coax her into sitting up, and she blinked blearily at us as she started to piece the world together. "Jane?" she asked. "What...where are..."

"You're at the Mercantile," I told her, squatting to be on her eye level. "You had a bad incident, so we kicked everyone out and closed for the day. How do you feel?"

She frowned as she pondered the question. "My head hurts. And my back..." Hissing as she moved, she reached around and rubbed the area above her tailbone. "And...something stinks..."

"That'd be the puke," said Tabitha. "You're going to want to give it a better mopping."

Bitsy puzzled over her briefly. "Aren't you...haven't I seen you around?"

"Tabitha Bradley," she replied with a strained smile. "I'm a pharmacist."

"No, not that...at Mystic Mountains, right? You...were you there Monday? With Katarina?"

She sighed. "Yeah, I was there. And you're damn lucky that Jane and I have been paying attention, since that stuff Katarina sold you gave you a seizure."

At that, Bitsy's mental fog seemed to clear. "A *seizure*? What are you talking about? It's been great so far..."

"Yeah, because you've been on the beginner and intermediate oils," I told her. "You just transitioned to the advanced level, right?"

"How did you know—"

"It doesn't matter. We think there's something nasty in the top-level stuff. Since Thursday, I've been running into people almost too dazed to remember their own name, and they're all Katarina's customers."

"But...no," she said bemusedly, shaking her head, "Oil of Life is fantastic. I showed you what it can do..." She held up her hands and looked at her fingers, but when they failed to illuminate, her frown deepened. "What...why aren't they..."

"Jane gave you some medicine to end your seizure, but it also neutralized Katarina's product," explained Tabitha. "You're better off without it."

Bitsy stared at us, aghast. "You took my *power* from me?"

"You didn't have any actual power," I said. "It was a trick—"

"It *wasn't* a trick!" she protested, her eyes welling. "It was real!"

"Bitsy," I said, keeping my voice level, "all that junk did was make your fingers glow. The other stuff Katarina can do...that doesn't come from an oil. She's been lying through her teeth and taking you all for fools."

I realized even as the words left my mouth that this was the wrong thing to say to a woman who'd been made to feel foolish in the most painful of ways. Her eyes hardened, and her confusion turned to fury. "They're right about you," she said through her angry tears. "You're an *awful* bitch."

"Bitsy—"

"Get out!" she screamed in my face. "You get out of here, and don't come back!"

Though her words stung, I stood and stepped away from her. "I'm going, okay?" I said. "Just wanted to be sure you were all right."

"How am I *all right*? You took my power away!"

"I'm trying to help you."

"Well, you can fuck right off," she snapped, and glared at Tabitha. "You, too. Y'all are just jealous, that's all there is to it."

"Goddess, give me strength," Tabitha whispered under her breath, then gripped Bitsy's shoulder. "Look at me. *No*, stop fighting," she said as Bitsy feebly tried to twist free, "and look at me."

Reluctantly, Bitsy scowled back at her.

"Your head is sore right now because you had a grand mal seizure," Tabitha told her. "Your butt is sore because you probably flopped to the ground as soon as it started, and you'll have bruises. This place smells like puke because the medicine Jane used to make you stop seizing also makes you sick to your stomach—right?" she asked, glancing over her shoulder at me.

"Sick and tired."

"Okay. Which is what you're going through right now," she said to Bitsy. "So let's think about this. You're mad at Jane for taking care of you and not at this Katarina woman, whoever she really is, for poisoning you? Is that where we are?"

"Katarina didn't *poison* me!" Bitsy exclaimed. "Oil of Life is—"

"What is it?"

Bitsy regarded her silently.

"I asked that at the seminar Monday, and y'all pooh-poohed me," said Tabitha. "'Oh, it's wonderful,'" she minced, "'it's magical, stop asking silly questions!' Sound right?"

"I...guess."

"Well, I've been trying to figure out what's in it. I've got a biochemistry degree, and I'm still not there. And that's just the beginner bottle—if Jane's right, the advanced stuff is completely different. How many people have you treated this week?" she asked me.

"Bitsy makes six," I murmured.

"*Six*," Tabitha repeated. "Not one of y'all knows what you've been taking, what it does to you, or how it might react with anything else in your system, and you're blaming *Jane*?" Thumbing one hand back at me, she continued, "That woman is *responsible*. She runs a clean workshop, we've gone over safety, and I've even tested some of her products for purity. Jane gives a damn. Katarina does *not*."

"Listen," I said when Tabitha came up for air, "maybe we can talk about this later. Bitsy's had a rough day. Do, uh...do you want a ride home?" I asked Bitsy. "I don't mind giving you a lift."

Though puffy, her eyes were cold as glaciers as she stared up at me. "I don't want *anything* from you. Get out. You can come box up your soaps and stuff tomorrow—we're done."

"Okay," I said, and retreated to the door. "I'm sorry, Bitsy. I really am."

"I'll get her back to her place," Tabitha assured me, and with that promise, I let myself out.

I was only halfway to my truck when my phone rang, and I swallowed my feelings as I looked at the screen. "Hey," I said, picking up my pace. "Did Annie bring you the sample?"

"Yacovi and Yven are working on it as we speak," said Liogh. "Annie and Pars are here. Come as soon as you can."

"What's up?"

The detective grunted. "Guess who's back in town?"

CHAPTER 15

Dad's home wasn't huge by most metrics. When he'd moved to Ragged Gap, he'd set up shop in a renovated two-story farmhouse—three bedrooms, two bathrooms, a barn, and plenty of room to hide his greenhouse and brew room, perfect for one. I hadn't done much to cramp his style, other than monopolizing one of the bedrooms and the smaller bath, and since I'd moved out, Dad hadn't bothered renovating.

Thus it was that poor Rose had spent much of the last week in my old room, complete with the movie posters and magazine pages taped to the walls and the headshop-chic sun and moon tapestry behind the bed. She was still up there when I arrived that afternoon, alternately spying with farsight and frantically sketching her visions. Annie had been sent up to babysit her and was hanging out in the hall with one of my grocery-store Harlequin paperbacks, on duty in case she needed anything. Yven, Rose's usual assistant, had relocated to the brew room with Dad, and the two were making the most of the sample we'd stolen from Bitsy. It wasn't much to work with, but between Yven's field kit and Dad's selection of reagents, they were doing their best to pick it apart in a hurry. This left Pars and Liogh, who had migrated to the kitchen and were assembling what appeared to be two dishes of chicken casserole.

"Dare I ask?" I said as I took in the scene—Liogh in a beige polo and Dad's red checked apron, Pars in a black T-shirt with my old canvas apron straining across his torso.

"We're being useful," Liogh explained. "Whatever Rose sees, we're not moving until closer to sundown, and since people get hungry and I hate to just sit, we thought we'd throw together a meal." They considered the two loaded Pyrex dishes, then asked, "Where would Yacovi keep water chestnuts?"

"I doubt he has any," I replied, pulling up a stool to a stretch of counter out of the way.

"Oh, well. We'll make do. Pars, there should be shredded cheese in the fridge from our grocery run."

As Pars topped the casseroles, I asked, "Did Annie tell you about Bitsy?"

"Seizure, yes?" said Liogh. "Yacovi was *very* interested. Has she recovered?"

"She's awake. Yelled at me for stealing her magical powers and threw me out of her store." My throat started to tighten, and I swallowed to fight it. "*Not* a happy camper."

The others looked up from their work, frowning. "That seems unfair," said Pars.

"Eh." I shrugged. "Think of it like this. The Mystic Mountains crowd has always wanted talent. Most humans think magic doesn't exist, but these are the true believers, right? Well, along comes Katin with her potions and lies, and they're conned into thinking it's really happening for them—they're going to be able to do magic just like she can. Then I hit them with neutralizer and explain that everything they've been experiencing is bogus, and they don't want to believe me. Easier to think I'm a jealous, greedy bitch, I guess."

Liogh winced in sympathy. "No one likes to think they've been conned. Annie told us about the woman you treated yesterday...Penny, was it?"

I nodded. "*True* believer. And I feel bad, you know? They're desperate for magic to be real. I could sit them down and tell them, 'Yeah, you're right, magic exists,' but then I'd have to follow that up with, 'You'll never be able to do a damn thing with it. Sorry!'"

"This situation is not your fault," they replied, and Pars nodded. "You could no more give those humans talent than you could teach me to throw fireballs. It's not going to happen."

"I know," I said, propping my chin in my hands, "but I tried to do the right thing, and now even my friend thinks I'm awful—"

"You tried to do the right thing. That is the important part. If it wasn't appreciated…" They grunted and opened the oven. "Live a little longer, youngling, and you'll learn that you can't please everyone."

Leaving Liogh and Pars to clean up the kitchen, I slipped out to the brew room, where Dad and Yven were working at opposite ends of a long table, racks of tubes and bottles lined up between them. "How's it going?" I asked.

Dad looked up at me through his safety glasses. "Slowly. You all right, girlie?"

"Fine," I lied. "Any thought as to what's in that potion?"

"Well…" He straightened and cracked his back. "You know my feelings concerning confirmation bias, but in this case…"

"There *is* Fingerflash," said Yven, carefully dripping clear liquid into a test tube with an eyedropper. "But not much. Significantly less than in the mid-level potion. Some alcohol, the usual essential oils to scent it."

"*Less* Fingerflash?" I frowned. "That sounds counterintuitive."

"On the contrary…hold on…" He jiggled the eyedropper until the last bit of its contents fell into the tube, then quickly capped the tube and gave it a vigorous shake. "With less Fingerflash, the users will notice that their apparent power is waning, right? They'll imagine something's wrong, and the logical fix would be to—"

"Take more of the potion," I finished. "Duh. So what's

in there that could leave people dazed or seizing?"

"That," said Dad, "is the million-dollar question." Holding up a fresh tube, which contained only a few drops of the unknown potion, he said, "The color's darker than either of the others, but it's not Fingerflash, so our mystery ingredient is probably purple as well, *maybe* black—but I kind of doubt it, considering the possibilities. There really aren't that many potions of the proper color."

"There's that stuff Liogh used to find blood remover in the woods," I offered.

"Sure, that's one, but it would be useless here. If you drink it, you'll never know—nontoxic, and it doesn't react that way. Now, I do know of a few potions that contain ingredients that can lead to seizures, but—"

Yven's unintelligible shout interrupted him, and I looked over to find that the test tube he'd been shaking had filled with bright yellow smoke. "What's that?" I asked, hurrying closer.

"This," said Yven, keeping his thumb over the stopper, "is a field test for gratenweed."

"Gratenweed?" Dad echoed, his brow furrowing. "What on earth would need gratenweed?"

"And, uh...*what* is gratenweed?" I added.

"Nasty little plant," said Yven. "It came out of an experimental greenhouse—an accident. It was originally used in a sleeping potion, but it's addictive, and it works too well. The first test subjects either slept for days or ended up in a sort of stupor." He arched an eyebrow. "Sound familiar?"

Dad beckoned for the test tube, and Yven passed it over for his inspection. "It's *highly* regulated," Dad said. "We've got a few legitimate uses for it, but mostly for healers treating trolls. Certain potions aren't as effective on them, and there's a sleeping potion still in use with gratenweed if the standard ones won't do the trick." Given Yven back his tube, he asked, "What's purple and includes gratenweed? Some new street drug I've missed?"

"I've got a theory," he muttered, putting the tube into a rack. "And it's not a new drug. Ever heard of Velvet Leash?"

Dad's jaw dropped. "*Damn.* I haven't thought about that one in ages…"

"I know, right? But it fits the profile—"

I pointedly cleared my throat, and the two of them seemed to recall that I was in the room and very much out of the loop.

Yven turned back to Dad. "Do you want to explain this one, or shall I?"

He looked my way, and I noticed a faint flush in his cheeks. "Well, Janie, as you keep reminding me, you're not a child. This is, uh…what's the word I'm looking for?"

"Kink," said Yven. He said something in what I took to be Pactish, and when I didn't react, he asked, "What's the English, Yacovi?"

"BDSM," Dad mumbled. "You, uh…"

"I know what that is," I said, saving him. "What does the potion do?"

"Based on my understanding of its use—and this is *not* firsthand information," Yven insisted—"it's a way for the dominant partner to take complete control of the submissive for a period of time. There's enough gratenweed in the mix to leave the drinker in a daze, and other ingredients make them incredibly suggestible. They can be guided by anyone, but when the brewer speaks, they're compelled to obey. The brewer's blood goes into the mix, you see—"

"*Ew.*"

He shrugged. "Not the weirdest potion in the books. And it's got a dark color, which again fits what we're seeing with Oil of Life. Now, because you have to brew it yourself to make it work properly, it's only ever made by sorcerers, elves, nymphs, or fauns, and since most of us tend to pair up along species lines, you seldom see it anywhere else. *Definitely* a niche potion."

"But doesn't the drinker have to knowingly take it?" Dad countered. "That's what I recall—recreational users raised a stink when it was put on the banned list because everyone who uses it does so willingly."

"Intention is a key component," Yven agreed, "but it's not as specific as you think. There was a study done about ten years ago. It's enough for the drinker to intend to drink the potion—they don't have to know that it's Velvet Leash."

"So," I said as the pieces snapped together, "Katin sells two potions that are mostly Fingerflash, then graduates her buyers to *this* one. They willingly drink it, maybe over the course of a couple weeks..."

"And they're left helpless and suggestible," said Yven. "Except your friend who had the seizure. How long had she been on it?"

"She might have taken her first dose Monday."

"Less than a week, and she used most of that bottle...yeah, I'd consider that a gratenweed reaction. It can linger in the body and build up."

"But why do this to a bunch of random humans?" Dad asked. "It doesn't make sense..."

Before the two of them could begin to hypothesize, Pars rapped on the door and pushed it open. "Red's come out of solitary. You might want to see this."

We followed him back into the kitchen, where Rose was slumped on my vacated stool, nursing a glass of orange juice and absently rubbing her forehead. She'd brought her sketchpad down, and Liogh was studying a drawing while Annie plopped a box of Wheat Thins in front of her.

Yven rushed to Rose's side, once again speaking incomprehensibly to my ears, and Rose raised her head and flashed a weary smile. She answered him in kind, I took it, and he stood behind her with his arm around her shoulders, pulling her against him as she recovered.

"See anything interesting?" I asked.

Rose nodded. "Our little fugitives are back, and they've got a whole compound going at that cabin."

"Huh?"

"Come here," said Liogh, turning the sketchpad toward me. "Do you recognize anyone?"

Rose hadn't taken a photorealistic approach in her rush to document her visions, but some of the faces of the people standing around outside the cabin were familiar. "Mystic Mountains folk," I told them, pointing to three of the figures. "What are they doing down there?"

Rose dug into the cracker box. "Brewing."

"*How?* They're human...right?"

"As far as I can tell," she concurred. "Not all brewing requires magic. I mean, half of what your dad does is pretty mundane, yeah?"

"So what are they making, beer?" I asked. "Moonshine?" North Georgia was apple country, but we had our share of small vineyards as well...

Yven pulled the sketchpad closer and shook his head. "No. Look at the setup here, under the metal awning. Double vat, condensation rig, and those colors—"

"Heat," Pars muttered, looking over his shoulder.

I craned my neck for a better look. "What?"

"Bottled Heat," Liogh murmured, stroking their chin, "and I agree. That's classic...but that would be the portion that requires talent."

"If they're making their own heroin..." Yven suggested.

"*Right.*" Glancing up and catching my confusion, the detective explained, "Heat is an illegal potion, highly addictive and still quite popular. It's made with a heroin base—"

"Not every time," said Dad, giving them a knowing smirk. "Some prescription opioids will do the trick as well. They don't call Oxy 'hillbilly heroin' for nothing. Anyway, Janie, once they've got their base, the initial part of the brew is purely with ordinary ingredients. Any human could mix it up."

"Mix it, bottle it, package it," said Rose, and turned the page. "This is the basement of the cabin. It's like a workshop in there."

The drawing showed four long plastic folding tables arranged into a thick rectangle, around which a group of women and men filled small bottles and loaded cartons. I couldn't make out any faces—the heads were bent over their work—but I suspected that more of Katin's customers had become her staff.

"That's her game," I said, tapping the paper. "Hook people on Oil of Life because of the promise of power, get them to willingly take the stuff with the bondage potion in it—"

"I'm sorry, *what*?" Annie interrupted.

"Wait—is that purple stuff what I think it is?" Pars asked Yven and Dad.

Yven nodded. "Positive for gratenweed."

"Wow, that's a new one..." He grimaced and folded his arms. "Right, so Katin's got herself an army of drones drugged on a sex potion and helping her make Heat. Delightful. No wonder Dirk went to Tampa—I bet he had product to sell."

"All I saw were sealed boxes trading hands, but I wouldn't be surprised," said Rose.

"How many people at the cabin?" Liogh asked.

She made a face. "Hard to say. Humans...at least twenty. I saw Dirk and Katin, of course, but there are younger people with them, including some kids. I'm *guessing* they're all sorcerers, but hell if I know."

"Any estimate as to the number of adult sorcerers?" they pressed.

"Eight or nine, maybe, plus Katin and Dirk. Say ten all told. It'd be simpler if they didn't look just like humans, but that's the best I can do right now. And that's assuming they're sorcerers—they could very well be masked."

"Perhaps," they allowed, "but what language were they

speaking? Pactish? Low Elvish? Would you know Nymphic if you heard it?"

"I'd probably recognize it, but I don't speak it yet," she replied. "And no, that's the weird thing—all I heard was English."

The detective frowned. "You're certain?" Rose shot them a look of deep incredulity, and they raised their hands in surrender. "Yes, dumb question, I believe you." Considering the assembled, they said, "All right. Assume Rose is correct about the numbers. With Mera and me...and Humphries?" he asked Pars.

"*And* Humphries," Annie interjected.

"That's three. If we can get in and set off a couple vials of knock-out before they notice us, we should be able to grab at least our primary suspects. We've got jurisdiction to take Dirk in for murder," they continued, "but what do we have on Katin? Unauthorized brewing and distribution? Anything else? I don't think we have evidence for accessory to murder..."

"What about kidnapping?" I said. "Forced labor? If she's got a couple dozen drugged people working for her against their will..."

Liogh rubbed the back of their neck. "It's criminal behavior, no question. The issue is jurisdiction. The crime seems to have taken place here, the victims are human—"

"They're still victims," I protested.

"I never said otherwise. But I can't just haul her before a tribunal on charges that she held humans captive outside the Pactlands. Had she kidnapped one of our citizens, that would be a different matter. And we can still get her for unauthorized brewing and distribution. But our criminal code is such that my hands are somewhat tied."

My anger began to spike, but I shoved it back down. "Because the victims are just humans."

"Because they're not Pactlands citizens," Liogh replied. "And the criminal acts were committed here."

"What if she'd killed them?"

They shook their head. "Wouldn't matter. Now, there *is* a charge the counselors could possibly throw in for threatening secrecy and general safety, but I think it would take more than what this group has done. Prosecution for that would need...I don't know, a large-scale display of magic on television or something."

"But you can't get Katin for kidnapping?" I pressed.

"You've got to understand something, Janie. The Pactlands was made as a refuge," Dad interrupted, drawing my attention from the detective. "We were facing extermination. So while our laws have evolved over the centuries, there are still certain...*gaps*, if you will, where humans are concerned. Homicide? Often criminal. Other crimes committed out here? Iffier."

"That's shitty," I muttered.

"Perhaps," said Liogh, "but it's what we have to work with today. Now, if the three of us—"

"Four," said Yven. "There's no reason that I can't offer backup."

Pars seemed unconvinced. "Are you sure? The last time—"

"I seriously doubt there are sirens here. *Four*," he insisted.

"He means five," said Rose.

Yven stiffened, but Liogh beat him to it. "Appreciated, but there's no reason that you should be along on a raid."

"I'm sworn," she shot back. "Got my badge. And I'm better at defensive magic than he is," she added, giving Yven a look that warned against disagreement.

"She's right," Yven admitted, "but—"

"No buts. Let's even these odds."

"Never heard of a farseer on a raid during my time at DPP," said Dad, "but then again, we didn't have one in the agency. I turned in my badge," he said to Liogh, "but if you're taking volunteers, I did my share of cross-training with Interdiction."

Liogh nodded. "Happy to have you back, Yacovi. If

you're certain…"

"I'm not decrepit yet, so—"

"And I make seven," I said, "so that's that."

"Forget it," was Dad's sharp, immediate reply.

"Uh…are we really turning away the pyro? Is that a good idea?" Annie asked.

"Janie is an underage civilian—" Dad began.

"So was I. So was Rose," she countered, and Rose emphatically nodded. "And neither of us could handle fire like I've seen Jane do."

Ignoring Dad, I said to Liogh, "This is my town. My people. And while I understand that you have your priorities, *someone* has to look out for the humans, too. That would be me."

My dad started to object again, but to my surprise, Pars cut him off. "She's got a point. Besides," he quickly added as Liogh tried to speak, "if the plan is to gas and grab, she's going to be back with us."

"The last time you brought an undertrained civilian on a raid, it saved your life," Rose murmured. "Come on, Liogh. We'll keep an eye on her."

The detective's mouth tightened, but after a few seconds, they sighed and scowled at me. "You stay well to the back, you listen to orders, and if I tell you to run, you go. Understood?"

"Yup."

"Good." Glancing at the oven, they said, "We've got about another hour on the casserole. Let's rest, check gear, and eat, and we'll set off closer to sundown."

"Dibs on the squishy den couch," I announced, and headed out of the room. But before I could go far, Dad grabbed my shoulder, and I turned to look at him. "Yes, sir?"

His face was tight. "Janie…"

"Don't."

"Janie, this is serious. I've been on raids. I *trained* to go on raids. Everyone else in there is agency personnel, and you—"

"I'm pissed," I snapped. "*I'm* the one with a dead faun in my yard. *I'm* the one who's watching people happily give themselves poison. *I'm* the one who walked in to find my friend seizing on the floor today, okay? So I'm going. And if you don't like that, then I'll call the Whitford PD and tell them I suspect human trafficking, and we can get the GBI involved."

Dad's eyebrows rose. "You want to sic human law enforcement on a band of sorcerers?"

"I want someone to look out for the humans caught up in this mess, and since the *obvious* victims aren't at the top of anyone's list…" Shrugging off his hand, I said, "I've got as much right to be there as anyone else in this house does."

"And I'm just trying to keep you safe," he said softly. "I don't want your name dragged into Laws' or DPP's files."

"I appreciate that, Daddy, but you saw Rose's drawings. I can't be the priority right now."

"You are *always* my priority."

"I'll be careful," I promised, then kissed his cheek and walked off to rest.

CHAPTER 16

The sun wouldn't set until close to eight that night, but darkness comes early in the mountain valleys, and Liogh didn't want to wait for true nightfall.

We left Dad's house a little after five, with Pars, Annie, and me in Pars's Jeep and the others in Liogh's. Each vehicle had been packed with a couple dozen vials of neutralizer and a bag of syringes, while both Pars and Liogh carried bottles of knock-out potion, an orange liquid that looked more like Tang than anything magical. Its bottles were strong enough to withstand regular bumping in padded cases but designed to shatter on impact, as the potion would vaporize on exposure to air. The resulting gas would make anyone who inhaled it quickly pass out— useful for riot control, Pars explained on the drive. "It doesn't hurt," Annie assured me as we sped toward Whitford. "Yven deployed it on my friends and me, and I don't even remember falling."

"Agency hazing?" I guessed, clinging to the arm rest as Pars took the curves at high speed.

"No, this was back in Richmond. We're on good terms now, I swear," she said as I looked at her over my shoulder from the front seat. "Really. He was following protocol."

"So how do we avoid inhaling it? Try to stay upwind?"

"Nah," said Pars, slowing as a doe raised her head on the weedy berm. "We've got enough of the antidote to go around. Before we get close, we'll do shots, eh?" he added, grinning.

I might not have been an expert brewer, but I knew

enough about potions to anticipate how gross that could be. "Please tell me it's more appetizing than the neutralizer."

"Oh, don't worry. Feels like cream going down, tastes like a combination of rosewater and sweet vanilla. Not the worst thing in the kit by *far*. It'll work for about two hours," he continued, "so we should have plenty of time to get in and out without worrying about the gas. What's my next turn?"

"Uh…Shady Lane. It's half a mile, on the right," I said, consulting my phone.

The route we'd mapped took us onto a ridge above the cabin, up a service road near a cell tower. Our plan was to park there, then make our approach on foot. Once the cabin was in sight, a little levitation would get the knock-out potion into position, and we'd climb down the rest of the way while anyone outside the cabin—and inside, hopefully—collapsed. While Liogh, Pars, and Dad incapacitated Katin, Dirk, and any other adult sorcerers on the premises, Rose, Annie, Yven, and I would administer the neutralizer and make sure the victims didn't choke on their own puke. After that, two of the agents would climb back up the hill and retrieve the vehicles, and the perps and victims alike would be loaded into the impossibly large storage areas for transport, either to Ragged Gap or to the Pactlands.

If all went according to plan, the knock-out potion would keep our targets unconscious for a couple hours. I wasn't entirely sure what was to be done with the humans we recovered, but I figured I could cross that bridge once we had a firm headcount.

As my weight shifted around a corner, my hip pressed into the unfamiliar hardness of the pistol holster I'd buckled on. I'd learned to shoot as a teenager, thought I'd never had cause to carry, much less go out strapped. But Dad had insisted that I take one of his .38s, even though I'd reminded him that I was a perfectly competent sorcerer.

"I'm competent, too," Yven had said, overhearing us, and made a show of buckling on his own holster. "Never hurts to have backup."

Annie wore a pistol on one thigh and a hunting knife on the other, while Liogh, Pars, and Rose, like Yven, opted for a handgun apiece. Dad, however, had pulled a shotgun from his safe and slung it over his shoulder, and no one had protested.

Soon enough—especially with Pars's driving—we reached the cell tower and parked, then quietly disembarked and grabbed our gear. As Annie passed me a vial of the knock-out antidote, Pars pulled a long staff from the back of the Jeep and rotated it in one hand, giving it a quick inspection. "Ever used one of these?" he asked me, taking a vial from Annie.

I shook my head, then shot back the antidote, which really wasn't terrible.

Pars did likewise and put the three empties in the trunk area before closing it. "A staff is great if you need to focus in a hurry," he said, showing me the conduit channels carved along the side. "I seldom use one these days, but it's not a bad idea to bring it out now."

"Blunt instrument?" I replied.

"That, and it makes a decent walking stick. The mountainside's a little steep."

I snorted. "Flatlander."

The others dosed up, and with Yven and Annie carrying the bags of neutralizer, we started down the slope toward the cabin. Liogh took the lead, picking a path through the trees but stopping every few steps. "What's their holdup?" I whispered to Rose, who walked ahead of me.

"Crunching, I bet," she whispered back, pointing to the leaf litter below us. "I don't know how much our footsteps echo up here."

I tried to walk softly and followed on, tracking the

cabin below us. Though summer-green trees still shrouded the property, I caught occasional glimpses of the metal roof or of a light. Voices filtered up from below, rendered indistinct by distance.

After about ten minutes, Liogh stopped and turned to Pars, who walked immediately behind them. With a nod, Pars pulled his bottle of knock-out potion from its case, and once Liogh had freed theirs, Pars muttered them both into the air. They bobbed over the trees for a few seconds as he chose a spot, and then they plummeted to the ground.

As soon as I heard the sound of breaking glass, a shout arose, but it died almost as quickly as it began. A few meatier thuds suggested falling bodies, and then a pair of doors slammed.

"If they're not unconscious in the cabin, at least they're cornered," said Liogh, and started downward again. "That stuff *spreads*."

The detective was right about that. As we descended through the orange cloud, we passed a number of birds and squirrels on the ground, then a deer. I squinted into the mist, looking for signs of life below, but all I could see was the rising potion fug until we finally reached the valley, where the cloud had somewhat thinned.

Littering the ground around the cabin were at least a dozen figures—men, women, and even a couple of girls no more than six or seven, who seemed to have been caught while playing with dolls beside a pair of old stumps. More squirrels dotted the grass and dirt, and one had passed out atop an overgrown holly bush. As I watched, a hawk fell from the cloud and landed in a weather-grayed hammock, which swung with the impact.

Just as Rose had drawn, the area was set up with brew stations, and it was a minor miracle that no one had collapsed onto a heat source. The cabin's doors were shut tightly, as were the windows—all but an upstairs window, I noticed, which was open just a crack...

"*Down!*" Pars bellowed, and shouted until a translucent shield rapidly ballooned forth from the tip of his staff. I'd barely taken a knee before I heard gunfire, and then a bullet ricocheted off the shield with a sound like cracking glass. The shield held, but the agents scrambled behind it, with Rose shoring it up and Annie and Yven unholstering their weapons to return fire.

As they readied themselves, Liogh said to Dad, "Amplify me."

Dad muttered, and when Liogh spoke again, their voice sounded like it was coming through a megaphone. "Division of Laws," they barked in Pactish. "Division of Plants and Potions. Come out with your hands raised and empty, or we're coming in."

We waited for a moment, the silence stretching across the lawn, and then I heard a voice I thought might be Katin's, similarly amplified. While she spoke in Pactish, it was heavily accented. "You have no business here. No jurisdiction. *Leave.*"

"We have jurisdiction," Liogh replied, "and the unconscious people I see here are the least of your problems. Surrender."

Another pause, and then Katin responded: "If you come any closer, we'll start killing hostages."

That threw a wrench into the plan. Liogh motioned for Dad to take the spell off their voice, then beckoned us into a huddle. "The cabin must be shielded," they whispered. "An ordinary structure like that should have been permeable, especially considering the amount of potion we dropped."

"What now?" Pars asked, maintaining his concentration on our shield.

"I'm inclined to take her seriously," said Liogh, "and if she won't kill, we know Dirk will." They hesitated, then asked Rose, "How many hostages do you think they have?"

"Give me a minute." She sat down and closed her eyes,

and Yven took up a position over her, gun drawn and aimed at the cabin.

"Leave," Katin called. "If you don't go, we start killing."

"Rose…" Liogh muttered.

"That's Katin at the window," she murmured. "Dirk has the gun. There are three—no, four other adults with her. That's her crew. Uh…I've got four children in the next room, they're scared…hang on…"

"I'm warning you," said Katin. "Count of ten. Nine…"

"Okay, I'm downstairs," Rose continued. "Um…maybe a dozen, rough count. Two sorcerers, looks like, and the rest seem glassy. At least ten hostages." She opened her eyes, withdrawing, and stared up at Liogh as Katin's countdown continued. "What do we do?"

I grabbed Annie's arm. "Can you get me to the porch?"

Her eyebrows shot toward her hairline. "Yeah, but—"

"Do it."

"Jane—"

"*Do it*," I demanded.

She gripped me in turn, and suddenly, the world was falling around me. Before I could scream, however, the ground seemed to rise up to greet my feet, and I found myself inches from the cabin door, tucked beneath the porch awning and well within the orange haze. "Plan?" Annie asked.

"Get out of here."

"Hell, no—"

"Annie, *go*," I insisted, and not waiting for her, I shouted in English, "Hey, Katin! I'm at your door. Let's talk!"

"What are you doing?" Annie furiously whispered.

"*Git*," I snapped, and with a last worried glance, she vanished.

The countdown ceased, and then I heard Katin above me, now in English and sounding rather confused. "Who are you?"

"My name's Jane Fortune," I said, fighting to keep my voice level. "I'm not Pact, but you've got some of my friends in there."

In the moment, I didn't feel like putting a more precise label on my relationship to the Mystic Mountains crowd.

When Katin didn't immediately answer me, I pressed her. "Come on, Katin. Or Katarina, if you like that better. Doesn't bother me. Look, the agents ain't happy, and neither am I, but let's see if we can't work something out without y'all shooting anyone. Okay?"

She said nothing, and I began to *really* think about what a potentially stupid thing I'd just done.

"Can I come inside and talk? Please? I...I'm not a hostage negotiator or anything. I make fucking *soap*. You want me to take this off?" I asked, unbuckling my holster. "Fine. I'm putting the gun down," I said, and slowly crouched to lay it on the porch, then nudged it out of reach as I rose. "No weapon. I'm not wearing body armor. Just want to talk."

"Jane," came Liogh's amplified voice, "get back here *right now*."

I sighed and leaned against the cabin wall. "Annoying, aren't they? Mind if I come in?"

The door unlatched.

Before I had time to reconsider, a man in a respirator grabbed me and pulled me inside, through a shimmering barrier—the shield against the knock-out gas, I assumed—then slammed the door. "Don't move," he said, and trained a pistol on me while the floor creaked overhead.

A quick count revealed four people in the front of the house, two men and two women. None of them looked to be more than about twenty-five, but that didn't mean much where sorcerers were concerned. Only the guy with the respirator had a gun, but since I was presumably dealing with people with at least a modicum of talent, I didn't give them any reason to start casting.

When the creaking sounds intensified, I cut my eyes to

the staircase to find Katin descending. She was still a pretty woman—it appeared that she hadn't masked before making her appearances downtown—but her blonde hair was a little oily and disheveled, and she'd traded the flowy blouse, stylish jeans, and gold jewelry for a red T-shirt and gray leggings. While I could see the contours of the saleswoman from Monday, the polished veneer had been stripped.

She paused at the bottom of the stairs, taking me in, then asked, "Who are you?"

"Just as I said, Jane Fortune." I spread my empty hands. "Is it Katarina Weller or Katin…"

"Waughnn," she said, and planted her hands on her hips. "Tell me why I shouldn't make an example of you."

"Because you're not the aggrieved party here," I replied, hoping she couldn't hear my racing heart. "Y'all kidnapped my friends. I want them back."

"Your *friends*?" She laughed incredulously, then glanced at one of the women. "Go get Love."

We held our positions in silence, ignoring Liogh's muffled commands, until she returned, pushing Stephanie in front of her. Stephanie's pink-streaked hair hung loose around her slack face, and her dark eyes focused on nothing.

"You think she's your friend?" Katin asked me. "She's *afraid* of you. They all are—they're either openly fearful or they whistle past the graveyard, talking about what a snobby bitch you are. Believe me, I've heard plenty." Her lip rose in a little snarl of distaste as she looked at Stephanie. "This one asked me to get rid of you. Asked if there was some way I could use magic to run you out of town. If you think she's your friend, then you're a fool."

"Okay, perhaps *friend* was a stretch, but these are still my people," I said. "You can't just drug them into brewing. What the hell is wrong with you?"

She didn't rise to the bait. "You said you're not Pact."

"I'm not."

"What about your little entourage out there? Sound Pact to me."

"They are. Most of them," I admitted. "But I'm not. Never set foot in the Pactlands, honest to God. Aside from a handful of people, no one there even knows I exist."

Her eyes narrowed. "Then how did you join up with them?"

"I mean, when some jerk dumps a dead faun in your yard, you take drastic action."

Dirk, who'd made it halfway down the stairs by that point, turned and retreated the way he'd come when I locked eyes with him.

Katin sighed, then muttered, "He's an idiot."

"Be that as it may, what was I supposed to do with that corpse, huh?"

"You're a sorcerer, right? Or are you masked?"

"Sorcerer," I said, deciding not to go into detail.

"Fine. You could have gotten rid of the body on your own—"

"Except for the part where there's an obviously murdered dude at my house, and I don't want to be the one to leave his family wondering what happened to him."

She snorted. "So you called in *those* assholes? Want to talk about leaving families wondering?"

I folded my arms. "I'm here, aren't I? What's your beef with the Pactlands? Why'd you leave?"

"Oh, we're in the same boat, sweetheart—I've never been. None of us have," she said, sweeping one hand around the room. "Native, every one of us."

"*How?*"

"I could ask you the same question."

"Fair." I shrugged. "My dad died, my mom didn't want me, and she dumped me here. You?"

Katin's expression softened. "Shit. I'm sorry."

"Yeah, well, nothing I can do about it. What's your story?"

She hesitated, glancing around the room at the other four sorcerers, then looked back at me. "Our parents were brewers. Not...*legit* brewers."

"Uh-huh."

"They worked for a guy named Mr. Silver," she continued. "We had a place out in Texas near the Midland portal, and all they did was brew product for him. 'Mr. Silver will take care of us,'" she said sarcastically, "'he'll protect us, we have nothing to worry about.'" Her mouth twisted into a sardonic smile. "Well, apparently, good old Mr. Silver, or whatever the fuck his real name is, isn't as good as they said. One night, a few dozen agents showed up and raided our home. Dirk and I grabbed as many kids as we could, and we ran. Guess those bastards had no idea that we existed, since they weren't there the next morning when we sneaked back to look around. They destroyed most of our brewing equipment, took our stock, seized our cash, and stole every one of our parents. I have no goddamn clue where my mom and dad are," she said simply. "Haven't seen them since I was sixteen, and I'll be forty-one next month. Dirk was just seventeen when the raid happened, and we had *grade schoolers* on our hands."

"Jesus," I whispered.

She nodded. "Yeah. So there we were, no parents, no money, minimal documentation. We'd all been homeschooled, and we seldom left the compound, so we had nowhere to turn for help. All of a sudden, we had to make it on our own, and I knew damn well we weren't going to be able to support everyone on, like, McDonald's salaries. Dirk and I did what we had to do to keep everyone fed, housed, and together. You may not like our methods," she told me, a note of challenge in her voice, "but this was about survival. No one in the Pactlands gave a damn, and the humans around us sure as hell didn't care about a bunch of kids scrambling to get by."

"What about the kids here now?" I asked. "Where did they come from?"

She gestured toward the sorcerers around us. "Time marches on, and when your family's stolen from you, sometimes you're eager to make a new one. We're the Golden Children," she said, stepping toward me. "We're not beholden to some rich bastard in the Pactlands. We make what we want, and we do it our way. And since none of us are Pactlands citizens, those cretins outside have *no* right to come for us."

"Maybe," I allowed, "but there's the slight issue of the unauthorized brewing—"

"And who gets to *authorize* us?" she retorted. "We're not bound by their laws, Jane! They have no say in how we conduct ourselves here. And they shouldn't have any say over you, either."

The earnestness of her tone surprised me.

"You're one of us," said Katin. "So screw the Pactlands. You think those people out there care about you? They don't. They'll take what they want from you and toss the rest away."

She had a point.

I was a dirty little secret, a half-blooded sorcerer without legal right to anything in the Pactlands. Yes, the agents had been kind to me...and Canna had sounded sincere when we spoke...but once this business was behind us, they'd pack up and go home, and I'd still be here. That was the cost of protecting Dad: my continued nonexistence. And even if I broke my silence and went public in the Pactlands, a small voice within me insisted, what good would that do? I was half *human*. They'd hate me for my father, no matter what I did. Hell, their laws wouldn't even offer full justice to the people I'd come into that cabin to rescue.

"Join us," Katin offered. "Help us get out of here, and we'll gladly have you. If a tenth of the things these idiots say about you are true," she said, cocking her head toward Stephanie, "then you'd be a real asset to the team."

"I've got my own business, thank you," I murmured.

She gave me a pitying smile. "Soaps and lotions, right? 'Fortune's Fancies'? Come on, you're better than that. We're practically gods here—why would you limit yourself to bath products?"

The insult, though teasing, helped snap me out of the funk of self-pity into which I'd been sliding. "Maybe I'm not brewing exotic potions, but I'm also not drugging and enslaving helpless humans."

Katin chuckled. "You mean the ones who hate your guts? Like this moron?" she said, pointing to drooling Stephanie. They're here for the taking. Who gives a shit about *humans*?"

In less than a second, the anger and hurt with which I'd been wrestling had erupted into a dome of white-hot flame that roiled around me, and the other sorcerers scampered back in alarm.

"I do," I told Katin, and touched the front door.

Fire blossomed around the frame, and the old shiplap on the wall quickly ignited. I'd thrown together a shield by the time the lone gunman shot at me, and though the blast made my ears ring in those close quarters, my shield held. As for the other three unarmed sorcerers, I anticipated magical attacks—Dad had taught me *that* much—but instead, they backed away with fear etched on their faces.

"Jane, *stop!*" Katin cried. "What are you doing?"

"The right thing," I growled. "*Run.*"

On balance, Katin and the Golden Children might have been able to take me, had they worked together. I was talented, sure, but I wasn't invincible, and they had the advantage of numbers. But what I realized, judging by the way the others scrambled for the back door, was that Katin's crew were sorely undertrained. She and Dirk had become de facto parents when they were just kids themselves. Obviously, they'd had a better brewing education than I had to that point, but perhaps there were other gaps in their magical training—and since no one was trying to put out my fire, maybe Dirk and Katin hadn't been the best teachers.

As Katin shouted for Dirk to grab the children, one of the sorcerers came at me with a kitchen fire extinguisher. When that did nothing, he raced up the staircase and returned with a pair of wailing toddlers in his arms, then bolted out the back. The other male sorcerer, he of the gas mask, was too terrified of the climbing fire to remember to put it on before he shot through the door into the drugged air, followed by the two from the basement.

Bless his heart, Dirk tried. Once the kids were evacuated, he took his turn shooting at me, first with a pistol, and then with a shotgun. But the same anger fueling my fire made my shield strong, and he decided to cut his losses rather than reload.

Last to leave was Katin, and we stared each other down across the den, the front of the house behind me aflame and the gas barrier shimmering behind her. Through the open door, I could see the freshly fallen sorcerers in the orange mist, which had dissipated but was still potent. "*Why?*" she asked as the wall crackled. "We did nothing to you!"

"You fucked around in my town," I told her. "Choose."

And she did. Taking a deep breath, she bolted through the barrier, but she made it only a few yards toward the woods before collapsing.

With that immediate danger neutralized, there was still the *tiny* detail of the house I'd set on fire. I recalled the flames into myself, which left everything behind me a well-charred mess. Amplifying my voice, I yelled, "Come to me! Now!"

It took my zombified neighbors a few minutes to shuffle into the smoky den from their holding room, and as they trickled through, I directed them out the back. Most didn't make it off the porch before passing out, and they piled up on the steps like logs. Still, better there than in the destabilized cabin, I thought, as I descended to the basement to look for other hostages. I found only two, Didi and Jerry, who remained sitting at the table, robotically moving filled potion bottles into cardboard boxes. They ceased their work at my touch, and I ushered them upstairs and out of the cabin.

The agents were still waiting behind Pars's shield when I came around the side of the building, and Dad cried out and sprinted in my direction. I braced myself just before he grabbed me, pulled me off my feet, and squeezed the air from my lungs.

Liogh, appearing a moment later with the rest of the crew, expressed verbally what Dad was trying to convey through suffocation. "What the *hell*, Jane?" they demanded. "What happened to listening to me and following orders?"

Breaking free of Dad's stranglehold, I straightened my shirt and wheeled on the detective. "Last I checked, you're not actually the boss of me. Your perps are out back, sleeping, as are the hostages. *You're welcome.*"

"Stay there," they ordered, then set off with Pars, Dad, and Annie to investigate.

I plopped onto the grass, suddenly drained, and Rose knelt beside me as Yven got to work with the neutralizer. "That was an insane stunt you pulled," she murmured. "Water?"

"Thanks." I took the bottle from her hand and drank half before surrendering it, then softly laughed. "Can't believe Annie went along with that."

"Oh, I can." Smiling at my bemusement, she said, "Annie told me she got a call from Pop last night. Uh...my great-grandfather, the future farseer," she explained. "Know what he said?"

"Powerball numbers, I'm hoping."

"'Trust Jane.'" Looking around at the sleeper-strewn yard, Rose said, "I'm glad she did. Are you okay?"

"I...think so, yeah," I said, and watched as she stood. "Who told your great-grandfather about me, anyway? I thought y'all were going to keep me quiet."

Rose cocked her head. "No one said anything. Farseers…we're tricky like that. But I wouldn't worry," she added with a little grin. "Pop's made a career of selectively distributing information, and he has *thoughts* about the draught. Take a breather, then come get some syringes," she said, and walked off to assist Yven.

Ten minutes later, when I'd shown no sign of leaving my grassy patch, Liogh returned. "How?" was all they asked.

"Undertrained sorcerers who couldn't handle fire," I replied. "And I sincerely hope you have social services in the Pactlands, since those kids are going to need help."

"Who are they?"

I sighed. "Katin said that Laws or someone raided their parents' compound when she was sixteen. They used to brew for Silver?"

Liogh nodded.

"Well, everyone in that house is native—they've never been in the Pactlands. Don't claim citizenship. And they're more than peeved that you people grabbed their parents in the middle of the night. Kind of traumatic, you know?"

"I can imagine."

"Doesn't excuse what they've done here, but maybe whoever comes after them with charges should take that into account. And the kids are innocent, of course, but you're about to rip *their* parents away…"

They offered me a hand and helped me back to my feet. "I'll make the necessary calls. Slight issue to deal with here first."

"Oh?"

Nodding to the burned cabin, they said, "That building will have to come down. Do you have a controlled burn in you?"

"Yeah," I replied. "Give me a few minutes. Or I could rebuild it—"

"That would take hours we don't have. Let's load up,

and then you and I will handle this."

After retrieving the Jeeps, squeezing the unconscious passengers into the holds—and injecting the Golden Children with additional sedative to keep them out—and pulling the evidence they needed from the cabin and its outbuildings, it was nearly an hour before Liogh came back to me for the burning. "I didn't think you had any power over fire," I said, readying myself to incinerate the place.

"I don't," they replied, then pointed to the shallow pond at the rear of the building. "I'm here to make sure the mountains don't go up."

The sun had set behind the western ridge by the time the cabin collapsed into ashes, and I watched in the twilight as Liogh summoned the pond from its basin and dumped it onto the smoldering ruins. With a flick of their wrist, they drew the water back into a hovering puddle, then repeated the process four more times before leaving it to soak into the blackened wood.

"Nice trick," I said.

"Magic is useful on occasion," they allowed, then nodded to the Jeeps. "Get in. We've got work to do."

CHAPTER 17

Tabitha sounded perplexed when she picked up that evening. "Hey, Jane. I got Bitsy home safely. Are you all right?"

"Uh…relatively," I replied, leaning against the back of Mystic Mountains. We'd parked the Jeeps in the employee spaces behind the building, the agents had sprayed the necessary potion to make their license plates impossible to remember, and Pars and Yven had tag-teamed to work a spell that made the vehicles temporarily unnoticeable—useful, as the agents had started pulling unconscious bodies out of the hidden holds like clowns from a Beetle. "Listen, I've got a big favor to ask, and tell me no if you've got better plans—"

"My plans are currently frozen pizza and Netflix. What's up?"

"Is there any chance that you'd be willing to babysit about twenty people until they wake? Shouldn't be more than half an hour or so."

Tabitha hesitated. "Come again?"

"Bunch of folks exposed to high-level Oil of Life. We've neutralized it, but they're sleeping off a sedative, and quite a few of them are covered in vomit, and I have no clue when some of them last *bathed*…hell, I don't even know everyone here."

She sighed. "Where are you?"

"Mystic Mountains. I'm letting myself in."

"How do *you* have a key?"

"Oh, I wouldn't go that far. But look, I don't need to

be here when they come around. Some of them hate my guts already. Would you mind meeting me here? Just…make sure they all wake up?"

"I'll do it," she said after a long moment, "but I want some real answers in return. Okay?"

"Okay," I said, eyeing Pars as he muttered a floating woman into position in the parking lot.

"You promise?"

"Swear."

"Good. See you in about fifteen minutes," she said, and hung up.

By the time Tabitha pulled in, I'd unlocked the front door, and she followed me back to the multipurpose space, where the agents and I had arranged the sleeping victims in rough lines. "What do I need to know?" she asked, folding her arms over her ratty Georgia Tech T-shirt.

"They were at a place near Whitford, drugged out of their minds on Oil of Life, and they've been given neutralizer," I said. "Katarina won't be back."

Tabitha's eyebrows rose. "Is she…"

"Alive but in custody."

"That works."

"So what do you want to know?" I asked.

Tabitha considered the unconscious would-be witches and made a face. "I'm thinking that might be a discussion for another day, yeah?"

"If you don't mind…"

"I don't." She gave me a long, appraising stare, her mouth tightening. "You look beat, Jane. Are you okay? Seriously?"

"Nothing a good night's sleep can't cure," I said, injecting confidence into my voice. "Thank you again."

"Sure thing, hon."

Before I quite knew what she was doing, Tabitha pulled me in for a brief but strong hug. "Uh…thanks," I said, chuckling wearily as we parted.

"Seemed like you needed that," she told me, then

pointed to the rear door. "Got a ride?"

"Yeah. I'll stop by tomorrow, okay?"

"Sounds good. I've got it from here," she assured me, and I let myself out.

Pars and Annie were waiting, having transferred their cargo into Liogh's Jeep, and they looked over their shoulders as I climbed into the back. "All set?" Annie asked.

"They're in competent hands. Did everyone else leave?" I enquired, suddenly afraid that I'd lost the chance to say goodbye.

"They just went to Yacovi's place," Pars replied, and shifted into reverse. "Let's swing by your house and get our things, and we'll caravan home from your dad's."

I tried to make conversation during the drive, but I was more wiped out than I realized. When I closed my eyes to rest them for a moment, I opened them again to find that we'd parked at Dad's house. "We used the spare key," said Annie, grinning as I pulled myself together. "You didn't budge. Are you going to be safe to drive?"

"Should be," I croaked, and let myself out. "Wow…sorry about that…"

Pars's heavy hand fell on my shoulder. "No need to apologize. Large-scale controlled magic will take it out of you, especially if you don't train for it. I remember how exhausted I used to get at your age." He chuckled as I yawned. "Baby's first raid. You'll sleep well tonight."

The front door opened, and Dad and the others emerged, laden with bags and boxes. "Just in time," said Liogh. "Did you bring everything from Jane's?"

"All traces," Pars assured them. "The suspects are still sedated?"

Yven nodded, then shoved his bag into the back of Liogh's Jeep. "Sleeping soundly as of fifteen minutes ago. We'll have them through the portal before they stir unless the road to Central is blocked."

Dad consulted his phone. "Traffic app says you're

clear. Safe travels home."

"Thank you for your hospitality," said Liogh, and they and Dad gripped each other's arms. "It was good to see you again, Yacovi. I hope we meet under better circumstances next time, eh?"

"Absolutely," Dad replied. "Hear that, Janie? No more corpses."

"Honest to God," I muttered, "you find *one* body..."

Liogh cracked a smile. "One too many for most people. And as for Jane," they added quietly, "her secret's safe until she's ready to come forward."

Dad stiffened, his brow wrinkling. "What secret?"

"Yacovi," they murmured, "did you truly expect me to believe you'd fathered *and* raised a child out here? You'd have brought her home if you could—I know you better than that. And I don't condemn you for what you did."

His shoulders slumped. "Did Jane—"

"She merely confirmed what I suspected. But you had to have known the risk in calling me—why did you?"

Dad looked at me, then back at the detective. "Because she was right. No matter what the guy in her yard did, he still deserves justice. And...and because I can't hide her here forever. Truth will out. It always does."

"Not today," Liogh insisted. "Not until Jane thinks it's time."

"Thank you," he said, and sighed deeply. "She's going to need to make her debut in the Pactlands one of these days, and if that means my sins catch up with me, then so be it, but—"

"Don't worry, Daddy," I interrupted, patting his shoulder. "I'm not going anywhere."

He turned and hugged me tightly. "Love you, girlie."

"Love you, too."

Katin wasn't entirely wrong, I mused, as the agents said their goodbyes and set off to the place I couldn't follow—not legally, anyway. Maybe no one in the Pactlands would ever give a damn about me. Stephanie and her buddies sure as hell didn't.

But Dad kept his arm around me as we waved goodbye, and for that night, that was enough.

Dad offered to change the sheets in my old room so I could sleep there, but I declined and made it home. I wanted the comfort of having my own walls around me, though the place felt strangely empty with Annie and Pars's departure. Deciding that I could leave cleaning and tidying for the morning, I crashed and slept until almost noon Sunday, when I woke to a quiet house—and a little peace. Katin, Dirk, and their merry band were gone, and Ragged Gap was that much safer. There still the matter of the Golden Children's youngest members, but that was out of my hands. While I hated the situation into which they'd surely awakened, there was nothing I could do to improve it.

Sometimes, the best solution is simply the one that causes the least harm.

Lovely as my blankets were, I couldn't stay buried all day, so I rose, made myself presentable, grabbed an unopened bottle of Dad's aged 'shine, and headed to the other side of town to check on Tabitha.

She sported sweatpants and an oversized T-shirt when she came to the door, and though her eyes were puffy, she let me in. "A small thank-you token," I said, presenting her with the bottle. "Since I assume you're not going out brunching today…"

Chuckling, Tabitha read the label and grinned. "*Nice.*"

"That one's a good year." I waited while she put it on a side table, then said, "So…dare I ask about last night?"

"I'm going to need coffee for that. Come on," she offered, and led me into her warm kitchen. The room had been designed with a touch of the cottagecore aesthetic: distressed white cabinets, refinished oak floor, potted ferns lining the long window, and bundles of drying herbs hanging from the ceiling. While Tabitha would never have used her own produce in her pharmacy, she'd made a study of folk remedies and recipes, and her herb garden offered a wealth of useful plants. Personally, I bought bags of the tisane she made for sore throats and stuffy noses every winter, and I knew that several of my customers sought her out as well.

Once Tabitha and I had been equipped with mugs, we sat at the wooden table, and she groaned before sipping. "It was...an experience," she began, absently pushing a few stray braids over her shoulder.

"That bad?"

"Yeah. Frankly, I'm glad you missed it. There was a lot of yelling once folks came to. Questions I couldn't answer. Threats to call the police—I don't think those were serious, but people were steamed."

"What did you tell them?" I asked as she paused for coffee.

"Most of them had little to no memory of the last few days. I said you'd gotten them out of a bad situation and given them something to counteract that crap they'd taken. Told them what I'd witnessed with Bitsy and what I'd heard from you and Ernie. They scoffed, then they tried to do that thing with their fingers, and then everyone promptly freaked out when they couldn't start the light show." She raised her mug again, cradling it in her hands. "Suffice it to say you're persona non grata at Mystic Mountains."

"Yeah, what else is new?" I muttered, and folded my arms on the table. "So."

Tabitha cocked her head. "So?"

"I promised you answers, didn't I?"

"You did."

"What do you want to know?"

She leaned back in her chair and drank in silence for a moment, then straightened and pushed the mug aside. "In the last week, for the first time in my life, I've seen real physical magic. Not intentions—actual items moving on their own. And I'm...not sure what to do with that."

"Okay..."

"But let's start with some basics. How long have you had power?"

"Born with it," I said. "It's improved with age and practice, but this is something you have or you don't."

"All right. Next question: are you human?"

I hesitated, which should have been answer enough, but I replied all the same. "Not entirely."

"Oh?"

"My mother was...*is*, I don't know...something else. They look human, but they prefer to consider themselves *other*."

She nodded. "Are you fae?"

I softly laughed. "Emphatic no. I've never heard of a real fairy."

"That's somewhat reassuring. And you're in Ragged Gap because..."

"Because it's the only home I've ever known. As long as I'm here, I might as well protect it, right?"

"I see." She stared past me at the wall, thinking, then focused on me again. "Guess that'll do."

"Really?" I frowned. "That's all you want to know?"

"Oh, believe me, I still have *questions*," said Tabitha with a wry grin, "but I mulled this over last night after I got everyone out of the store, and wisdom counsels that it's a bad idea to probe too deeply into the affairs of magical beings."

"You know me," I replied, shrugging. "Not exactly the vindictive world-destroying type."

"I appreciate that, but all the same..." Reaching across the table, she took my hand. "I *do* know you, Jane. I also know what's said about you. And I...I think you mean well," she said, holding my gaze. "You're young, and maybe you're a little too quick to set things on fire, but I believe your intentions are decent."

I could feel myself flushing. "Sometimes, things need to burn."

"No quarrel here. Fire can be a wonderful cleansing tool. But speaking of tools, you know how it's said that if you have a hammer, every problem looks like a nail?"

I nodded.

"Maybe if you have a blowtorch, every problem looks like kindling. Just a thought," she said, and gave my hand a squeeze as she released it. "A few minutes before you showed up just now, I saw a post on one of the local threads about a cabin burning to the ground last night. It's a wonder the whole area didn't catch fire. No one even noticed until a neighbor about a quarter mile away walked outside at dawn and saw smoke curling. The fire department says the fire was almost dead when they got there—nothing worse than a bit of smoldering." Smirking, she asked, "Know anything about that?"

"Want to guess where Katarina made her camp?"

"Kind of figured. Anyway, *I'm* certainly not saying anything about the matter, but, uh…be careful with that blowtorch, okay?"

"Yessum." I finished my coffee in a long gulp, then pushed back from the table. "Can I bring you takeout? Pretty sure I owe you at least lunch."

"Nah. I'm going back to bed, but I'll take you up on it down the line," she replied. "Thanks again for the hooch…and about that—" she began, her eyes widening.

"It's perfectly normal moonshine. Just aged well."

Tabitha relaxed. "Good to know. Maybe you should go back to bed, too, hon," she said as I put my mug in the dishwasher. "Give yourself a break after whatever happened last night."

I smiled and shook my head. "My salve won't make itself. I meant to go hiking last weekend and look for the last of the goldenrod. Think I'll get around to that while the weather's nice."

"Then I'll wish you happy hunting," said Tabitha, and

saw me to the door. "Should you find any, put me down for a tub of salve, won't you? And I need more of that lavender soak."

"On the house," I promised, and left her to her rest.

I stayed away from town for the rest of the weekend and into the next week. The foraging hike did me good, and between cleaning after my guests and making up for the time I'd lost in the workshop, I kept myself busy. Thus, I was surprised when someone rang my doorbell on Tuesday evening around eight, and floored when I checked through the window and saw Stephanie standing on the mat.

My first instinct was to arm myself—if Penny and Bitsy were any indication as to how she would feel at the loss of her artificial power, I could expect her to take a swing at me *at best*—but I forced down my anxiety, reminded myself that I could flambé her if it came to that, and opened the door. "Hi," I said, quickly checking her for the bulge of a hidden gun.

"Hi," she mumbled.

She looked little like her regular self, the polished but slightly funky businesswoman with the pink-streaked ponytail and tailored pants. Her hair was down and flat, her jewelry and makeup missing, and she stood before me in a baggy sweatshirt and jeans.

"Do you want to come in?" I asked.

Stephanie stepped inside and glanced around, but I had nothing more exotic or intimidating than a droopy Christmas cactus in the foyer. I closed the door, steered her into the den, and gestured toward the couch, and Stephanie sat.

Taking the cushion at the far end, I folded my hands in my lap and stared her down. "I'm not sorry for what I did," I said simply. "At all. And if you can't understand why I did it, then that's your problem."

Her dark eyes began to well, but she nodded.

"I'm not leaving town," I continued. "Sorry Katarina couldn't swing that for you. You do realize she kidnapped you, right? Used you?"

"I remember," Stephanie whispered.

"Remember what?"

"Moments. They're all kind of fuzzy, but..." Her tears began to fall. "She *changed*, Jane. She was so wonderful and kind and warm, and it was all an act."

"Yeah," I replied, unmoved.

"Someone came to my house Thursday and told me to get in a car. I did. And...I remember being there with her, and I was making...*something*...and she said horrible things. Told me to drink more Oil of Life when she fed me. I...I don't even know if I slept..."

"It's over."

Stephanie's face contorted as she tried to hold back her sobs. "You set the house on fire."

I nodded.

"And you got me out."

"I did."

"*Why?*"

"Because burning the place down was the easiest way to flush her and her people—"

"No, no," she interrupted. "Why did you save me?"

I stared at her, momentarily taken aback. "What sort of monster do you think I am, Stephanie? Why would I leave you there to burn alive?"

"I...I guess..."

"I went into that house to *rescue* y'all! If it was just a matter of nabbing Katarina, the folks with me could have handled that. I wanted to make sure you idiots got out alive."

Her lip trembled. "We're not idiots—"

"Then you just made some really dumb choices," I countered. "But it's over now. She's long gone, and you can go back to your yoga and crystal healing and whatever."

She sat there for a moment longer, composing herself, then stood and sniffled. "It wasn't real, was it? The magic that oil gave us?"

"It *was* magic," I said, rising, "but not like she led you to think."

"Then how could Katarina do all of those things?"

My eyebrow rose. "You're the one who believes in magic, right?"

"Yes, but—"

"I'm only going to tell you this once," I said, crossing my arms. "The stuff Katarina can do—the stuff *I* can do—it can't be taught to people like you. People without the talent for it," I clarified as her mouth started to open. "There's no potion you can take, no weird oil you can rub on, no mantra you can chant, that will give you the abilities you're chasing. You're born with them or you're not, and that's as honest as I can be with you."

I waited, but when she didn't rush to object, I continued. "I'm not here to threaten you. Not trying to run you out of business. You want to keep being the alpha bitch of the woo-woo brigade, go right ahead. But if you could grant me a modicum of respect instead of trash-talking me with your posse, that would be nice."

"You don't have to be so mean," she muttered.

I glared back at her until she looked away. "When I was thirteen, I came to you because you were cool and claimed you knew about magic, and I was young and awkward and desperate for friends. I showed you the tiniest bit of actual magic and asked for your help, and you kicked me out. Remember that?"

She had the grace to blush.

"Maybe if I'd promised you power, you would have tolerated me. But I didn't think to lie to you like Katarina did. I was just a lonely kid, and I've more or less stayed away ever since, like you wanted. So please, Stephanie, tell me how I've been mean to you."

"You rub it in!" she blurted. "You rub it in our faces, and you don't care!"

"How? By helping people who come to me and ask? Would you rather I send abused spouses to you for love charms?" Shaking my head, I returned to the front door and held it open. "You want to do the right thing? Tell your followers the truth. Tell them I'm not a jealous asshole who stole their power for fun. But you know, I'm not holding my breath," I said as she slipped past me. "Because that would mean telling them that you were duped in the first place. What *have* you told them? That I ran Katarina off because I'm such a horrible person?"

She paused, her features stark in the white security light. "I'm letting them make up their own minds."

"Big of you," I said, and closed the door.

I waited until I heard her drive away, then stepped into my kitchen and collected myself.

Tomorrow, maybe I could make an appearance. Start mending fences. Pick up my products from the Mercantile, assuming Bitsy hadn't thrown them into a dumpster already.

Tonight, however, the lonely teenager within me still longed for a friend.

I picked up my phone, scrolled through the contact list, and dialed.

Two rings later, a cheery voice answered me in Pactish. "Jane! Hello! Please tell me no one else is dead."

"Hi, Canna," I said, leaning against the counter. "Not this time. Sorry for keeping Pars away last week…"

"That's the job, it's not your fault. Now—Maliul, *no*! For the last time, leave your sister's doll alone!" She waited while a child's voice mumbled, then sighed. "I love my kids, I swear, but sometimes…anyway, I'm so glad to hear from you! How are you, dear?"

"Better now," I replied, and smiled to myself at the sound of happily shrieking children and Pars's deep laughter in the background. "Is this a good time to chat?"

ACKNOWLEDGEMENTS

Hello again, dear reader! Here we are at the start of a new trilogy. As always, thank you for reading, and I hope you enjoyed. Come back soon—there's plenty ahead for Jane.

(If, by chance, this is your first Pactlands book and you're *slightly* confused, never fear! You might want to jump back to Hall of Thorns and The Wild Hunt, the two series before this one. Each series can be read alone, but they do work best in sequence.)

My thanks go to the Novel Chicks, who continue to put up with my shenanigans, and to Adam Domby, whose generous feedback is greatly appreciated.

And yes, here's to you, Mom and Dad.

ABOUT THE AUTHOR

When not writing fiction, Ash Fitzsimmons is an appellate attorney and an unrepentant car singer.

Find her online:
www.ashfitzsimmons.com

www.ingramcontent.com/pod-product-compliance
Lightning Source LLC
Chambersburg PA
CBHW030249200626
46816CB00002BA/573